BLACK SILK

BLACK SILK

VELVET VOWS TRILOGY
Book One

LETIZIA FIRMANI

Black Silk
Paperback Edition

Love N. Books Press
An Imprint of Wolfpack Publishing
1707 E. Diana Street
Tampa, FL 33610

www.lovenbookspress.com

Edited by My Brother's Editor

Paperback ISBN 978-1-969876-06-6
Ebook ISBN 978-1-969876-05-9

To those who needed an anchor to escape the abyss holding their soul captive.

&

To everyone who's been patiently waiting for the blonde main male character to finally get his moment—this one's for us. The time has come.

Playlist

Listen on Spotify:

"The Summoning" – Sleep Token
"You Put a Spell on Me" – Austin Giorgio
"Monsters" – Ruelle
"End Of Time" – Zara Larsson
"Skin and Bones" – David Kushner
"Lethal Woman" – Dove Cameron
"Cravin'" – Stileto, Kendyle Paige
"PASSENGER PRINCESS" – Nessa Barrett
"Just Pretend" – Bad Omens
"True Romance" – Tove Lo
"I Wanna Be Yours" – Arctic Monkeys
"I Will Follow You into the Dark" – Death Cab for Cutie
"Heavenly Bodies" – Arankai
"Morally Grey - Nation Haven Edition" – April Jai, Nation Haven
"But Daddy I Love Him" – Taylor Swift

Author's Note

Content warnings: This book contains scenes that include: drinking, swearing, sexually explicit content (including dom/sub relationship, dirty talk, breath play, impact play, edging, bondage, praise, and use of sex toys), blood, violence, murder, death, fire, suicidal ideation, prejudice, and emotional abuse and controlling behavior by a parent.

If you think there are other triggers that should be disclosed, please contact me at letiziafirmani@gmail.com.

Always remember that your mental health matters, and if any scene in this book becomes too much for you, put it down. You always come first.

Just know that the MMC in his book is a cutie who will tie you up and make sure you have a great time any chance he gets.

BLACK SILK

One

TALULLA

If that buzzing doesn't end in the next five seconds, I won't be able to stop myself from smashing the culprit to a pulp, which would be unfair since, technically, the lamp didn't do anything wrong. But sitting in this obnoxiously large office with very tacky furniture already has me on edge for unknown reasons.

"Miss Popescu." The dean finally breaks the exhausting silence as I nervously grip the armrest of the seventies-style chair. I seriously don't know how someone can think that pea green is a good color for anything. "I don't know how to say this, but..."

"But?" I cross my arms over my chest as the quietness continues to fill the room. He's fidgeting with his tie while tapping his index finger on the desk. "Am I in trouble or something? Because I've been a saint of a student lately."

"No, you're not in academic trouble—per se."

Tilting my head to the side, I notice how his jaw is clenching. "What is it, then?" I finally ask.

"The check for your tuition bounced."

"That's impossible. I talked to my parents just the other day." No, he wouldn't dare. Not like this, not out of the blue.

"Talulla, you are an extraordinary student, and most likely, you'll be a PhD candidate in your field, but if we don't get the payment by the end of the week, I'm afraid I will have to terminate your enrollment for the semester, if not the entire year." Joining his hands, he rests his elbows on the desk, leaning forward to get closer to me.

"There has to be something I can do! I'm a TA. I have multiple scholarships...I bet there's more I can do to get—"

Dean Jefferson cuts me off. "It's true. You have all those things going for you, which cover part of your living expenses, and your scholarships cover half of your classes. But you're still missing $25,000."

My eyes widen at the realization that I am indeed fucked. "I'll get the check to you by Friday."

"I'm sure this is all a misunderstanding. You are a terrific student, Miss Popescu. I'm certain everything will be okay. Talk to your parents."

"I will. Thank you, Dean Jefferson."

As I leave the office, I dial my dad's number, walking toward my best friend, Cassandra. She's sitting on our usual bench in front of the Victorian-style library. The terracotta-colored bricks of the building look particularly pale as the September sun in Palo Alto keeps shining brightly. This is probably our last year together at Bear Creek University. We're both finishing our master's in history. Cassie is a witch, which comes in very handy when a vampire roams around campus, and I'm too busy with papers. The phone rings, and after three tones, my father, Emil Popescu, the most feared vampire hunter in the world, picks up.

"Hi, *copil.*"

Child.

Not son or daughter—just child.

The tone of his voice is firm, as always, and he sounds detached because that's how my Romanian father is with me. Because he's disappointed. He wants me to quit school and take over the "business," and I've told him many times that I will after I'm done with my studies.

"Hi, Dad."

"I guess you are calling for something," he says as I sit beside Cassandra, making sure she can hear the painful conversation I'm about to have.

"I'm sure there was a mistake, but Mr. Jefferson, the dean at my school, told me my tuition for my final year hasn't been paid. Actually, the check bounced."

"That would be correct." The words seem to have no effect on his tone. His reply is monotone—indifferent.

"It's my last year," I groan as I look for something to punch that isn't a wall.

"I am well aware."

Cassandra is looking at me with wide eyes as I anxiously bite my lip to the point of drawing blood. "Can I talk to Mom?"

"No."

Licking off the ironic liquid from my mouth, I try to ask, "Dad, do we have financial problems I'm not aware of? Because I'm pretty sure money has never been a problem in this family."

"No, I have simply voided the check."

I sigh, and my heart pounds in my chest so hard it aches. "May I ask why?"

"You know exactly why, *copil*."

"Dad, it's my last year. We had a deal. I finish school, and then you get your perfect vampire hunter."

"I have waited for you to finish school. You finished school." His faint accent makes the monotone replies sound even colder.

I take a deep breath in, trying to remain calm. "I am doing my master's."

"You got your degree. There is no need to waste more

time when we both know what you are destined to be. I have already given you enough spare time."

"So your way of getting me back is by not paying for my schooling?"

"Yes." Well, that was way too quick of a response. Shit.

"What if I don't come back?"

"Then I guess you'd better find a way to pay for your living expenses because, as of now, you are completely cut off." If he sounded monotone and indifferent before, he was definitely annoyed right now. With me. His daughter.

"You won't actually do it."

"As a matter of fact, I would, and I already did. If this is truly what you want, you can pay for it on your own." The line cuts off.

I'm fucked.

I'm fucked.

I am so *fucked*.

"How much do you need?" Cassandra asks, leaning toward me but keeping a safe distance. She always leaves enough space—for protection. She tends to get visions when she touches people, and that makes her very closed off, but having her around is still comforting.

"Twenty-five grand."

"Holy fucking shit," she breathes. "By when?"

"Friday," I reply, holding my head in my hands. I stare at the mosaic of stones on the ground, the little tiles forming abstract shapes. Maybe if I start counting them, I'll forget about everything else. I can focus on this one task and avoid the problem altogether.

Cassandra clears her throat, and I snap back out of my trance. "Let me call Asmo. We're gonna figure this out."

"Can we go get coffee? I'm going to pretend everything is fine and go to class."

"Sure," she simply replies, clearly restraining herself from revealing what she really thinks of the situation.

We make our way to the closest coffee stand and order two cups to go, the sudden quietness turning my anger into full numbness. "Okay, go ahead. Say it," I finally break, unable to look at her any longer.

"I can't believe how fucked up your dad is."

"He's...well, something."

Her response is fast and snappy. "He's a dick."

"He grew up in an environment that made him this way."

"You're trying to find an excuse for him? Really?" Her icy-blue eyes pop out as we make our way through campus. There's only a slight tingle on my fingers, even though the coffee I'm holding is scorching hot. It's one of the benefits of being a vampire hunter. I'm able to resist pain better than most humans. We sit under an oak tree, searching for shade as we wait for our classes to start, and the sudden coolness of the ground balances the warmth of the hot cup in my hands. I stay silent as I look at the people walking around us. Some are calm, some are late for class, and some are crying as they look at their papers.

"I guess I just wish he could accept that this"—I point at the main building in front of us—"is what I love."

"Can your mom make him change his mind?"

"She wouldn't go against him on this. I don't think so, at least."

As if on cue, a tall, slim, blond guy with a buzz cut approaches us—Asmodeus, Cassandra's wizard childhood friend. Just a friend, nothing else. That's what she repeats to herself and to me every time I point out how he's clearly interested in her.

"Hello, ladies. I heard someone needed a knight in shining armor."

I look around. "Where's this knight you're talking about?" I tease as he sits down beside Cassandra.

"Always a pleasure, Talulla." He laughs before adding,

"I took the liberty of asking around to see what was available, and I think there's something we should look into."

"Which is?"

"Underground fighting."

Cassandra snaps her head in his direction, her silky black hair whipping through the air. "Absolutely not."

"And why not?" Asmo asks. "She's literally a walking weapon. It's brilliant." He flashes a bright smile, pointing at me.

It's true. I am stronger and faster than a regular human being and have been training my entire life to kill. My body count is in the triple digits—of staking vampires, not the other body count. That would be exhausting...

"Asmo, I can't believe I'm saying this, but you are a genius."

"See, Cassie? Problem solved." He turns to look at his friend, the corners of his lips lifted, waiting for her approval.

Cassandra rolls her eyes at him. "Problem not solved. Unless you plan to have her fight nonstop from now until Friday, she won't ever get twenty-five grand."

"We get a loan from the organizer."

"Because that isn't sketchy at all." She raises her eyebrow, crossing her arms over her chest.

"Cassie, we are two witches and a vampire hunter. I'm pretty sure we can handle ourselves."

"Mom, Dad, it was great chatting with you, but I gotta go to class, and then I have to help Mr. Wagner with marking papers," I interrupt their little banter.

"Is that your way of telling us you're banging your professor?" Asmodeus asks.

My feet come to a full stop as the question hits me more dramatically than it should. "Jesus Christ. No, dude. Absolutely not." I shake my head profusely.

"He is cute. You could—" Cassandra tries to say before I stop them both.

"Gross. Not my type, and I don't really want to add to the list of possible reasons for getting kicked out of my program and, well, school. It's very much against *all* the rules."

"I mean, you are an adult, and you have a lot of the same interests..."

My head continues to shake.

"Fair enough. You still need to get laid."

"I need to get this money and finish my program and then find a job and live my life."

"Good plan," Cassandra finally relents.

I salute them and realize Cassandra is looking right past me. As I turn, I see a blond man walking in the distance. The sunrays hit his figure, making his hair look pearly. The brilliance makes me gasp because, as I continue to stare, I realize his skin doesn't belong to the sun but to the moon. He's perfectly dressed in black trousers, a black button-up shirt, and a black trench coat. He passes a hand through his hair, and I subconsciously lick my lips when the light hits his chiseled jawline. He inhales, and I swear I see a corner of his lips lifting up before he slightly turns toward us.

The most beautiful man I've ever seen in my life is looking at me...and he's a vampire. Before I can get a better look at him, he sharply turns away and continues his walk inside the building.

"I thought daylight rings weren't really common anymore," Asmodeus says to break the silence.

"They're not. I haven't seen a vampire wearing one in...well, I've actually never seen one in real life." My eyes are still glued to where he walked in, as if a pull of some kind was keeping my sight there, hoping he'll step right back outside.

"Why is he here?" Cassandra says out loud, making Asmodeus and me turn, realizing she knows who the vampire is.

"Do you know him?"

"I...well, not me specifically, but my brother worked on a case with him a couple of years ago while he was in Europe."

"Okay, well, I don't have time to stake anyone in the middle of the day before a class I'm already late for. Mr. Wagner will end me."

"Go. We'll take care of this."

"Yes, think about all the reasons why I shouldn't do underground fighting and something totally illegal to pay for my tuition, because my Eastern European daddy is disappointed in me."

"That's first on my list, don't worry."

Two

FLYNN

Dean Jefferson has been talking nonstop since I sat down in this absolutely terrible-looking chair. Is this man legally blind? It would explain the choice of color of...well, everything in this office. What has me somewhat stuck to my seat is the faint, sweet smell that seems to be lingering in this exact spot. Fruity, a bit flowery? Roses—it reminds me of roses. I rub the armrest with my index finger and casually bring it to my nose. I don't understand what it is about the scent that is making me so curious. The tingle I get goes from my nose to my throat and then straight down to my cock. I shift my legs to hide my uncomfortable situation.

"When I got your email, Mr. Lancaster, I was shocked at how generous your offer was. Are you sure this is okay with you?"

"I know Bear Creek has a research lab working on Da Vinci's life, and if I can help in any possible way, I would like to do just that."

"Ms. Sinopoli's studies are truly fascinating, and Mr. Wagner, the head of the department, will make sure everything goes as smoothly as possible. This is a tremendous institution, Mr. Lancaster. Your possessions are going to be in great hands."

"I have no doubts about that," I reply politely. The reality is that I don't really give a shit about what they'll do. They're history nerds. I know they won't ruin anything. What I care about now is that girl. She looked so familiar. Could it be? Same eyes, same facial structure...

Yes, what a fucking delight.

Emil Popescu's daughter in the flesh. Now, this is what I call a fabulous turn of events. The person who interests me is the one who was standing beside her, though. Cassandra Drusus has an address I need—the address of the witch I came here to find. The one with the cure.

Is this possibly a desperate attempt? Yes, but I'm so tired of this non-life.

That girl's eyes on mine felt like fire, and her smell... intoxicating. The dried blood on her lips was potent. I haven't drunk from a living body in a long time, but I was ready to take her right there, in the middle of the day, in public. This is exactly why I need to stay away from her.

My smirk calms down as I am forced to continue this unbearable nonsense of a chitchat with the dean. Finally, after an hour and a half of agony, he points me toward Mr. Wagner's office. Let's hope he's not as loquacious as this mortal who should stop attaching a toupee to his head with cheap dollar-store glue. Because this might be the day I start biting necks again.

I knock on the office door and am greeted by my sweet, new obsession.

"You." Her voice feels like silk caressing my skin, and her eyes are the color of the sea, a blue so intense I want to dive into them.

"I'm looking for Mr. Wagner," I say, looking down at her and trying to decide whether her hair resembles a more honey or caramel shade. It's so vibrant and serene. Can a hair color feel that way? Somehow, it does. Her scent is a mix of soft flowers and some sort of fruit—a bit sweet and delicate. It reminds me of spring and warm weather...strawberries and roses. The same smell I was obsessing over only moments ago in the dean's office. What was she doing there?

"Why?" she asks before a man in his late thirties gets up from his desk and walks toward us.

"Mr. Lancaster, it's a pleasure to meet you," the man says, extending his hand to shake mine. "I'm Eric Wagner, and this is my TA, Talulla Popescu."

"Ah," I start, getting her attention. I was right indeed. Emil's daughter is standing right in front of me. "A pleasure to meet you, Miss Popescu." I extend my hand to hers. "I'm Flynn Lancaster."

As my skin touches hers, a tingle in my chest rises and travels straight to my fangs. I caress my teeth with my tongue to alleviate the sensation. Not just thirst, but desire. It's a weird feeling. Her warm essence ignites something within me, something I haven't felt since I was human. I want to embrace her in my arms and mold her to me. Talulla turns my hand, looking at the band around my index finger. "Nice ring."

She's assessing me, just like her father would, yet she seems...different. "Family heirloom," I reply, the corners of my lips lifting into a smirk.

"Of course." Her eyebrow rises, and she releases my hand quickly.

The human behind his desk is frantically searching for something, and as he looks at his watch, he brings his attention back to the other two people in the room. "I believe I forgot some documents in my car. I'll be right back," he explains, making his way to the door.

"Professor, I can go get them for you." Of course, she offers her help. Because why wouldn't she? Such a good girl, ready to help any chance she gets.

I swallow the growl that builds inside me when I see Mr. Wagner's hand resting on her arm before he replies to her, "Not necessary. I parked right behind the building. It will take me a minute. I'll be right back." And he had better take his fingers off her before I bite them off. "Make sure to entertain Mr. Lancaster."

"Yes, please entertain me, Miss Popescu."

She narrows her eyes at me as Eric leaves the office, running. "Is he always so nervous around adults?"

"How do you even have a daylight ring?"

"Straight to the personal questions, I see. You could have offered me a drink first, little hunter."

"I'm going to kill you." Her eyes narrow on me, but mine can't stop looking at her plump lips, bruised by her nibbling.

"Do you always flirt this much with people you've just met?"

She puts her hands on her hips before replying, "What is your problem?"

"I don't have one. I'm perfectly content, actually." I laugh, and as I tilt my head to the side, I ask, "What were you doing in the dean's office earlier? Were you being a bad girl?"

Her jaw tightens, and the sudden change in her mood makes me realize something did indeed happen to upset her. "None of your business," she replies as Mr. I-Can't-Stop-Touching-My-Assistant returns to the office with a folder in his hands.

"Found them!" He waves the papers in the air, and I take that as my cue to get ready to leave.

"Great. Let's go then."

Eric simply nods, and Talulla passes him his bag. She even holds his bag for him? Really? God, this is so much to witness. How is it that one of the most powerful vampire hunters is here holding bags to get a little gratification? She clearly can sense my eyes on her because, as

Eric moves toward the door again, I see her opening her mouth.

"Are you going to be a problem?" she whispers, just so I can hear.

Clever girl.

I inhale her presence once more, and will you look at that? Is that what I think it is? My little hunter seems to like my company just as much as I like hers. She might be good at hiding her impulses from others, but she certainly can't hide them from me, especially when I can smell exactly how she feels about me.

"It was a pleasure talking to you, Miss Popescu," I say out loud, extending my hand once more, and she takes it.

Eric clears his throat, noticing our hands, which remain interlocked for one too many seconds. "Miss Popescu, you can go back to marking the papers while Mr. Lancaster and I go assess some pieces he's donating to the department. I need them done for Wednesday's class. I can't wait to make some first-years upset."

"Fascinating," she whispers, slowly walking back to her seat and never taking her eyes off me. "I'll have them done by tomorrow, Professor." Her voice is loud once more, so Eric can hear. She wants me to see her as a predator, and maybe, just maybe, I'll let her believe she is not my prey.

Mr. Wagner leaves the room, and I take a second longer before I follow him outside. "As much as I'd love to feel your hands on my body, no, I won't be your kind of problem. I don't really play the vampire game anymore."

"Sure."

"I'm just here to donate some artifacts, little hunter. Nothing more."

"Don't call me that," she says, her voice sounding almost like a growl. I like it.

"So feisty."

"Very."

"Please say hi to your father for me." I wink at her and make my way toward the exit, but before I close the door behind me, I pop my head inside one last time. "I do need to ask Cassandra Drusus a question, so I'm sure I'll see you very soon."

Her jaw locks, and her nostrils flare at the mention of her friend. She's worried for her, even if she knows exactly how powerful her friend is. Tough exterior but soft soul. A soul I should not want to know, but after spending only a moment in her presence, I almost can't find a good reason not to be around her.

Change of plans. I want Talulla's hands on me, and I always get what I want. At least, before I let myself die. My last wish before my deserved afterlife in hell.

Three

TALULLA

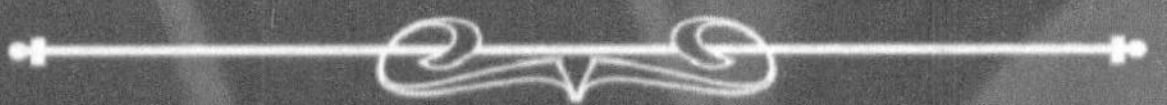

Flynn Lancaster.

What does a vampire with a faint British accent and incredibly expensive taste in clothes want from Cassandra?

A vampire I can't seem to get out of my head. When I touched his icy skin, I felt warmth. How can a lifeless being give me such a reaction? His velvety fingers sent electric shocks all over my body. He felt...soothing, and that scares me. Very much. Especially now that I have to focus on my money problems. I can't spend my time investigating a random vampire with a daylight ring.

I lock Eric's office and make my way to my dorm, feeling drained from the emotional roller coaster I experienced today. I shoot a message to Cassandra to meet me at my building and then realize my mother sent me a text. My poor mother.

Mom
I'm trying to find a solution, sweetheart. He won't have that power over you. I love you.

Me
Don't worry, Mom, I'll be okay. Love you too.

Nora Popescu is the best mom I could ever ask for.

She's sweet and caring and has never had me wanting for anything in life. There's just one thing she can't bring herself to do—leave my father. She is a firm believer that keeping him content is the only way I can have my own life.

The reality is that she grew up in an even worse environment, and my father swept her away from it like a knight in shining armor. He did save her, and he always treats her with respect, but my father is a vampire hunter, and that meant giving me a vampire hunter education before I could even crawl. Tough love—that's what he always calls it. Denying me things I like so I can focus on what is really important: *the cause*. The absurd idea that we must exterminate vampirism once and for all. We, as in my father and me. He had me knowing exactly how powerful I would be from a young age.

The only vampire hunter in existence who can't be compelled.

A vampire hunter trained by the best and with the best abilities.

Now I'm ruining all his plans by wanting to stay in school and be nothing like that. Don't get me wrong, I still end up killing vampires who get in my way. But I never kill a being who isn't giving me any problems, even if it's a lifeless being. Most of them didn't even want to be turned—they didn't have a choice—and that's what my father seems to forget.

Sometimes, I feel like I'm just like a newborn vampire, turned against my will. I was made into a weapon through no choice of my own, and now I'm going to use my abilities to cheat and earn money to get out of that life once and for all. *The end justifies the means.* Isn't that what Machiavelli said?

I reach my door and find Cassandra and Asmodeus waiting for me. The blond wizard is gazing down at her, adoring her from afar. Cassie really needs to realize how gone the guy is for her.

"You're fighting tonight, and Asmo was able to get you a meeting with the organizer."

My jaw drops.

"Based on your performance tonight, he's willing to lend you an advance that will cover your tuition, which you will then have to repay by continuing to fight."

"That is—"

"So wrong," Cassandra finishes the sentence for me.

"It is, but it's also perfect. Thank you, Asmo."

"Don't thank me yet. I don't love the idea either, but I know you'll win very easily."

"I guess this organizer guy didn't really say how long I was supposed to fight to pay back the advance."

"He did not."

"We'll worry about that later," Cassandra adds, and I nod.

"Cass?" I ask before adding, "Why does Flynn Lancaster want to talk to you?"

Cassandra's eyes go wide. "Did he approach you?"

"He came to Eric's office while we were working because of some artwork he's donating, and well...he said he'll see us soon because he has to ask you a question."

"That is...odd."

Asmodeus's stare darkens at the thought of a vampire around Cassandra. "You gotta call Set," he says. "Maybe he knows why he's looking for you."

"I'll shoot him a text and see. In the meantime, we should prepare a plan for tonight."

"Easy. We go there, I fight whoever, the organizer is impressed, I get a hefty check, and we're out."

"I have a weird feeling about this. I don't know." Cassandra comes closer, touching my arm. She wants to get a vision. She never touches anyone unless it's Asmodeus. Me? Very rarely.

"Anything?"

"Nope. But I do feel like something is coming, and I'd just feel better if we were prepared."

Asmo brushes her shoulder, trying to give her a sense of comfort. Cassandra's eyes close, and Asmo keeps a reassuring hand on her. Then, the moment of silence gets interrupted by her phone. A photo of her and a guy with the same sharp features but with dark eyes and light hair appears on the screen. I always saw them as so similar, yet so different. Two sides of the same coin. Set is calling us back.

"Hey, Set. You're on speaker," Cassandra informs him.

"Hey, Cassie Bear, what's up?" His voice sounds a little far and echoey. He's driving somewhere.

"Flynn Lancaster is on campus and told Talulla he needs to speak to me."

"Oh shit. Flynn is there? He didn't tell me he'd be in town," he replies, his tone remaining calm.

"Set, why does a vampire I don't know want to talk to me?"

"I know this sounds crazy, especially saying this with Talulla there, but he's not bad at all."

"He's a vampire," I state.

"A vampire who won't hurt you unless you give him a reason to do so."

I snort. "That makes no sense."

"Flynn is old. He isn't like the newbies you find here. He hasn't touched a warm body in ages."

I clear my throat, trying to stop imagining him possibly biting my neck as his only solution for nutrition. "He...doesn't feed?"

"He does, just not like you'd expect."

"What would he want to know from me, Set?"

"Maybe a name. He might be here on business."

I replay my earlier interaction with him in my head, trying to think of a possible reason why a vampire would need to ask anything of a witch. "He's here to donate some artwork to the university."

Set chuckles from the other side of the line. "He's clever, Talulla, very clever. That's clearly not why he's here."

"I know that, Set. I'm not that stupid," I hiss.

"Never said you were, Talulla. You're many things, but stupid is not one of them."

Set always treated me like part of the family, even if Cassandra came into my life only a few years back. He's like the brother I never had.

"Can we trust him?" Cassandra asks.

"Trust him? Tricky question. He's a vampire, so always be cautious, but see what he wants. It can't hurt. What I do know is that he's an honorable man. He won't touch you. Asmo?"

"Yes, bro?"

"Keep them safe."

"You know it."

We reach the address that was sent to us just twenty minutes before the fight is supposed to start. It's an old, abandoned warehouse with a packed parking lot. Even if secluded, this number of cars is still suspicious. I wonder why the authorities haven't checked this place yet. As I step inside, I laugh at the scene in front of me. The seating section is shrouded in dark lighting, and there is a big spotlight on the ring, which is right in the middle of the room. People are filling their seats, laughing, and drinking cheap beer. The smell of tobacco and sweat fills my nostrils, and as we approach the little cubicle on the left side, a sense of unease rushes through me.

I'm nervous, and I shouldn't be.

I can do this quickly. But that's the problem. I need to make sure not to accidentally kill my opponent.

"Ah, you must be Asmodeus," a man with a thick Italian accent says before turning toward Cassandra and me. "Which one of these two is the fighter?"

"The blonde one," Asmodeus replies with a smirk on his face. "Her name is Talulla, and as I told you on the phone, you'll love her."

"Pleasure to meet you, Talulla. I'm Paolo, and I really hope we can do a lot of business together."

I shake his hand and nod. "Same here. Is there a locker room or somewhere where I can change?"

"Yes, of course. Follow me. It's in the back."

We walk through the crowd, and I can feel so many eyes on me—on us. We look out of place. Well, at least Cassandra and I do. Asmodeus is in his element.

"Are you sure you're up to it, kid? The other guy tonight is big." Paolo looks at me with concern in his eyes. He's probably in his fifties, with faded tattoos on his arms, and not in the shape he definitely used to be when he was my age. He wears a wedding band on his ring finger, indicating he's married and probably a father too.

"I'm a tough cookie. I'm not going to disappoint you," I reply, smiling at him.

"Well, I definitely hope so. If you win, come find me after the match. If you don't..." He turns to look at Asmodeus and Cassandra. "Take her out of here through the back and don't make a scene. I don't need the paramedics and police around here."

"Will do." Asmodeus nods. Cassandra stares in silence with clenched fists.

"Okay, then," Paolo says before turning on the lights in the locker room. "This is your spot. No one will bother you in here. You can change, and there are showers in the back too. Be ready to fight in ten."

"Perfect. Thank you, Paolo."

"Don't thank me yet." He exits the room, leaving us three alone in this space.

"I don't like this at all. We should find another way," Cassandra says. "What if he's in the Mafia or something?"

"First of all, he probably is, but that's okay because I'm here to fight and not to do other illegal activities. Second of all, we are supernatural creatures. I'm sorry, but I'm pretty sure we can handle ourselves."

Cassandra's hands are still closed into fists. She's nervous. She's been feeling like this all day, and I don't know how to make her feel better.

"How about if we still feel like something is off after this fight, we leave and don't even look for Paolo? We can figure out another way to get the money."

She sighs. "Fine." Then she turns toward Asmodeus. "Let's get two seats close to the ring, just in case."

"Yes, good idea," he replies before turning to me. "Don't kill him, Tal, but fuck, I can't wait to see you fight."

"I'll be careful, I promise."

With that, they leave, and I change into boxing shorts and a sports bra. It's very tight around my chest, but it's the only way not to have my damn boobs jiggling around and giving everyone a free show.

A knock on the door lets me know it's my time to step into the ring. I crack my neck, and after checking the tape around my fingers, I decide I look legit enough to be seen. This is it. This is my way out of my family's business and into my new life. An illegal way, I know, but desperate times call for desperate measures.

I don't even see the people around me as I lock eyes with my opponent, who is already in the ring. He's easily six feet five and completely covered in tattoos, with tanned skin and a missing tooth that shows as he smiles at me. He's a professional. His crooked nose gives it away.

"Come on, little girl. Let's have some fun," he says as I step into the ring.

"Jeff, I want a clean fight. Don't kill her, please. I don't need the headache," Paolo yells from the side. "This is not a boxing match, but if the opponent taps out, it's over. Are we clear?" he adds, waiting for us to nod. Then the ref in the ring checks our shin guards for possible hidden objects.

The whistle blows, and the fight starts.

Jeff walks slowly toward me with a cocky pace, thinking he can end this in a matter of seconds. What he doesn't know is that *I* will be doing that.

He tries to grab my arm, but I crouch down quickly, use my momentum to grab his ankle, and make him fall to the ground with no effort. The audience laughs, and I can hear many people mocking Jeff for letting a girl fight him.

"That was not nice, little girl." He gets up, and his movements get faster, but not enough to ever touch me.

"Don't call me little girl," I say before I knee him in the stomach and then elbow him on the back of his neck, making him fall like a bag of potatoes. I turn him onto his back, and with no effort, I press my foot on his neck, making him choke on his own spit.

Jeff taps out not long after that.

I laugh as the people cheer my name. I give Jeff a hand to help him up, but his pride is too wounded to accept it.

I look over at Cassandra and Asmodeus, who are clapping, and then, for some weird reason, I look at the entrance. There, I find Flynn resting against the doorframe. As soon as our eyes lock, he gives me a small nod and then heads out.

Odd.

I walk to the locker room and wait for Cassandra and Asmodeus to find me. I put on a big hoodie without even bothering to change. I just want to talk to Paolo and leave this place. As if on cue, a knock on the door gets my attention.

"It's us."

"Come in. It's unlocked."

Cassandra, Asmodeus, and a very happy Paolo come into view.

"Was that good enough for you, Paolo?"

He walks to me with an envelope. "Here's a check. You're a true surprise. We have a deal. Here's how it's going to work. When I text you, you come to fight to repay what's in there. It's as simple as that. I'll try to give you at least a day's notice."

I tilt my head a little. "Why are you helping me?"

"You look like my daughter, Talulla, and I can tell when my daughter needs help. This is strictly business, but it's in my blood. If I can find a way to help someone in need, I will do that. Don't take advantage of it, though. I do not like people who treat me poorly."

"Understood." I nod and thank him once again before he heads out.

"Flynn was here," I tell them as we head out of the locker room.

"Well, let's get this over with. If he has to ask me something, let's do it now so we can continue with our lives."

We head outside, and there he is, still in his dark trousers and black button-up shirt that mold perfectly to his body.

"I'm impressed, little hunter," he says as we approach him, not moving one inch.

"Don't call me that. How did you know where to find us?"

He touches his nose and smirks. Then he turns toward the two witches at my side. "Cassandra Drusus, what a pleasure to finally meet Set's sister."

"What do you want?" Asmodeus asks, cracking his knuckles.

"Cute." Flynn points at the blond guy beside me. "Does he bite on command too?"

"Flynn, what do you want?" I ask, and I can see how happy he is to hear my voice.

"I do like the sound of my name on your lips, little hunter."

"You have a death wish," Cassandra says, laughing at what he just said. He does have a death wish. He's pissing me off so much I want to strangle him right now.

"I need to find a friend we have in common."

Her eyebrow rises. "And why would I help you find this friend?"

"That's none of your concern."

"If you want us to help you, you could at least answer a simple question," Asmodeus says, crossing his arms over his chest.

"I'm sure Set can—"

Cassandra's phone rings. She picks it up as soon as she sees who's calling. Her face falls as she hears what happened, and then she stares at Flynn.

"What the fuck did you do?" She lunges at him.

I look at him, and he's clearly confused by what she's insinuating. "Cass, what happened?" I ask her, trying to keep her from cursing Flynn.

"He drained someone," she accuses.

"What the fuck?" Flynn's confusion continues. "No, I

did not." His eyebrows squish together, and his hands are up in the air, pleading his innocence.

"A werewolf was found dead on campus. Completely drained."

"Okay, first of all, I don't drink from dogs," he starts. "Second of all, I was here watching the fight, and before that, I was with Mr. I-Wanna-Fuck-My-Assistant the entire afternoon."

"The fuck did you just say?" I bark at him. "Mr. Wagner would never."

"Oh, he would," Flynn says. "You, though, I don't think you would."

"I mean, he kinda does check you out," Asmodeus adds.

"Can we focus on the real matter here? A werewolf was drained, and we need to find out who did it."

"Cool. How about I get what I want, and then you guys can go do whatever you children do at your age?"

"You're insufferable."

He smirks at me. "And you are quite the delight." Then he turns to Cassandra. "Now, where can I find Evanora Hart?"

Cassandra's head tilts a little. "Why do you need a potion mistress?"

"Because she has the recipe for something I really want, and I have a lot of money to spend."

"Evanora doesn't like strangers showing up at her place," Asmodeus states.

"Good thing I'm not a stranger, then."

Four

FLYNN

I finally persuade Cassandra to give me Evanora's address, but before I let them go, I slip my number to Talulla.

"In case you find evidence and need to stake me."

"Can I do that without the evidence?" Her comebacks are quick, and I like that a lot. I like a creature who needs a scolding.

"I'm sure you can do just about anything, little hunter." I start walking away before she has the chance to reply to my statement, but she's feisty and doesn't let me go that easily.

"You really need to stop calling me that."

"And why is that?"

"It's...I don't like it." She crinkles her nose.

"Your mouth says one thing, but..." I inhale, enjoying the sweet scent coming from her—her desire. "Your body says another. Besides, I like to name my pets."

"I'm not your pet, Flynn."

I chuckle at her firm tone. Her blonde hair is shining in the moonlight, and I can see her blue irises sparkling as she looks straight up at me. She's so small but so strong and angry with the world. She needs to take out her sorrow and pain on someone, and if she feels comfortable doing it with me, then so be it. Let me be her punching bag. Let me be her salvation. Let me be the anchor that pulls her out from the deep abyss obfuscating her soul.

"Not yet. You're still an animal, but you will be my pet after I tame you."

She slaps me in the face so hard I almost feel it. "You're an asshole."

"You're gonna be punished for that one, Talulla." I massage my cheek, letting her know she did, in fact, do something to me. Too bad I actually enjoy pain, and I can tell she does as well.

"You two stop flirting. We gotta go. One body has now turned into three. All drained." Cassandra enunciates. That's odd. Very odd. What vampire would find joy in drinking tasteless blood from a creature that could rip his head off?

"Seems like you've got some work to do," I say before adding, "and I have a witch to go visit."

"You and I are not done, Flynn Lancaster."

"I certainly hope we are not. I am having so much fun."

She's said my name only a handful of times, and it's already one of my favorite sounds. I feel the fabric between my legs getting tighter the more I stand in her vicinity.

"I'm going to murder you."

I could let her end my misery. Dying at the hands of Talulla Popescu is a good way to go if things don't go according to my plan. "I'm counting on it," I reply, winking at her and then walking away from my absolution.

The drive to Evanora's house is almost an hour long. I have all the time in the world, but the pull I feel to go back to Talulla's campus is strong. Three supernatural creatures died in the span of a couple of hours.

Drained.

It could just be a sloppy vampire, but why would a vampire go for another supernatural creature and risk dying indefinitely? It makes no sense. Not my problem. I should not make this my problem. I'm getting the potion, and I am leaving. That is the plan, and I will stick to it.

I pull onto a dirt road and slow down, trying not to ruin my car. Of course, a witch would be this secluded. After a couple of minutes, I finally see a Victorian-style house in the distance. This is it. The moment of truth. As I park the car and get out, I look at my surroundings and make sure there are no wards up. Evanora is well known for those, and I know I have to make myself be seen to even have the chance to walk up those steps that lead to her front door.

"Evanora?" I call out. "It's Flynn Lancaster. I have a question for you and a lot of money to spend."

A laugh fills my ears as if a siren is right behind me. Freaking witches and their spells. "Well, this is a surprise."

"Is it? I'm sure Cassandra called you as soon as she gave me your address."

A light on the porch lights up, and then the door opens. "Come in, Flynn Lancaster. I haven't seen you in ages."

As I step into her home, I see plants of every type filling every inch of the house. Then, from where I suppose is her kitchen, Evanora stands with her arms crossed over her chest. She looks older than the last time I saw her—probably in her late forties. Her dark curly hair is now mixed with some gray. Her skin looks almost bronze in the dim lighting. She is still as beautiful as she was fifteen years ago.

"You haven't changed a bit, Evanora. Still as bewitching as ever."

She laughs before raising an eyebrow. "Flattery never

worked on me, Flynn. You know it very well," she says, shifting from one foot to another. "What can I help you with?"

She lets me sit down at her kitchen table as she puts a pot of tea on the stove.

"I have a request for you, and I know it might sound strange, but I would like you to hear me out before you say no."

"Go on."

"I've been alive for a very long time. In a state of non-death for almost as long, and I feel like it's time for me to put a stop to this purgatory."

"What are you trying to say?"

"It's time for me to die, Evanora. Indefinitely."

"If you want me to kill you, that's never going to happen."

I cackle a little at her quick response. "I knew you would say that, but I had something else in mind."

"Which is?"

"I know you have a recipe for a potion that would make my imminent suicide a little easier."

"Flynn—"

"My last wish in this non-existence is to have one last moment as a human. Being turned was something I didn't choose, and I've been alone long enough to know it's time for me to make a decision."

She takes a seat at her kitchen table. "That potion worked only once, and I don't even know if that vampire actually stayed human. It's not—"

I interlock my fingers, resting my hands on the table. "I know it might not work. What I'm asking you is to just try."

"And what happens if I fail?"

"I'll accept the fact that a cure isn't in the cards for me and find another way to end my misery."

"Why don't you just stake yourself?"

"Because, for once, in my many years on this earth, I'd like to feel something again."

Her eyes fill with water. Being vulnerable with an old friend, with her, is the only way I'll have her agree to what I need.

"You feel many things, Flynn. You always say that you don't, but you do."

"It's not the same," I add to her statement, taking out an envelope full of cash and putting it on the table. "Let me know if this is enough."

She waves her hands before collecting the tears she wasn't able to stop. "I don't need your money."

"I know, but someone will have to spend it when I'm gone. Use it for the ingredients."

"The potion—it will take time to gather everything and then brew it."

"How long?"

She taps her chin a few times, probably trying to predict a time frame. "A month at least."

I nod. "I'll stay in the area."

"Before I agree to it, I have one request for you."

"Go ahead."

"You have to promise me you won't get murderous with me if it doesn't work and will try to enjoy this last month you have if this is truly what you want to do."

"That's two requests." The corners of my lips lift into a smile. "I won't kill you, Evanora. You know I don't kill people who try to help me out."

"I know, but you do tend to kill people who piss you off."

I slide my tongue against my fangs. "You could never upset me. You know better than that."

"Cassandra is friends with a Popescu. Don't forget that. Nora's daughter."

"Oh, I know." I chuckle at the mention of my little hunter. "I had the pleasure of meeting Talulla."

"And you're still here. Must have been your lucky day."

"Definitely a very lucky day indeed." A smirk grows on my face.

Five

TALULLA

Our drive to the morgue is silent. Asmodeus is behind the wheel, Cassandra is beside him, and they glance at each other every few seconds before turning to look at me.

"What is it, guys?"

"Oh, nothing," Cassandra says before smiling at me.

"Three people died, and you guys are keeping things from me now? Rude."

"Tal, did you notice anything that happened today?"

"What do you mean?"

"You know we notice things, right?" Asmodeus says, raising an eyebrow at me.

"Yes, and?"

Cassandra sighs. "Are you attracted to the vampire?"

My eyes widen. "What? No, I am not. Are you insane?"

"It's okay if you are, Tal," Asmodeus adds, chuckling.

"Guys, Flynn is just a pain in my ass that I probably will have to deal with."

"You seemed to enjoy the back-and-forth," he says.

"What are you two trying to insinuate?"

"I'm just saying that Flynn can clearly keep up with you, and he certainly likes to do so," Asmodeus states.

"He's a vampire."

"We are all supernatural creatures. What's the big deal?"

"The big deal is that I am supposed to kill his kind!"

"Yeah, but you aren't really on duty much anymore," Cassandra adds.

"Are you on his side now? Really? You don't even like the guy," I reply to her. "We don't know anything about him."

"I haven't made my opinion on him yet, actually." She laughs. "And Set seems to kinda like him, so he can't be that bad."

"Can we just try to sneak into the morgue, see what's up, and never talk about this again?"

"As you wish." Asmodeus laughs.

I rest my back on the seat and try to breathe as I look out of the window. What would my father do if I ever ended up with a vampire? I can literally picture his face. Completely emotionless. Hard. Cold. And probably calling me a disappointment. A failure.

I wonder if my mother would find a way to accept me. They know I wouldn't be able to be compelled and that it would be my decision. All of it would be my decision. Something I want and not something that was forced upon me.

Is that what I need?

I feel like I've had to accept whatever was given to me without second-guessing, and yet here I am, still not wanting any of it. Taking a life, even if it's from a creature that should not exist, always takes a toll on me. Who am I to decide who lives and dies?

The car comes to a stop, and before we get out of the vehicle, Cassandra hands me a potion.

"What's this?"

"Transfiguration potion. We'll look like three employees, so no one will question us. It won't last long, especially with your crazy immune system, so we gotta be quick."

"Gotcha." I drink the liquid like a shot, and they do the same. "Let's go."

My phone rings as we approach the door. "Turn the damn thing off, Tal," Asmodeus whispers.

"Sorry." I turn it off, seeing it's Mr. Wagner, probably requesting something stupid in the middle of the night. "It was—"

"Wagner. We know. He tends to call at the worst possible time."

"Facts."

We get inside and go straight to the fridges. We open them one by one until we find the three bodies. We are used to corpses, but these are empty shells. They look like porcelain dolls. Frail and ready to shatter into a thousand pieces if they fall to the ground.

"They're so pale," I say, examining the skin.

"I mean, they are dead," Asmo says before Cassandra smacks him on the arm. "What? It's true."

"You literally have no tact."

"Why would a vampire drain three werewolves? It makes no sense."

"Let's take pictures of the medical records and go. The potion is almost over."

We make sure not to touch anything without gloves, take photos, and leave the premises just in time as the potion wears off.

As we get to my dorm, I listen to the voice message my professor left on my phone.

"Talulla, I left some paperwork in my office. I need it to finish the acquisition of the pieces Mr. Lancaster is donating to the university, and you're closer than I am. Please bring it to me. It's in a red folder on my desk. I'll be up all night. You know how I am."

"That has to be against school rules," Cassandra says

as she keeps her ear close to my phone so she can hear as well.

"He does this all the time. It's fine," I sigh. "You guys go in. I'll be back in ten minutes."

"Just bang the poor man and get it over with," Asmodeus laughs.

"Again, not trying to get expelled here." I shake my head and make my way to the history department. I use my keys to get into Eric's office, and I find the folder right there on his desk. Good, easy. I don't want to stay here for long. I lock the office and start walking toward the professors' wing, apartment 317. I've been there way too many times to bring stupid things the man forgets. I can tell he's fond of me, but he's also always very careful to never cross boundaries by doing things that could make him lose his job.

I knock on his door, and he opens up a moment later. He's wearing sweatpants and a tight white T-shirt. He's in shape for someone who spends his life with his head in a book.

"Talulla, thank you so much for the folder. Come in, please."

I quickly do as he says before I reply, "I need to get some sleep. Is there anything you need me to do before tomorrow?"

"No, no, all is set," he stutters. "Everything is perfect. I just—"

"What's wrong, Professor?" Weird. He's weird. There's no doubt about that. But tonight, he seems quite distracted, and it's odd hearing him hesitate.

"You know you don't need to call me that here. I'm Eric to you."

"I know," I reply, feeling uneasy at the thought of calling a superior by their first name. "Is everything okay?"

"You tell me, Talulla. Mr. Jefferson told me about your situation."

"I see."

"Is there anything I can do to help?" he asks as his hand squeezes my arm.

"It's all good. My father just didn't move enough funds to the right account. It's all taken care of."

"You know you can ask me anything, right? I might be your boss, but I care for you, Talulla. You're remarkable." His hand now brushes my hair.

"I know, and I truly appreciate it, but as I said, it's all fixed. I will bring the new check to the office tomorrow, and everything will be as it was before."

"Okay, good. I'm glad," he says, opening the folder. "Oh, and you're still attending the fundraiser with me, correct?"

Fuck, I forgot about the gala. I should probably prepare my speech with Cassandra soon. "Yes, of course. I haven't forgotten about it."

"Wonderful."

"Can I ask what Mr. Lancaster is donating?"

Eric's eyes sparkle at the mention. "You won't believe it. I can't wait to analyze it personally."

"And what is it?"

"It's a collection of Leonardo da Vinci's sketches and thoughts."

"There's no fucking way."

"Talulla, language!"

"I'm sorry, Professor. It's just...why would he donate it?"

"Because he knows our department is working on Leonardo da Vinci's life, and he is a very generous man."

I laugh at the thought of Flynn as generous and then realize Eric has no idea why I'm laughing. "Sorry, I—he seems so young. It's weird to be in possession of something so valuable and to just give it up."

"Mr. Lancaster might look young, but he definitely understands the importance of what he's donating. He's been very clear about how we treat his possessions."

"Will I be able to see it as well?"

"Of course. It will be exhibited at our school museum."

"I guess I won't be able to work on it."

"Ms. Sinopoli's lab will be working on it. I'll make sure to try to get you a pass to see it up close, but you won't be able to touch it."

"Thought so." I nod. "I gotta go now, professor."

"Eric."

"Right, Eric. I gotta go. I'll see you tomorrow after classes."

"Good night, Talulla, and thank you."

I leave the professors' wing and make my way to my dorm. A sense of unease fills my every pore. I quicken my pace as I examine my surroundings. Someone is following me, and I know exactly what it is.

A vampire.

A new one too. Too cocky to be an old one.

Thank fuck I always have a stake with me. Force of habit, I guess.

I quickly grab the wooden weapon from the back of my boot and come to a stop. "Come out and play, bloodsucker."

A guy around my age comes out of the bushes, his fangs nice and visible. "You look like a pretty treat."

"I am more like a full meal, and because of that, I think I might have to kill you."

"We could have so much fun, love." The vampire advances, truly thinking he has the upper hand in this situation. Too bad they never do—not with me. Not when it's one-on-one, and I've been doing the staking for much longer than he's been doing the sucking.

"Are you the guy going around draining werewolves?"

His head tilts to the side. "How do you know about those?"

"I know a lot of things, bloodsucker."

"They were easy meals," he says, sniffling and then coughing. Odd.

"Did you just cough?"

"Allergies," he replies, advancing on me.

"You're a fucking vampire. You don't have allergies," I state as I quickly swerve his moves and stake him.

I take a potion Cassandra made for emergencies and let a few drops fall on the dead body, watching it bubble and then disappear quickly.

I get back to my dorm and find Cassandra and Asmodeus on my bed, looking at the medical records.

"Guys, I think I might have just killed the vampire who was behind those deaths."

They look up with wide eyes. "Did you just kill Flynn?" they ask in unison.

"No, I didn't kill Flynn, but after I left Eric's apartment, a vampire came out of nowhere and said he drank from them."

"Well, that was easier than I thought," Cassandra mumbles.

"He did do something weird before I staked him, though."

They wait for me to continue. "He was sniffling and coughing as if he were sick."

"Vampires don't get sick."

"I know that. That's why it was odd."

"I'll tell my mother what happened, but hey, at least we can go back to studying now."

"Well, you ladies have fun with that. Hanging out on

the campus of a school I don't actually attend is starting to make me want to go back to school."

"Drop me off before you go?" Cassandra asks him.

"Of course."

As they approach the door, I get a message.

> **Paolo**
> Fight the day after tomorrow at 11 p.m.

"I've got a fight in two days."

"Cool, we'll be there." Asmo nods as they leave. Before they step out of the room, my best friend pops her head back in. "We should go to the game tomorrow. It might be a good chance to speak with some werewolves and let them know we took care of it."

"Great. Can't wait to drown in all that testosterone."

"Wear some school spirit wear."

Six

TALULLA

Am I dragging my way out of my dorm to go to a football game surrounded by half-drunk university students? Yes, I am, but only because my friends asked me to and I don't have anything else to do right now. That's the only reason. And maybe because I'm hoping to see shirtless men.

Asmodeus and Cassandra are waiting for me on a bench right in front of my building. "Is the history department hoodie the only Bear Creek merch you own? Don't you have a football jersey?"

"Says the one wearing the matching T-shirt." I raise an eyebrow at her. "You know very well I don't own a damn football shirt, just like you don't. And why are you getting all worked up when Asmodeus is literally wearing a black shirt?"

"He doesn't go here."

"Yeah, well, this is what I have. Take it or leave it."

"We're such nerds," she replies, laughing.

We make our way to the school's stadium and take seats on the bleachers. Bear Creek is facing Arizona State. Do I know anything about football? Absolutely not. This is all I know, but looking at football players isn't so bad. Having night encounters with them? Also not so bad if you make it a singular occasion you're never going to repeat.

The game starts, and while everyone looks at the

players on the field, I look at everything else. It's hard to analyze everything when there are so many people in one place, but that's how I was brought up. Always look at your surroundings and make sure no vampire can take you out. Maybe that's why I still have a stake in my bag, which I never remove.

As I get lost in thought, I realize the game has ended and that we won, which is great but also unfair, knowing we have three werewolves on the team. Of the three who died, two were also part of it.

We reach the locker room, the steam of the showers filling the big empty space, and a mix of sweat and cologne hits my nostrils. "God, they stink," I whisper as we take a seat, waiting for our target.

"Well, well, well, who do we have here?" Scott Reyes, the quarterback of the team and also a werewolf, comes out of the showers with a towel hanging so low I can literally imagine everything. It might also be because I've seen everything of this man already. It's difficult to forget that when he looks like a machine, which he does. "Talulla Popescu, if you're looking for round two, you might just be in luck. I think I broke up with my girlfriend earlier today."

"You know I don't go back for seconds," I say before introducing my company. "These are Cassandra Drusus and Asmodeus Gratiadei."

"Ah, yes, the detective witches. Looking for our serial killer?"

"Actually," I start, "we wanted to let you know I took care of it last night. Your pack is safe."

"You did?" he asks, his hands rubbing a towel on his wet hair. I can't help but admire his muscles moving and contracting as he continues to dry off. Maybe I do need to get laid. The thing is, I'm a little tired of meaningless sex.

I blink a few times, trying to get out of the trance I'm in. "Yeah, it was a new vampire. Odd, really."

Scott stops moving and looks straight at me before he asks, "Then why did my brother find a fourth body at the back of a club in a dumpster earlier today?"

"What?"

"Yeah, Tal. These bloodsuckers are going crazy."

"Which club?"

"Crystal Cave."

"That's impossible, Scott. My father's associates go there every night."

"If you're talking about Stefan and Andrei, I haven't seen them in weeks."

My eyes widen at his statement. I know they go there. It's one of the clubs they always make sure is clean. Always. "It makes no sense."

"I've been going hunting every night, Talulla. We all have."

"Why didn't you tell me?"

He laughs. "I don't need a vampire hunter. My pack can handle this."

I ignore his cocky comeback and look at my friends. "We should interrogate some vampires there. Might be our best option at this point."

"You're reading my mind." Cassandra smirks at me.

Scott grabs my wrist as I try to make my way out. "I thought you had retired."

"I have, but this is my school, and I can't just let this happen when I have the power to stop it. Especially when my father makes it his life's mission to piss me off."

Asmodeus is the one talking now. "Do you really think he did it so you would end up hunting?"

"It wouldn't be the first time."

"He let people die, Tal. I don't think he would go to this extent. I'm sure he has a reason for it."

Sure, he does. He always has a fucking excuse, but Emil Popescu always has an ulterior motive. He's that persistent. He knows I'll go there tonight, and he'll make sure to have someone ready to report that his once-adored daughter did indeed fall for his trap. Because it is a trap, but I can't risk other people dying just because he needs to prove something.

"God, he's so infuriating," I whisper as I make my way out of the locker room. My friends follow closely behind in silence.

We return to my building, and after separating for the rest of the day, I go back to my room and work on my thesis for a few hours before I get ready to meet Cass and Asmo again to go to the club.

When we get to the door, the bouncer recognizes me right away and lets us through. When I would hunt on a regular basis for my dad, I used to come here a lot. Now I don't anymore. There's no time.

It takes me less than a minute to spot Scott's older brother, Kaden, the alpha of the Reyes pack. He's sitting in a more secluded area on a dark leather love seat. The dim lighting makes it hard to distinguish the color. Kaden is another one of those random encounters that happened once. Maybe I should be glad that work and school take up most of my time lately. But as soon as he sees me, he's on the move.

"Haven't seen you here in a while, Talulla," Kaden says as he approaches us.

"I've been very busy," I reply, looking around the club. It's filled with people dancing, with the aroma of spilled liquor hitting my nostrils right away.

"Too busy to spend time with your favorite werewolf?"

"I don't see your brother around here, Kaden," I joke, looking around as if I'm actually looking for someone else. My eyes do fall on someone else. A vampire. Not any vampire—Flynn.

He winks at me as I turn back to look at Kaden, who is now holding his hand against his chest. "You wound me."

"We're gonna go grab a drink and look at all the exits," Asmo says before moving away from us.

"Wanna dance?" Kaden asks, wrapping his arms around my waist and moving me to the dance floor. I simply nod as I follow his lead and hook mine around his neck. I inhale his scent, a mix of sandalwood and sweat. Not terrible, but also not what can help me forget my problems. "We could have so much fun together," he says, pressing my body to his.

"What would your mate say about that?" Yes, because the alpha in front of me almost forgot this small detail about werewolves and how they're destined to be with another werewolf. It's a bond they can't avoid. They see each other, and no one else exists anymore.

"What if you are my mate?"

I snort. "Does that line really work on women?"

"It's not a line, Tal. We are so good together. It has happened in the past that alphas have mated with other creatures."

Then, for some reason, I do something unexpected. I play along with what he's saying, almost hoping to be heard by *someone*. "Oh yeah? And what would you do if I were your mate?"

"I'd probably do anything you'd ask me to." His hand slides up and down my back, getting very close to my ass.

His other hand travels up my belly, his thumb brushing awfully close to my breasts.

My mouth opens slightly. I haven't been touched like this in a while, and it's nice to feel wanted like this, but for some reason, it also feels terribly wrong because he isn't what I need right now. Not even one bit. "Good, because I'm trying to find some information about those deaths from your pack."

He rolls his eyes, chuckling. "Well, the cause of them is staring at us right as we speak."

"That was quick. Must be a new record for me."

"And he's walking straight in our direction."

"What?" I ask as he spins me around. Flynn Lancaster is walking in the middle of the dance floor with a glass of whiskey in his hand. He moves like a predator, his eyes locked on mine and his jaw clenched. Is he upset? It doesn't matter, because all I can see, even in this dark space, are his icy-gray eyes, so cold yet so deep. He exudes menace. The kind of danger I would dive into face-first without even thinking twice about it.

"If you wanted to grab my attention, Talulla, it worked."

I stop moving but keep my arms around Kaden's neck. "I'm working, Flynn. I know it might be hard to believe, but not everything revolves around you, unless you're the one behind all those deaths. Then yes, I was trying to gain your attention."

He chuckles, his arm brushing my back and sending shivers all over my body. "I don't drink from dogs. I have a much finer palate."

"Hey, don't touch her!" Kaden yells at him, but Flynn's eyes are on me. He doesn't pay attention to anything else but me.

"I might drain this one if he keeps touching you,

though." His jaw is still clenched as he lowers his face to mine, his cheek touching my own. "I thought your father's pets hunted here," he whispers into my ear. My eyes close as his tobacco and vanilla cologne overrides every other smell around me. It takes me a moment to come back to my senses and get back to the situation in front of me.

I tell Kaden to wait, and, grabbing Flynn's hand, I walk us toward the bar. Feeling his fingers interlocked with mine is supposed to feel wrong, yet I can't help but notice how such a small gesture makes me feel at ease. "I'm helping the Drusus coven, you Neanderthal. No need to go all alpha on me. I don't even know you."

"And rubbing your ass all over an actual alpha is your way of doing things?"

"Another member of his pack was found dead earlier today, and who I rub my ass on isn't any of your concern."

I swear I hear him growl. "Talulla."

"Stop making that face, Flynn. You're gonna get wrinkles."

"What are you doing?"

"None of your business."

"You made it my business when you decided to walk into a cave full of vampires who can't wait to taste the daughter of Emil fucking Popescu."

A wild smirk appears on my face. "Worried about me, fangs?"

"I'm worried about the massacre you'll leave behind and that I'll have to clean."

"If you're nice, maybe I'll stake you as well," I reply, winking at him and then walking back to the middle of the dance floor, where not only Kaden is waiting for me, but a vampire as well.

I lock eyes with Flynn once more as I let the vampire rub himself all over me. My hands roam all over my body, squeezing my tits a little to give him a show—a show he can't participate in. He's sitting at a table, and I can't help but notice how his knuckles look even whiter than usual as he grips his glass so tight I know he'll break it at any moment.

Good. He can be jealous.

Who does he think he is, asserting his territory over someone who isn't his?

I turn away from him and face the bloodsucker who has been keeping his face way too close to my neck. "Hey," I say, showing off the fakest smile ever.

"Hello, pretty treat," the vampire replies, continuing to sniff me, and for a moment, I feel his tongue trace my neck. Gross. "Wanna continue this dance in a more private place?"

Ah, gotcha. "We can go out that door." I point to the exit where I know Cassandra and Asmodeus are waiting.

"Perfect plan," he replies, holding my hand and moving through the crowd toward the door. He's too focused on getting his meal to even notice that Asmodeus slips me a stake right as he steps outside the door.

The problem is that I miscalculated the bastard. Because as soon as we get outside, we're not alone to play our little game where I ask him questions and he doesn't reply to any of them, so I end him.

No, I am surrounded.

FLYNN

I don't fully understand what's happening to me anymore. The more I see her, the more I crave to make her mine. I down another glass of whiskey before I turn to look at the bane of my existence. Did she really have to wear those leather pants? God, she's cruel. Don't even get me started on the little fabric she calls a shirt. That show she gave me earlier almost sent me to heaven.

I look around, and there she is, walking toward the back door with a fucking vampire. I guess she did find what she came here for. That's what she does, after all. She kills my kind, and I should probably get that fact tattooed on my forehead. Maybe that will convince me to stop playing with fire.

Her friends are at the door, waiting for her, the blond moron giving her a stake. I wonder how she would feel on top of me with that stake ready to pierce my heart. Yeah, I might need to go to a vampire therapist or something. I clearly have a problem. I stop looking at her and glance at the rest of the vampires in the club. There were about ten, all sitting at a table.

Shit.

They're not in here anymore, which means...

I run to the back door as fast as I can, and Cassandra stops me right as I'm about to go outside. "Let her work, Flynn."

"Do you want her to die?"

"What are you talking about?" Asmodeus asks.

"There were ten vampires sitting at a table over there." I point to the opposite side of the club. "They're not there anymore. Now, I'm sure she's good, but that many vampires are a lot even for me, so please step aside before your friend becomes dinner."

"And why would you help us?"

"You might be right to be worried about what I am, but know this one thing," I say, getting closer to the Drusus witch. "I never asked to become this. Now move."

Cassandra swallows some air and moves to the side, following me as I walk onto the scene.

Talulla is right in the middle of a circle, stake in hand, ready to attack at any second. "Well, well, well, thank you for waiting, guys. I see you've got a very pretty meal out here."

"Who are you?" one of the vampires asks. They're all in bloodlust. They probably haven't fed in days, and when vampires don't feed, they tend to go a little insane.

I run in front of him and tighten my hands around his throat. "I'm your worst nightmare." Then, I do exactly what I said I'd be doing. I grip his neck so tight I draw blood. My fingers sink inside his body, and then I pull backward, tearing his throat out of him. He doesn't even get to scream.

The head still dripping from my hand, I turn to look at Talulla with a smirk on my face. "I thought you wanted to play, little hunter. Let's play."

That's all I have to say before the other vampires start to attack us. One after the other, they fall dead to the ground. The witches help as well.

I turn to look at Talulla once more as she dances with the stake in her hand, a hypnotic melody of deadly moves.

She's ready to pierce the vampire under her when another one comes out of nowhere and jumps right onto her back. His hands tighten around Talulla's body, making it hard for her to do anything.

I don't even realize I'm moving until I'm holding the bastard who tried to sink his fangs into her neck, ready to rip his skull open.

"Wait," Talulla says, gasping for air. "We need to ask some questions."

I growl but rein myself back from delivering the killing blow. My grip remains tight as she gets close to us. "Why are you attacking werewolves?"

"Why would I tell you?"

My grip tightens once more. "You might want to answer her. I really don't like impertinent imbeciles."

"We didn't attack them, okay? It was just one guy who did."

"Well, I staked that one guy last night, so tell me why another body showed up today."

"I don't know," the vampire replies, and my grip tightens once again.

Grabbing the vampire's jaw, I turn his face toward me. "Let's see if you're telling the truth," I say, getting ready to compel him. "Do you know who's behind those deaths?"

The vampire's pupils enlarge for just a moment, letting me know the compulsion is actually working. "No, I don't."

Crack. My hands move so quickly that he has no time to say anything else.

"Why did you do that?"

I raise an eyebrow at Talulla, who has her arms crossed. Is she upset? "He didn't know anything."

"I know, but I was ready to stake him."

The corners of my lips lift into a smirk as I look at her hand, gripping the wooden piece so tightly. My cock begins to throb in my pants at the sight. "You can stake me any time you want, darling," I say, starting to walk away from them. "Especially if that is how you look when you hold it."

Seven

FLYNN

I might have had to get myself off a few times before I went to bed last night after spending all that quality time around Talulla. Do I have a death wish? Because every time I think about the sight of her doing her thing, I can't help but want her to touch me like that. I'd take anything she gives me.

The rental I'm staying at is right in front of the university campus. In the beginning, I thought it would be a good idea to keep my facade in place for a couple of days, but now? Now I know I have a certain vampire hunter very close to me, and there's no way I'm changing anything about it. I'm staying right here. The reality is that I really should not want to do what I want to do to her. I never felt this predatory *need* to learn about my prey. Yet here I am, making sure I can spend time with her to do just that. Maybe she'll stake me for real if I ask her nicely. She has no idea how old and strong I am, but I know I would do just about anything to feel her skin against mine once more. No matter in what way. So I come up with an excuse to get close to Talulla and find the detective witch with the hope of seeing my new world with her.

Cassandra is sitting on a bench. As the fall breeze arrives, she seems to be the only person wanting to study outside and not at the library. I sit beside her, not saying a word and waiting to see how long it takes for her to notice.

"Are you going to stay there and say nothing for long, or do you actually want something?"

"You don't like me much, do you?"

"I don't know you. It's different." Her eyebrow rises, and then a slight smirk appears on her face.

"I just wanted to thank you for the information you provided. Evanora was very helpful."

The witch crosses her arms over her chest. "Are you going to tell me why you needed her?"

"It's...private." I click my tongue in the hope she'll drop the interrogation.

She narrows her eyes at me. "Sure, it is."

"Did you kill anyone else after I left last night?"

"No. You two made such a mess we ended up having to use like five potions to clean all that bloo—" Cassandra stops talking, and I turn, noticing her eyes widening.

"You okay there?"

She looks up at me with the same wide eyes. "Listen, I know this sounds weird, but I gotta go. Can you do me a favor?"

I raise an eyebrow at her, curious. "Depends."

"I don't know how long I'll be, and Talulla has a fight later tonight. I don't like her being alone there."

"And you trust me, a vampire, with her?"

"I don't know if I can trust you yet, but I trust my brother's judgment."

"Set is a good man. Same place as last time?"

"Yes."

"Are you going to tell me what's up?"

"I just—I need to check something. I think we missed something about those bodies, and I need to be sure."

"Way to be cryptic."

"Just make sure Talulla isn't alone in there. I know she

can handle herself and literally told me she doesn't need us there, but I have a weird feeling about all of this, and..."

"She won't be alone."

"I know it sounds overprotective and all that, especially when you saw exactly what she's capable of doing, but I really—"

"I'll be there," I cut her off before she begins to hyperventilate.

She exhales. "Thank you. I'll see you around."

Well, I did want an excuse to see Talulla, and Cassandra just gave me a very good one.

After the detective witch leaves, I sit on the nearest bench and contemplate what I could do before the event tonight.

Stalking Talulla could be an option, but I should probably get a refill of blood for my fridge before I do something like that.

I can literally smell her essence everywhere on campus. I could find her in a matter of minutes and then go on with my day. Then what? Do I just watch her as she goes about her day? Keeping my distance is getting hard very quickly. The predator in me is making this obsession impossible to attenuate the more time passes.

"Mr. Lancaster," a familiar voice says from behind me. I don't even have to turn or do anything to confirm my suspicions. I would recognize his repugnant smell anywhere I go.

"Professor Wagner," I say, slightly turning my head since Eric finds it acceptable to sit right beside me. If he only knew he was sitting beside the most dangerous predator in existence, he might be more inclined to keep some fucking distance.

"Did we have an appointment?"

"No, we did not." My tone is cold and detached.

Maybe he'll get a hint if I show him a nice, full smile. Fangs and all.

"Then, may I ask what you're doing here?"

No, you can't, but now I have to reply to you mostly because, for some reason, Talulla seems to be okay spending time around you, and I can't commit murder in public. I mean, I could, but the cleanup and the compulsion wouldn't be worth it. But if I lure him to that opening right there, into that dark alley between the main building and the library, maybe, just maybe, I'd have fewer people to worry about. My throat starts itching the more I think about how I could easily suck him dry and still be able to get my five minutes of stalking in before I go to the blood bank and buy some groceries. "I like admiring the architecture around here. It reminds me of London."

"Minus the gloomy weather and constant cold."

I snort. "Yes, minus those things." I turn to look at him and realize he's looking straight ahead, at nothing, really. "It's nice to get a change of scenery when everything looks the same in this country."

"Americans do tend to make a lot of the same things," he agrees, and then he turns his neck toward me, the action making his jugular vein even more visible. The dark blue line almost pulses as I continue to stare at it. I need to go before I rip his head off his neck.

"Well, it was a pleasure seeing you, Mr. Wagner, but I do have somewhere to be."

He checks his watch before replying, "And I have a meeting with my assistant that I'm already late for. Goodbye, Mr. Lancaster."

I growl as he starts pacing toward his department building. Tardiness is something I really do not like, especially when the one waiting is *her.*

I wait until he walks inside before following his scent, my tongue pushing on my fangs and making me bleed. I haven't fed from a human neck in a very long time, and yet, here I am, ready to drain him right in front of a vampire hunter just because he was late to their appointment.

Well, I could lie to myself and say that's the only reason, but it isn't. It certainly isn't as I stare at Talulla waiting, arms crossed over her chest and leaning against the office door. She's wearing a tight band T-shirt, and I almost run to her as I realize she's wearing a lacy bra with no padding underneath. Yes, because I can clearly imagine her nipples as they slightly peek through the fabric. Goddammit, Talulla, why do you have to wear something like that when you look like a fucking goddess?

Who am I? Where did the composed control freak go? Gone. So very gone because Eric just showed up, and his eyes go right where they don't belong.

I need to feed.

Badly.

I quickly stalk out of the building and make my way to my car. The blood bank I've been using is about half an hour away from Bear Creek, so I need to find a way to calm down before I go back in there and rip a man to shreds.

After putting on some music, I start the drive. My hands clench so hard I can feel the steering wheel bending as I leave the parking lot. As I get farther from the bane of my existence, I finally relax, feeling the knot in my throat softening. What an ironic turn of events.

After parking my car, I make my way to the blood bank's entrance, sensing something behind me. I inhale and realize a werewolf is close by. I turn and see a guy who resembles Kaden, the alpha from last night.

I should probably pretend I haven't seen him, but after the little massacre game I had to play last night, I want to make sure the dumbass doesn't get himself killed.

The Drususes could easily track me here, and it would be harder to explain if I were seen in the vicinity of another dead werewolf.

After seeing him walk into an alleyway, I mince toward the closest building and wait to see his next move. He knocks on the back door of a bar, and a woman comes out right after. I make a mental note of the name of the bar, Boozy Business. Ah, clever.

"You have the cash?" the woman asks. As I look at her, I realize she's a witch. The crystals around her neck give it away.

The werewolf hands her an envelope. "Here," he says, scratching the back of his head. "Are you sure this is going to work?"

"It has never failed before," she simply replies, handing him a paper bag. "Have them drink it as soon as you can. You don't want it to go bad."

"Will do. Thank you." The werewolf nods and starts walking my way.

I quickly jog back and finally enter the blood bank, knowing I'll have to share this little detail with the detective witch later. It might be something important to the case. He might be the person behind it all.

"Welcome back, Mr. Lancaster," a joyful voice greets me at the counter.

"Good afternoon, Laura. I hope your day is going well," I reply, trying to keep my polite face on. The middle-aged lady continues to beam at me.

"It is now that you're here, Mr. Lancaster. You bring the sunshine inside."

"Can't say I've heard that one before." I chuckle at the irony of her words, tapping my fingers on the countertop.

"The usual?"

"Yes, please," I say, handing her a cooler bag.

"I'll be right back." She walks to the back and takes

her time to fill it up. It takes her about five minutes to return with my bag nice and full.

I get my refills of O positive, and Laura gets her envelope of cash. Simple as that. Would I thrive to get something rarer? Yes, but it's harder to hide when one is so much more common than the others.

We have a pretty good deal. She can't afford to send her daughter to university, so I basically pay for her tuition with the cash I bring her, and well, probably much more than that. It's a quick ten-minute business exchange, and then I'm out of here, and she goes back to her job. No questions asked, and I like it that way.

On my drive back to my apartment, I make a quick phone call to the local museum where I decided to donate some artwork. They told me I could visit any time I wanted, and I have a pretty good idea of who I want to bring with me when I do that.

It's the perfect excuse to spend some time with my little hunter outside her everyday life.

I go back to my place to change, and then, when it's time, I drive to the warehouse and enjoy the show. I stay in the back, not giving too much attention to the people around me. The only thing I'm looking at is my beautiful Talulla. As she steps into the ring, she turns, and for a moment, our eyes lock, and I forget everything else. In a room full of men, in pure chaos, she was still able to find me. Her stare keeps me locked in place, yet I am ready to jump into that ring and claim her mouth. An invisible thread pulls my heart directly toward her. I'm her new lifeline, and she is my North Star.

Eight
TALULLA

> **Cassandra**
> Change of plans. I'll meet you at your dorm after your match. I sent you a surprise, though.

I have no idea what Cassandra means by surprise, but I'm sure I'll find out as soon as I get out of this locker room.

As I step into the ring, my eyes travel from the big man in front of me to the icy-gray ones fixated on my very being.

He's here. In the crowd.

Flynn Lancaster.

Again.

He's staring at me as if I were the only person in the room, and for some forsaken reason, I like the audacity of this vampire. I feel seen and alive around him, and it scares the shit out of me.

"Are you ready to get thrown around, baby?" The guy in front of me tries to regain my attention. I chuckle at his words. For someone so ripped, he clearly has very little in his brain.

"Are you ready to be taught a lesson, big guy?" I can see Flynn giving me a devilish smirk, still paying attention only to me. Nothing else. He wants me to know I'm the only thing around he cares to look at. I feel completely vulnerable as his eyes travel over my body. I wish he were in this ring right now so I could have an excuse to have his hands on me.

No, Talulla, that is literally the one thing you know is wrong. The only thing that you were brought up with that would get you kicked out of the family. Completely.

Would that be such a bad thing? I feel kicked out of it already anyway. I never really felt part of it.

The bell rings, and the fight begins. I can't get distracted. I have to win the match, get the money, and give the vampire a little show on who he'd be up against if he decided to give me—or anyone around here—a hard time. Even if after last night I don't know what game he's trying to play. But I can't think about that right now, not when I have to focus on trying not to hurt the man in the ring too much. Trying to hold back my strength is even harder than actually throwing a punch. I know how dangerous this game I'm playing is. But I'm doing this for my freedom. I take part in illegal fights for a bit, gain enough money for my tuition, and then, done. I find a job in my field, and I don't have to ask for any sort of help anymore.

I stop the first punch, then a kick, and then another punch. The guy is getting frustrated that I am doing nothing but stopping his moves. Little does he know he's getting tired very quickly, and my stamina is fucking phenomenal.

As he steps back, trying to regain normal breathing, I attack. An easy punch to the stomach, an elbow to the nape of the neck, and then a foot to the ankle, making him lose his balance. I press my foot on his neck, making him choke for a moment.

"I don't like to be called baby," I say as I add pressure onto his neck, and he taps, ending the match and making me the winner. Maybe the amount of pressure on his neck was a little much. I offer my hand to help him get up, but the man refuses, swearing his way out of the ring. Ouch. I guess I broke another guy's honor. I smile as he yells from the back of the building. Oh well, I tried to be nice, but he didn't want to be nice back.

As I step into the locker room to get cleaned up, I hear a knock on the door. It's him—Flynn. I know it's him. I can feel the pull I felt the first time I saw him, the same kind of feeling I had as he watched me fight in the ring. The kind of connection that snapped into place as he walked into my life.

Not good.

So not good.

Very, *very* dangerous. Cassandra will kill me for it.

"Come in, blondie," I say, trying to remain as calm as possible. My heartbeat quickens in my chest. Why am I so nervous when I'm around him? I could kill him in seconds, yet here I am, feeling my cheeks burn.

The corners of his lips lift up. He absolutely can hear my heartbeat. "It's truly amusing to see how many people underestimate you."

No mention of my warmed state. I appreciate that. I could blame the fight, but I didn't look very tired at the end of it. I shrug. "Not every person knows I can actually fight."

"I find it a bit unfair to your opponent. Not everyone has your qualities."

"What qualities?"

He snorts before replying, "You're a hunter. A damn good one."

"It's not like I'm proud of it. I hate doing this, but I need the money."

"What does a university student with a TA job need with all this money? You're making me question so many things, dear Talulla."

I huff. "It's a long story."

Flynn slowly steps closer to me, making no noise. Like a cat. A predator trying to get to its prey. "I have a long time, and I love to listen."

"Don't you have some other girl to bite? It would make it easier to just stake you."

He shakes his head, disappointed by my comeback. "I don't feed like an animal. I have self-restraint."

My eyebrow rises. "Sure, you do."

His face is now only inches away from mine. I should pull away. I should stake him once and for all, even if I'm out of the business. But I can't. The connection I feel is too intense, and it scares me. "You haven't answered my question."

I sigh. "I just..." The words seem to stop coming out. My lips fall into a thin line. Why do I find this embarrassing?

"Just what?"

"I don't like being interrogated. It's not like I'm happy with what I'm doing." My stare lowers to the floor.

"I can tell, and this is why I'd like to know why you're putting yourself into a situation you clearly don't enjoy."

"I need enough money to pay for my tuition and living arrangements. My scholarships aren't enough, and, fuck...even work isn't enough."

"You're telling me Daddy Popescu doesn't have enough funds for his favorite daughter?"

I laugh at his words. "Daddy Popescu definitely doesn't think of me as his favorite daughter. Not anymore, at least."

He tilts his head. "How come?"

"Listen, it's great chatting with you, but I gotta talk to the organizer and go home. I have classes in the morning."

"Let me take you back to your dorm."

"Why would I let you do that? You're a vampire, and

I'm a vampire hunter. I grew up learning every possible way to kill your kind."

"And yet, here you are, doing quite the opposite." He reaches for a strand of my hair and slowly moves it behind my ear. His touch is so soft and smooth. His skin feels silky on mine.

My lips part slightly as his hand gently cups my cheek. "I like to think I'm out of business." I feel paralyzed, completely immobile, as his fingers continue exploring my face and neck with touches so light I feel like I might be dreaming. My eyes close as the silence envelops us.

"But you could rip me to shreds if you wanted to," Flynn states, letting his hand fall from my face, which makes me open my eyes wide.

"I could, but you haven't given me enough reasons to do so. And I don't want to."

"A vampire hunter who doesn't want to kill an abomination? Now, this is a first. Especially after last night."

"I told you. I'm not interested in that life anymore. I'm retired. You're not an abo—You know what, never mind."

I can feel the amusement pouring out of his stare. "It's in your blood," he simply replies.

"Well, then maybe I was adopted because I don't care. I never did. I don't want to do this. Taking unnecessary lives is just wrong."

"Ah, that explains the missing funds. Daddy is very unhappy about your new values, isn't he?"

"I don't want to talk about it," I reply, gathering my things and getting ready to leave the room.

"I apologize for the touchy questions. I didn't mean to upset you. I just want to get to know you."

"It's fine. You didn't know."

"Then tell me something that makes you happy. I can't bear the thought of seeing you leave in a bad mood."

"What's going to make me feel better is seeing Paolo very pleased with my match and telling me I'm almost done repaying my debt." I wave and start pacing toward the door. Flynn remains still behind me, and for a moment, I ponder the idea of forgetting what he told me two minutes ago and leaving without him, pretending he didn't just see me enjoy every second of his hand on my skin. I wonder if he can be as brutal as he is gentle. "Well," I say, looking over my shoulder. "Aren't you gonna take me home? You're my surprise after all, aren't you?"

His mouth curls into a smile. His eyes darken as my words reach his ears. "Unquestionably." He slowly walks to me. "I wouldn't be able to live with myself if something happened to such an innocent girl."

I snort and shake my head at his words. "Shut up."

He places his hand on the small of my back as we walk through the crowd, which is now busy watching another match.

I stop at the front, where I find the organizer of the night, hoping not to gain too much attention.

"Talulla, *bella mia*," Paolo says, getting a reaction from Flynn. "Great, clean match tonight. Well done. You are a natural."

"Thank you, Paolo."

"Ever thought of, you know...doing this the legal way?"

Flynn's arm is now wrapped around my shoulders. "She's not interested."

My eyes snap to the tall blond man beside me. His stare is deadly, his eyes so dark they look like a pool of black coal ready to burst into flames.

"What my friend here is trying to say is that I have other priorities. I do this just for fun and, well, for the money."

Paolo looks at Flynn, then me, and smiles. "Of course,

bella. You know where to find me if you change your mind."

"She won't."

"Flynn, calm down."

Paolo laughs before handing me an envelope. "I wrote down what you made tonight and the balance." He winks at me. "Take him out of here. I don't want to see all the men here crying seeing you got...claimed."

"I am not clai—"

"Talulla, let's go. Paolo is a busy man," Flynn states as he pushes me out the door.

As we step outside, I wiggle free of his embrace. "What was that about? That was absolutely uncalled for."

"It's already enough that I didn't rip anyone's throat for looking at you as if you were an object."

"Because you don't do the same thing?"

"You, my dear Talulla, are definitely not an object."

I roll my eyes at him. "I am not sleeping with you, Flynn."

"You definitely shouldn't sleep with me."

"Then why the possessive act in there?"

"Because every single man in that building was looking at you, and I didn't want to even give them a small reason to try to bother you. That's all."

"I should've called a cab for a ride. Gosh, you're unnerving."

"The witch asked me to be here. Now, stop acting like a child."

"And why would I believe that?"

"I ran into her earlier while I was looking for you. She told me you'd be here and begged me to make sure you'd get home because she was going to do some coven stuff."

"I wonder if they found some new clues," I whisper to myself. "Wait. You were looking for me?"

"As you may know, I am donating some pieces to your

university, but I am also making a deal with the local museum, and I was wondering if you'd like to see their current exhibition when people aren't around. Be my tour guide if you will..."

"Wait, seriously?"

"Yeah, they called me, and after seeing what I am offering, they basically begged me to visit the museum and told me I could go anytime."

"That—are you sure?"

"Talulla, I wouldn't be asking if I didn't want your company."

"I-I don't know what to say."

"How about something like, 'I'd love to escort you to this museum and spend hours upon hours talking about each piece they have displayed.' That would be nice."

"You would want to hear me talk about history for hours?"

"Why not? I can probably tell you if your books are accurate or not. I might have lived a few of those moments."

"Well, this definitely makes me feel a little better about not being able to analyze the Da Vinci sketches, at least."

"What do you mean?"

"Oh, nothing. I'm just blabbering. I'd love to visit the museum with you."

He seems to hesitate for a second, but then a small smile appears on his lips. "Good. I'm looking forward to it."

"Why? You could have anyone, and yet, here you are, trying to gain the attention of a vampire hunter."

"*Retired* vampire hunter. Don't forget that part, Talulla. It makes all the difference."

"I can kill you. I literally killed ten of your kind just last night."

"Actually, if I remember correctly, I helped a bit

there." He snorts. "You absolutely could kill me, and I'm sure that if it ever got to that point, I'd deserve it."

We stop in front of a black car with tinted black windows and all. "Of course, you drive the Batmobile." I roll my eyes.

"I gotta stay in character." He chuckles as he opens the passenger door for me. "I am vengeance, after all."

As we drive off, silence falls once again. I have so many questions, and yet nothing comes out. To try to look busy, I open the envelope and read the remaining balance. Not as good as I thought it would be. I swear under my breath.

"Is everything all right?" Flynn asks, looking at me for a moment, then back at the road.

"Yeah. I just thought I'd be making a better impression tonight."

He shakes his head. His jaw clenches hard as his hands tighten around the steering wheel.

"What?" I ask, narrowing my eyes.

"You're making me want to end your father, and I don't love the idea of ending my chances before I even get the opportunity to take you out."

"It's my fight, not yours. Besides, we're just going to the museum, nothing else."

"You have fought long enough, don't you think?"

I sigh. "Can we talk about something else?"

"What would you like to talk about?"

It takes me a moment to think about something. "What artifact are you most proud of having in your collection? The most valuable one you own."

Flynn's lips lift up. "There are many things I am very delighted to have, but I think the piece I find most precious is Dante Alighieri's diary, where parts of the *Divine Comedy* are written."

"What the fuck?" My jaw drops.

He laughs at my reaction. I am shocked. "Yeah, and I

don't let many people know about it, and I would never give that up."

"Yeah, no shit."

Flynn clicks his tongue. "Language."

"Okay, Grandpa, I didn't take you for such a prude."

"Oh, my sweet, sweet Talulla, I'm definitely not a prude. I should do something about your unnecessary impertinence."

"What are you gonna do? Punish me?"

His eyes darken at my words. He parks the car and immediately rests a hand on my thigh, slowly tightening his grip. "Is that what you want from me?"

"You wish, buddy."

My words die on my lips as he keeps his hand on me and takes a deep breath in, inhaling my scent. "Your self-restraint is truly admirable, little hunter." Then, he releases his grip before getting out of the car and opening the passenger door for me. "I'll walk you to your door."

I simply nod, unable to say anything after what just happened. I was ready to move his hand. I was ready to jump on him...and not to stake him. The way he makes me feel is primal. Ancient. My family might find it inhuman, but I see it as almost...holy.

As we reach my door, I turn to face him. He's already looking at me as if I were the most delicious dessert in existence. As if I were a glass of water and he was a man lost in the desert.

"I'm not gonna invite you in," I manage to say before he pins me with my back against my door.

His lips brush my ear as he says, "I'll pick you up tomorrow evening." I am once again as rigid as a statue, but the feel of his soft lips tickling my skin is the sweetest and most delicious sin.

I clear my throat, trying to regain a normal heartbeat.

"I should be back here around 5:00 p.m. from work. So is 7:00 p.m. okay?"

He nods. "I almost forgot...You might want to tell the Drususes to ask around why one of the pack members was doing business with a witch uptown."

"Who did you see?"

"I suppose it was the alpha's brother. Saw him at the back entrance of a bar called Boozy Business."

"Were you spying on them?"

"I was there for other reasons and just happened to see him. Now, go inside and tell Cassandra all about it."

"They're not in my dorm."

"Yes, they are. Good night, little hunter." Then he disappears into thin air, and I stay there against the wall, trying to understand what just happened.

I unlock my door and find a nervous Cassandra pacing up and down my room. Asmodeus lies on my bed.

"Asmo, at least take off your shoes, for fuck's sake."

"Talulla, you're home, finally," Cassandra says as soon as I drop my bag on the floor.

"What's up?"

"I don't think it's a vampire."

"What is?"

"The killer."

"The vampire I killed confessed to drinking from them, though. How is it not vampires?"

"They want us to think it is, but that is not what killed the werewolves."

"What Cass is trying to cryptically say is that whoever is behind this wanted us to think it was the vampire you killed, but we checked the police reports. We looked at the body again. We made sure to check everything."

"And?"

"The draining happened postmortem."

"I don't understand."

"I think it would be good if Flynn looked at the body. I'm going to see if Set can find a way to get access to the bodies for a bit," Cassandra states as her hand rests under her chin. "He might recognize something we didn't yet take into consideration."

The thought of his lips brushing my ear comes rushing back. "Sure, I guess."

"You're not opposed to the idea of a vampire helping us?"

I shake my head as a smile arises on my face.

Asmodeus laughs. "Did something happen on your ride back home?"

"No, nothing happened."

"You were ready to rip his head off only yesterday, and now, after one car ride, you're okay with him looking at a case we are working on?"

"He helped Set in the past, didn't he? I'm sure he won't mind helping the Drusus coven again." I shrug my shoulders, giving them a simple justification.

"He came looking for you earlier."

I tap my foot on the floor nervously. "He told me."

"What happened on the drive between the warehouse and the dorm?"

"Nothing. He asked—"

"He asked you out."

"No, he just asked if I wanted to visit the local museum with him. No big deal. It's nothing major, and no, I'm not going to sleep with him. It's not even a date or anything like that..."

"Oh my fucking god." Her jaw is on the floor, a mixture of shock and excitement.

"Cass, it's fine."

"Girl, you're fucking glowing. You like him."

"I-It's not possible. It's complicated, and I can't get distracted. It's just a museum visit."

Asmodeus walks toward me. "With a vampire who has been drooling all over you since he saw you the other day. Tal, he's not going anywhere. He's a predator, after all."

"I don't even have the time to breathe between schoolwork, my job, and now the fights."

"Time is all he has, Talulla." Cassandra laughs.

"I-I should not be wanting this. This is wrong on so many levels. I am not letting myself fall for it."

"Love works in mysterious ways," Asmodeus says, looking at me, then at his oblivious best friend.

"He can't feel love, Asmo. He's a vampire." That's exactly why this can't work. It will never work, right? He has no heartbeat. How can he feel things when he has no life in him? He's a predator. That's what I grew up learning. Yet, here I am, questioning the possibility of this even remotely being imaginable.

"I always thought that was only a theory," he replies, and I see my other friend agreeing with him in the corner of my eye.

I shake my head, hoping to do the same with my thoughts. "Let's focus on the medical records. Maybe there's something that could help us get some sort of clue."

"Way to change the subject," Cassandra says, handing me a folder with the printed shots we took the other night.

"Flynn said something before he dropped me off. He said he saw who he thinks is Kaden's brother getting something from a witch."

"What?"

"Yeah, he saw him at the back entrance of a bar called Boozy Business."

"That's random."

"Or too coincidental."

"Okay, I'm sending Set to check the bar and see if he can find out why Scott was there."

"Did you realize how quiet the university has been about these deaths?" Asmo suddenly says.

"Probably for their image," I reply as I continue to scroll through the pages. "Can't ruin the reputation of a highly respected school."

"Hey, do any of you know what this level here refers to?" I point to the chart on one of the pages.

"That's the toxicology report. Apparently, there were traces of acetaminophen in his urine."

"Acetaminophen? Like Tylenol?"

"Yeah, I suppose so."

"Why would a werewolf be sick?" I question as they look at me, just as confused as I am.

"Four werewolves," Cassandra states. "All four werewolves had acetaminophen in their systems."

Then, I tilt my head to the side as I replay my encounter with the vampire last night. He was sniffling. "He was congested too."

"Who was?"

"The vampire I staked the other night. He was sniffling as if he was congested, and he said he did drink from those werewolves."

"What if he caught whatever they had by drinking from them?" I say.

"We have to go tell the coven."

"I'll tell Flynn tomorrow. Maybe he knows about supernatural colds."

"Look at you still thinking about your vampire."

"He's not my vampire."

"Not yet."

Nine

TALULLA

Drifting to sleep doesn't come easily as I continue to think about the werewolves and, well, Flynn. I want to kill him, I do. I also want to listen to him talk about his life and enjoy his eyes on my body. He makes me feel as if I mean something, as if my life is more than just an imposed destiny I don't aspire to achieve. How can a lifeless being make me feel so alive? He's a predator, and he thinks I'm his prey, but I am not. I can't let myself fall for someone who is destined to leave me behind.

It's hard to go on with my day when I'm nervously counting the minutes until I can go back to my dorm to get ready. Another couple of hours with Mr. Wagner, and then I'll be free to think about Flynn. It should be easy enough.

"We're going to go through a lot of papers today, Talulla."

"That's okay. I just have—"

"I hope you're free tonight 'cause it will take us a while."

"Actually, I can't—"

"Start marking, Miss Popescu."

"Yes, sir."

I start working through the papers as fast as I can, looking at the time every five minutes. It's now almost

7:00 p.m., and I'm supposed to be meeting Flynn in a couple of minutes.

"Mr. Wagner?"

"Yes?"

"I finished marking all these, so I should—"

"Great. Start with these, then."

Another pile of papers is presented to me. Great. Now I'm going to have to text a vampire and tell him I can't make it to something I really was looking forward to, and he doesn't seem like the type who likes this kind of disappointment. But that's what I am, aren't I?

Me
Hi, fangs. I hate to do this, but I have to reschedule. I'm stuck marking papers.

Flynn
It's 7:15 p.m., Talulla. You should have been done hours ago.

Me
Academic life is unpredictable. I'm sorry, I really am. I was looking forward to it.

A knock on the door makes me jump out of my seat. No...It can't be him, right? There's no way.

"Office hours are done. Come back tomorrow, whoever you are," Eric yells.

Then the door opens. "I don't think so," Flynn says as he steps into the room.

"Flynn, what are—"

"Mr. Lancaster, I didn't know we had an appointment."

"We don't. I have one with Miss Popescu, though. One she's very late to."

"Flynn—I mean, Mr. Lancaster—I am so sorry," I try

to say, but he interrupts me before I even have the time to apologize.

"See, when Talulla let me know she was still working, it shocked me. Her shift ended two hours ago, yet she's still here."

"Talulla knows what she signed up for when she decided to become my TA. If she wants this life, this is what she needs to learn."

"Mr. Wagner, Miss Popescu was requested to give me a private tour of the local museum. I'm sure you can understand the importance of this matter, as I am a very important investor in this institution. She is also the key to the finalization of my donation."

"She's just a grad student."

"Miss Popescu comes with me now, or the deal is off, Mr. Wagner."

"That seems a little excessive, Flynn."

"I don't think so, Eric."

"Flynn, please," I whisper.

"And another thing. Miss Popescu is in the new documentation I sent this morning, but I am sure you haven't read it yet, so let me enlighten you. She will have free access to view and work on the Da Vinci sketches."

"She doesn't have the qualifications yet."

"She's the only one I truly trust with them, so if she is denied anything, I will take everything back. Have I made myself clear?"

"Crystal."

"Let's go, Talulla. We're already late."

"Y-Yes."

"Talulla, we're gonna have to talk about this...situation tomorrow," Eric whispers to me, thinking Flynn can't hear him as he steps outside to wait for me. Too bad he does, and he comes rushing back in.

"Don't you dare threaten her, Mr. Wagner. I am not

in the mood to clean up your remains." Then, Flynn looks past him at a picture frame on the bookshelf. His head tilts a little before he looks back at Eric.

"Flynn, let him go. This is ridiculous. You're acting like a caveman." A smirk appears on his face, and then he drops Eric's shirt collar.

"Mr. Wagner, look at me," Flynn says before forcing him to look into his eyes. "You're going to forget about this little encounter. I came to pick Talulla up, and you were happy to let her go."

Eric turns to look at me. "Talulla, please. Go. It's already so late."

"Good boy." Flynn finally walks toward me and leads me out of the office.

I remain silent until we reach his car. I don't know how to feel about what just happened. Eric might have overstepped, but Flynn did worse, and for some reason, I don't even have to tell him he did. His locked jaw and blank stare say enough.

"You don't have to play the protector for me, Flynn. You know I can handle myself."

"Haven't you thought that maybe I do it just because I want to?"

"You can't threaten my professors."

"This is why I made sure he wouldn't go around telling anyone what we are," he replies, turning his face toward me and smiling. "Even if I have a slight suspicion that he already does."

"What? That's impossible. I've been so careful."

He shrugs as he opens the passenger door for me. "Maybe he knew from before."

"No, there's no way."

"Well, what I do know is that it might have looked like I compelled him, but I didn't, and he went along with it."

"But why wouldn't he say anything to me?"

"Maybe he just doesn't care."

"How can a human not care when they find out about the existence of the supernatural?"

"You're asking a lot of questions about something I really do not want to talk about tonight."

"It makes no sense," I whisper under my breath, not giving him attention.

"You keep pondering about that. I'm gonna start driving to our date."

"What were you looking at when you were trying to compel him?"

"Hmm?"

"You looked at something."

"Ah, yeah, the picture he keeps in his office. The person beside him...do you know who she is?"

"That's his dead wife." My tone is cold, almost detached.

He snorts. "Okay, no need to say it so morbidly."

"I didn't say it morbidly and wait...did you say date? This is not a date."

"Ah, there she is."

"Is this a date?"

"How about you decide what this is?"

"You call having to endure my crazy obsession with history a date?"

"Any time spent seeing you smile is quality time in my book, so I don't see why it couldn't be."

"Don't people eat on dates?"

"You have no faith in me, kid. I know how a date works, thank you very much."

"Don't call me kid. It's weird," I start saying, crinkling my nose.

"Ever watched *Casablanca*?"

"Are you comparing yourself to Humphrey Bogart now?" I raise an eyebrow at him.

"I would never," he replies, a hand on his heart.

"I'm not dressed for this. Oh god, no, I need to—"

"You need to stop overanalyzing every little thing and just let me take care of it—of you."

"I was raised to overanalyze and dissect every situation in every room I walk into, Flynn. I can't just stop."

"How about a compromise?"

"Shoot."

"You continue to overanalyze and think about your professor knowing what I am and what you are and thinking your attire is not proper when I truly do not give a shit what you are wearing, but when we get to the museum, you turn off your brain and enjoy the night."

"It's just weird that he didn't ever bring it up."

"Almost there, honey bear. You'd better overthink quickly because, in a couple of minutes, this discussion will be over with."

"Did you just call me *honey bear*?" I punch his arm. "Do not ever call me that again."

"If I get to be touched by you, I don't know if I can stop."

"You truly have a death wish."

"Maybe I do."

"You should've let me change."

"You are done overthinking for the night," he says as he parks the car. "We arrived at our destination."

"You are peculiar, you know that?"

"I am whatever you want me to be," he replies before he gets out of the car at vampire speed and opens my door. As he offers his hand to help me out, he lowers his head so he can whisper to me, "And you look absolutely exquisite in jeans and a T-shirt."

As the corners of my lips lift up, I narrow my eyes at him. "You know I can open my own door, right?"

"You are capable of doing many things, Talulla, but

doesn't it feel nice when someone wants to do things for you?"

"Not if that someone is doing it for other reasons."

He shows himself so put together, so sarcastic, but I can see in his body language how much he would love to teach me a lesson, and maybe, just maybe, I'd let him do that. Then his hand lands on the small of my back, and he makes it clear he wants to continue with his planned evening. "You have so many walls up around you. I am only trying to make it clear you don't have to have your barriers up when you're with me."

"We literally met the other day, and you're still a vampire. It's a little hard to just—"

"If you really cared about my...condition, I wouldn't be here now, would I?"

"Touché."

"Let's go. I thought you were hungry," he says as we continue to walk toward the entrance.

"We're at a museum. What kind of food—" I stop in my tracks as I notice what's waiting for me inside the museum. A round table sits right in the middle of the main exhibit, with a white tablecloth draped over it. Plates and candles are set on top. A candlelit dinner in a museum. For me. From a vampire.

"You okay over there?"

"I..." Words can't seem to come out. This is the perfect date. This vampire stranger took one look at me and was able to create the perfect date. "You did this for me?"

"It seems like it now, doesn't it?"

"But why?"

He tilts his head to the side in confusion at my question. "Because I wanted to."

"You could have any woman, dead or alive, and you pick the one who could kill you to do this?"

"Isn't there a saying that goes, 'Keep your friends close and your enemies closer?'"

"Flynn."

He's face-to-face with me, his fingers pulling my chin up so he can look at me when he speaks next. "I really don't want to be your enemy, Talulla. Quite the opposite, really."

"But I'm just...me."

"Just?" He chuckles at my statement. "Your inner strength and will to pursue your dreams even if the person who should love you the most tries to crush them is so inspiring."

"I'm just in survival mode. I've always been in survival mode."

"You use the word *just* a lot. I see you, Talulla. I see how tired you are of showing everyone that you have your place in this world."

"And you got all that from the last few days?"

"I'm very observant."

"Is that your way of saying you've been stalking me?"

The corners of his mouth curl up. "You like it." His piercing stare is making me burn from the inside. I've never felt so wanted by anyone in my entire life, and then this vampire shows up out of nowhere. I can't stop looking at him, just like he can't stop looking at me, and I am scared. I'm so scared of what he's doing to me. Because he did get one thing right, which is that I absolutely like the way he is around me at all times and how I feel about it. I feel alive. With a purpose. A will to continue what I'm doing.

"Okay, fine, let's do this."

Ten

FLYNN

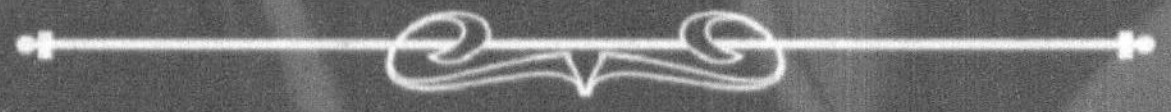

The way her eyes light up as she lets herself go is something I want to witness for the rest of my existence on this planet. I keep my hand on the small of her back, and I feel her body slightly tremble as my thumb moves up and down. She tries to contain herself so much, but it's obvious what she wants, and I'm going to give it to her—on my terms, obviously. Talulla needs to know she can count on me and let herself go. I'll be there, ready to catch her, venerate her, and fuck her.

God, I tremendously want to reach for her jeans and have my way with her. Her panties are already soaked, and all I've been doing is trying not to rip her clothes off. The shirt she's wearing is an oversized band tee, and it's tucked into a nice pair of high-waisted jeans that are doing very naughty things to my imagination right now. If she were to pay a little more attention to my trousers, it would be very apparent how hard I am. I could press my crotch to her back, and she would feel every inch of it. But I won't. Not yet. Not when I can tell how terrified she is of the feelings she has.

Her father made her think she needed to be a weapon, a warrior, a robot with no emotions. Just death. Nothing else. But the reality is that she craves stability, and I want to give her that. I want her to smile just like she is right now as she looks at this place filled with paintings and historical pieces.

"You're staring," Talulla says as we reach the table.

"I'm enjoying the view, that's all."

"I'm a mess, Flynn. You should've let me change."

"If you really want to take those jeans off, I'm not going to stop you."

"Pig."

There it is. The provocation.

I quickly get behind her and do exactly what I said I wouldn't do. I press my pulsing cock against her ass. One hand grips her hip, and the other goes around her throat, keeping her in place. "Here's a reason to call me a pig. Feel what you're doing to me."

"I—"

I move my hips forward to let her feel exactly how hard I am, and her words die on a choking sound. "Cat got your tongue?"

Then she does something I wasn't expecting. She starts moving, creating a deadly friction against my pants. My grip on her throat tightens, and I see how aroused she's getting as her reflection in the glass covering a painting creates its own kind of artwork. Then, as quickly as I started this, I end it. "Take a seat, little hunter. Your food is gonna get cold."

She's still panting as I help her sit, and I get to my seat on the other side of the table. "What are you going to do? Just watch me eat?"

"You worry a little too much about what I do with my spare time."

"Flynn."

"Take the cover off your food, Talulla. I have my own drink right here." I point at a goblet to my right.

I see one of her eyebrows rising. "You drink blood from a glass?"

"Is that so weird?"

"So you really don't feed," she states, as if she needed to confirm that more to herself than anyone else.

"I don't feed from a neck, no."

Tilting her head slightly to the side, she asks, "Why?"

Her neck is exposed now, and usually, I'd feel the need to rip someone to shreds just from seeing their jugular vein so visible. Not with her, though. Do I want to taste her blood? Obviously, I want to. The aroma of it is spellbinding. Her essence calls to me like a siren calls to a sailor, and I am a slave to her song.

"I thought we talked about this already."

"It's just so...peculiar."

Crossing my arms over my chest, I say, "Not everything your daddy told you is the truth, Talulla. Not all vampires want this kind of life."

"Why wouldn't you want to be a vampire? You can live forever, and with your daylight ring, you can live a normal life."

I chuckle at her words. "Normal life." The laughter continues. "Now, that's funny."

"You know what I mean..."

"Do you know what happens when a vampire bites a human?"

"The human feels a state of ecstasy until they either die from the loss of blood or just pass out."

"And they also fall completely under the control of the vampire."

"What do you mean?"

"If I bit you, you'd be doing whatever I tell you to. You'd be unconscious even if you were awake. It's... sickening."

Now she's laughing. "You're telling me you wouldn't want a girl in your bed doing exactly what you want?"

"I want the girl to do what I want on her terms. It's different."

"Elaborate."

"I'm a predator that doesn't want to be one. I want the other person to have an escape at all times. And where's the fun if the other person is following my orders because of the high of the bite?"

"I think I actually understand what you mean. I feel like I'm stuck with an image of myself that doesn't accurately represent who I am. People think I'm supposed to be a certain way, but I'm the complete opposite."

"That's right." The corners of my lips lift into a smile. She sees me for who I am and still wants to spend time with me.

"You are a unique vampire, Flynn Lancaster."

"Just like you are a very unique vampire hunter, Talulla Popescu."

She uncovers her food, and her jaw drops as she sees her favorite meal presented to her. *Mititei* and fries. "What the...how did you know?"

Crazy how big a reaction I get by giving her ground meat rolls. I wonder what her reaction would be if she got another kind of roll... "I might have made a phone call."

"This is perfect." She digs in in no time, and then her jaw drops once again as she sees the sauce I am presenting to her. "And you got me mayo?"

"Cassandra and Asmodeus were very specific about the mayo and no ketchup thing."

"Ketchup ruins everything. Mayo, though...mayo makes everything better."

I smile as she does a little happy dance in her seat before dipping a fry in mayo and bringing it to her mouth. "Noted," I simply reply as I pour myself a generous amount of blood into my glass.

We continue to eat in silence, and then we start exploring the museum. "I can't believe you get to do this."

"Visit a museum with the most beautiful woman I've ever seen? Honestly, I can't believe it either."

She rolls her eyes at me, and, fuck, it's the most exquisite view of her. I want her to do that while I'm so deep inside her that she sees stars. "I meant that you can just pay to have this place to yourself. And stop that."

"Stop what?"

"The compliments, I-It's a lot."

"It's the truth."

She shakes her head profusely. "I'm not that at all."

"I'm pretty sure I know what I'm talking about. I know what I've witnessed in my long life, and you are the most beautiful thing that has ever caught my eye."

"Can I ask you something?"

"Anything."

"How did you get...turned?"

My body goes rigid. I've never told this story to anyone, and it still feels as fresh as if it were yesterday.

"You don't have to tell me. It's okay," she adds as she realizes I've been silent for a little too long.

"I was twenty-five when it happened."

"So young."

"It was during the first war. I was recruited, and I needed money to care for my family. You see—"

"You were married."

"Yes, I was. Does that bother you?"

"How can it bother me? You've been alive for so long. I wasn't expecting you to be a virgin, Flynn."

"I wanted my wife to have the life she deserved, so I went to battle, and as I was ready to call it quits, I got wounded...very badly."

"Oh my god." Talulla's hand covers her open mouth.

"That's when an unknown man came to visit me. It

was the middle of the night. I was in a tent, ready to let myself go, and this man took my arm and bit me. Then he fed me his blood, and the last thing I remember is the sound of my neck breaking."

"Holy shit," she exclaims as her hand covers her mouth. "Did you ever see the vampire again?"

"Vladimir wanted a friend. I learned to forgive him with time, even if I would have preferred to have a choice in how my existence went."

"Is he still in your life?"

"No, he hasn't been for a while."

"And your wife?"

"My wife passed away peacefully with her new husband a while back. She lived a long, happy life—a life she deserved to have."

"That's so wonderful to hear."

"Is it?"

"Yes, even if you weren't there, you were still able to give her what she needed. I think it's beautiful." Talulla's acceptance is remarkable.

I see her true interest in my past, and all I want to do is kiss her. I don't even realize I've moved until my hands end up on her cheeks and I'm lowering myself to her. My lips touch hers so gently, so softly. Then her arms go around my neck, and the kiss intensifies. She's so full of fire——a fire she needs to let out. "I've never looked at it that way. Thank you for letting me see a new side of it."

"You're welcome, Flynn. You suffered a lot, but you still found a way to be a good person."

I chuckle at her words. "That, I certainly am not."

"In your own way."

"Talulla, just like you kill vampires, I have killed many beings. In front of you as well."

"You don't want to, though."

"That doesn't make me a good person."

"It makes you human."

"Is it human that I wanted to rip out Eric's throat earlier?" Yesterday, I kind of planned exactly how I could take him out without anyone even noticing.

"You didn't, though."

"You need to get your red flag detector checked because that's what I am, Talulla. I'm vicious."

"I kill your kind. Aren't you the one who should have his red flag detector checked?"

"Maybe I like pain," I reply with a devilish smirk on my face.

"Maybe I like pain as well. Ever thought of that?"

Oh, fuck me. She did not just say exactly what I wanted to hear her say.

"We'll see about that," I whisper in her ear as we continue our walk around the museum.

"Are you gonna take me home at some point?"

"So impatient. I thought you liked talking about these things," I say, gesturing to all the artifacts around us.

"I do. I just don't want to bore you."

"Is that what you call your soaked panties?"

"They are not!"

"You forget one thing, little hunter," I say from behind her. "My sense of smell is very, very good."

"Asshole."

"I might have to punish you for that."

"I'd like to see you try," she replies, crossing her arms over her chest.

"Let me take you back home then."

The smile that appears on her face is rather demonic. It's too bad she will learn really quickly what I want from her...and it's all of her, all the time.

Eleven

TALULLA

As we reach my dorm, I turn to face him before I unlock the door. "Are you going to come inside?" He's pressed against me, and the pressure of his body on mine is already sending me to places I didn't know existed.

"Do you want me to?" he asks as he brushes a lock of hair off my face.

"Yes."

"Then open the door," he replies, his lips lifted into a smirk.

I do that, and as soon as we walk into my room, he sits on the chair in front of my bed and leans back. He then tilts his head, his smirk never leaving his face. My heart quickens, and I know he can hear it. "Take off your clothes, Talulla."

I raise an eyebrow, and my hands land on my hips. "What makes you think I'm going to do that?"

"Because I asked you to, and more importantly, because you want to."

"You're just going to stare at me while I do this all on my own?"

"Yes," he says, crossing his legs. "I think I will do just that."

"Don't you want to help?"

"So impertinent."

That comment makes me laugh out loud. "What are you going to do about it?"

He reaches me so fast I almost don't realize it until he whispers on my lips, "You're going to take off your clothes, and you're going to touch yourself, Talulla."

"Flynn—" is all I'm able to say before he cups my core and gives it a little squeeze.

"Do as I say, Talulla."

The corners of my mouth lift up as I slowly take off every piece of clothing I'm wearing. He's back on the chair, enjoying the show. Death Cab for Cutie shirt? Off. Super tight blue jeans? Slowly coming off as well.

Flynn's eyes are locked onto my skin and my movements, his Adam's apple going up and down as he swallows air. I'm down to my bra and lacy thong when Flynn suddenly gets up again and paces toward me. "Turn." His spicy, vanilla-scented cologne becomes stronger and stronger as he moves. I don't know what's making me dizzier, the perfume or *him*.

I do as he says, and his velvety fingers leave a trail of shivers down my spine. He unhooks the bra, and I let it fall as his lips gently caress the nape of my neck. "Do you know how hard it is not to fuck you right now?"

"Then do it." My voice comes out as barely a whisper.

He kneels, leaving kisses down my thighs. Then, he proceeds to slowly pull my thong off. "Your skin, the way you talk and walk, your fucking smell..." He sighs. "You're intoxicating. Addicting."

"Like a drug?"

"Exactly like a drug."

"That seems unhealthy." I could tell him just how much he does that to me too, but I'm sure no words are needed when I've already melted into a puddle.

"It might be, but I don't plan on changing a single thing about it." He lets me turn to face him, still on his knees, now looking up at me. This image of Flynn on his knees venerating me is something I did not think was possible.

"Liking what you see?" I ask, brushing his hair back with my hand.

"Everything. I'm liking everything," Flynn replies, grabbing my hand and positioning it between my legs. "Now, you're going to lie on your bed and make yourself come."

"Are you going to watch me?"

"Yes, I am."

My heartbeat quickens as I slowly back up to the bed. He walks back to the chair and sits down, making himself comfortable to enjoy his private show. Flynn's icy-gray eyes lock with mine as I slide my hand between my legs. I can already feel the slickness dripping from my core. I start circling my clit, and my hips move in response as I try to find the perfect pace. Biting my lower lip, I close my eyes as I slide a finger inside me. A soft moan escapes my mouth, and my eyes go back to Flynn. He's inhaling my scent, and his lips curl into a smile as I continue to fasten the pace. He's so focused on me, so I give him a little show, making my moans louder as I get closer and closer to my climax. Then, as I pinch one of my nipples, I add another finger and continue to thrust in and out of me. I'm panting when I feel my orgasm arrive. "Flynn, I'm coming," I say in a soft voice, followed by a loud moan and spasms of pleasure.

He's between my legs in less than a second, his tongue sliding inside me as I come down from my extreme state of ecstasy. Then the wave of pleasure comes back, and I move my hips as he continues to drink from me.

"Good girl," he says, leaving a kiss on my clit before coming back up and licking his lips. "Divine," he growls.

"Did you enjoy the show?"

"Very much." He smiles. "Did you enjoy coming for me?"

"Very much."

"Good." His lips brush mine before he adds, "Because that was the last time someone else's hand touches your skin."

"What?"

"I am going to make you come from now on. Only me, Talulla. No one else. Not even yourself unless I tell you to."

"That is a little ridi—"

"You come when I say you come, Talulla."

"How will you know if I touch myself when you're not around?"

"Because I trust you."

My eyes widen at the quick response. "That is a lot of trust you're giving me, Flynn."

"Besides, I would be able to smell it on you."

"And what happens if I slip?"

"In that case, you're going to suffer the consequences."

"Are you going to finally punish me?"

"Yes, I will."

"And what about now?" I say as my fingers circle my clit once again. "Aren't you going to fuck me?"

"It seems like you want to get punished, and my cock is a reward," he says, grabbing my hand and positioning it above my head. He then lowers his body on top of mine. "Enjoy your last night alone, Talulla, because when you wake up tomorrow morning, you're going to be mine."

"What if I don't want that?"

"You should have thought about that before you walked in front of me and became my entire world."

"Does that mean you're also going to be mine?"

"I've been yours since that very day, Talulla."

Twelve

TALULLA

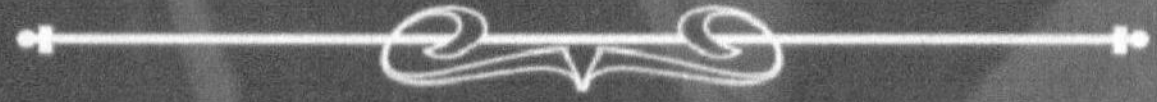

As I walk toward my classes the morning after, I still replay the past night in my head.

I'm already yours, Talulla.

How can I already feel so intensely about someone I'm supposed to want dead?

The walk to Mr. Wagner's office is a little more nerve-racking than usual, but as soon as Eric sees me, he lets me come in and take a seat.

"I was worried I wasn't going to see you today, Talulla," he says, taking off his reading glasses and putting them down on his desk.

"We had class, and I always help you after. Why wouldn't I be here?"

He snorts before replying very quickly to my question. "Because of last night's unfortunate discussion."

"That was uncalled for. I am so sorry, professor."

"You're apologizing for him?"

"I—yes. He tends to be a little intense."

"Talulla, you're a vampire hunter, and he's a vampire."

My eyes widen as his words settle in my brain. He does know what I am. He knows what Flynn is as well. "I..." Getting the words out seems to be harder than expected.

"I've known since your first day. You're safe."

"Why didn't you tell me?"

Eric moves his chair right in front of mine, and as he sits down, he says, "I didn't want to worry you. I know how hard it is to keep everything hidden. I understand how hard it is to live your life, and I didn't want to make you think I was a threat."

"And are you?"

"What?" His head tilts a little to the side.

"A threat. Are you a threat?" I repeat, my tone rising slightly. I've been his assistant for a long time, and not even once have I had even the slightest suspicion he knew what I was—what I am. I, one of the deadliest people on the planet, trained to analyze and work under pressure, didn't realize my own professor knew my secret. I feel like this would disappoint my father even more if he knew.

He laughs at my question. "I think we both know I am no match for you, Flynn, or anyone else from your *world*."

"That isn't a real answer, Professor."

"I would never be a threat to you. I fully understand your struggles, and I wish I could help you more with your...family situation."

"Thank you. I appreciate you saying that. I'm dealing with it. It's all good."

"Is it?"

My head tilts a little. "Yes, I work at a gym a few nights a week." It's not entirely a lie. "It's not much, but it gets me what I need."

"Good, I'm glad," he says before going back to his papers. "But please talk to me if you ever need more. I might not be able to do much as a professor, but as a friend, I can lend you some money."

"I truly appreciate the thought, but I know how much you make, and you also can barely make ends meet at the end of the month. It's okay, really. I'm doing okay."

"Okay, I'll drop it for now, but my door is always open."

"Thank you, really." Then I look past him and see the picture Flynn was looking at last night, and the question comes too naturally. "Professor," I start. "How do you know about the supernatural?"

Eric looks at me and then turns to look at the picture I'm staring at, his eyes widening for a split second. "My late wife," he says, clearing his throat. "She did a study on the existence of the supernatural, and, well, she found it." He starts fidgeting with his bracelet. "And this is how your *friend* wasn't able to compel me last night."

"A charmed bracelet?"

"Yeah, my wife gave it to me a bit before she got into the accident. I never take it off. I feel like it's a way to keep her with me, you know..."

"Yes, I understand."

"Well, enough of this," he says, clearing his throat once more. His voice is trembling now. "Now, back to work."

The following hours fly by, and I don't even realize how late it is until I get to my dorm and two witches and a vampire are waiting for me inside.

"Well, I didn't know my room would get this crowded on a fine Friday evening."

Flynn keeps his hands interlocked behind his back as his eyes burn into mine, his tongue tracing his soft lips. I can almost imagine them on mine. Just the thought of it makes me nearly fall to my knees, and he knows it. He knows the effect he has on me, just like I know the effect I have on him, even if I still wonder why this is happening. His smile grows, and as I stare at his now poking fangs, I truly wonder how they would feel sinking into my flesh.

Asmodeus clears his throat, and I almost jump at the sound of it, my head snapping in his and Cass's direction.

Cassandra's eyes are wide open, probably because of the little staring competition Flynn and I had going on, and with good reason. It's one thing to discuss the situation, but it's another to see it with her own eyes. A vampire hunter with a vampire—it's just unheard of. But that's the thing, isn't it? I don't know if what we feel is only momentary or if it's going to last.

"Nicely done, Flynn." Asmodeus chuckles before Cassandra's elbow ends up in his stomach. "Ouch, Cass."

Flynn hasn't said a word, yet I know how much he wants my friends gone. But if they're here, there's a reason. The vampire cracks a smile and makes sure to show his fangs to Asmo. It's his way of saying, "Don't piss me off."

"Okay, well, what's up? Why are you all here?"

"Right," Cassandra starts before scrolling on her phone to find something. "We went back to the bodies with Set and did some tests."

I'm back in detective mode. "Okay?"

"The werewolves took a potion before they died."

"A potion?"

"Yes, something that made them feel sick and then slowly killed them."

"Jesus fuck."

"Language," Flynn finally speaks.

I raise one eyebrow as I turn to look at him once more. "What is it with you and swearing?"

"I like swearing," he replies before getting close to my ear. "On certain occasions."

"Okay, can we focus here for a moment?" Cassandra snaps her fingers. "Then you two can go on with your sex session."

"There's not gonna be—" I get interrupted right away by Flynn's hand on my mouth. *Rude. And kinda hot. Dammit, Talulla, focus.*

Asmodeus continues for Cassandra. "There's a pissed witch around, and we need to find out why."

Flynn tilts his head. "It's not Evanora."

"We weren't implying it was her." Cassandra crosses her arms over her chest. "And it's not even the witch who dealt with Scott. Set went to check on her. The pack bought some protection potions. Nothing sketchy at all, unfortunately."

"Then I don't understand why we're all still here," I reply, grabbing a denim jacket and heading for the door.

"Actually," Flynn interrupts me, and I turn to look at him, his icy-gray eyes penetrating mine. "I had a different plan for us this evening."

"Oh?"

Cassandra and Flynn look at each other as if they're having their own conversation, which is truly starting to get old. The fact that they clearly talk behind my back pisses me off. "Right, yes, of course. How could I forget? You guys go. We will keep you posted."

"Wait, what?"

"You heard me," Cassandra replies.

"What is happening?"

"What's happening is that you're going to get ready to have a nice evening out with a vampire," my witch friend replies, tying her long, black hair in a high ponytail before she heads toward the exit.

My hands are up in the air. "I'm so confused right now."

"Just have fun and don't think about anything."

"Listen to your friend. She's a clever one," Flynn adds.

"I—"

She doesn't even let me finish. She opens my door and steps outside. "Bye! I'll send updates, I promise."

"Bye."

FLYNN

I reach for her arm and pull her to me. I've been wanting to throw her onto the bed and fuck her since she got to her room.

"Are you going to tell me what's happening?"

"Nope."

"Where are you taking me?"

"You're gonna have to get ready to find out." I look at my watch. "You have about forty minutes. Then we have to hit the road."

"Is this your plan for making me yours?"

My mouth curls into a devilish smirk. I make sure she sees my eyes because she clearly forgot a little detail about last night, and I have to make sure she says it loud and clear. I move so quickly she doesn't even realize it until her back hits the wall, my hand making sure she doesn't hit her head from the impact. My body presses against hers. Her warm scent mixed with flowers and...strawberries? I can't get over it. This is all I need for the rest of my existence. "Wasn't I clear enough last night?" I whisper in her ear, and I can almost feel her core throb as my voice reaches her skin.

"You said..." she starts, but is unable to finish.

"Yes, what did I say before I left last night?"

"That you're mine."

"Before that, you little brat. Don't disappoint me. Come on, you can say it."

"I'm not gonna say it, Flynn."

"You've gotta learn how to follow orders, or you won't get your reward."

"I grew up following orders. What makes you think

I'm going to enjoy following yours?"

"Because I am not going to make you give up on your dreams."

"Flynn..."

Lifting up her chin with my fingers, I rest my lips on hers. It's soft and gentle, and her warm skin is making me feel the sweet pain of hunger in my throat. "Whatever you want, it's yours. I'm going to make sure you have it."

Then I see a single tear trailing down her cheek, and I force myself not to lick it off. But I do catch it with my thumb. She needs reassurance. She needs someone to remind her that she is strong and capable of getting what she wants. Her eyes close as my fingers touch her skin. I have the same effect on her that she has on me, and I didn't think this feeling was possible for me—not like this, not anymore. Not after all the pain I've felt and caused over the years. She is here, capable of ending me at any moment, yet she shows herself as the most vulnerable being on this earth, for me. Talulla's stubborn personality, her anger against the world, just falls when she's with me. She can be herself and let herself go.

"I'm yours, Flynn," she finally speaks. Her voice is so soft I can barely hear it. "You already knew that."

"Go get changed. I have a big surprise for you."

"Any hints on what I should wear?"

The corners of my lips lift up. "Comfortable shoes—maybe sneakers—a T-shirt, and I don't know, something short."

"You're in a suit, and you want me to wear what I wear every day?"

"First of all..." I take the blazer off, showing the tight black T-shirt I'm wearing underneath. "I'm clearly wearing casual attire."

"You call your brand clothes casual?"

"I didn't think you disliked my wardrobe."

"I..." She sighs. "I like what you wear. I just feel like I have nothing in comparison."

My head tilts slightly. "I like what you wear, Talulla. You don't have to change for me. It's a casual place we're going to, and the lights will be off most of the time anyway, so you could be naked, and no one would know." I smile. "Well, I would definitely know."

"Okay, well, I'm not going to wear another band shirt. I'm sorry to disappoint you, but I have to attempt to look the part if I have to bring a model-looking vampire everywhere."

I pretend I didn't hear or notice that the girl wears this band's shirts all the time. It's too bad she's in for a real surprise tonight. "Model-looking?"

"You!" she screams into her hands. "You look very good right now, and I don't."

"You're kidding me, right?"

"No, I am not."

"Where is the confident Talulla who knocked out a seven-foot-tall man in less than a minute?"

"That's different. You're *you*," she replies, gesturing at me.

"Let me make myself very clear right now." My hand is now around her throat. "I only want you, Talulla, as crazy as it might sound. I want to be around you. I want you to be around me. You make me feel alive, and no one has ever done that since I was turned."

"A miniskirt will do, then?"

I lick her lips as my hardening cock presses to her core. "That'll do."

Thirteen

TALULLA

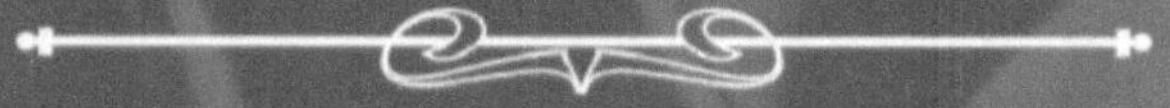

I quickly get to the bathroom, take the fastest shower of my life, and get ready. For once in my life, I'm excited for something I don't know about. I'm excited to go on an adventure with my own personal vampire. Yes, mine. All mine. That model-looking blondie is all mine, and I can't believe it. I feel like a ten-year-old girl getting a puppy.

I put on a lacy bra, making sure it's the good one with the wire under my breasts. I don't need these girls to go anywhere. I choose a matching lacy thong, a stretchy black miniskirt, and a tight, black crop tank top that shows off my assets very, very well. Easy, comfortable, and basically the only thing I own that, in the dark, could match his perfect closet.

I can't believe he's wearing a T-shirt and not one of his usual silk shirts. A tight one too. I can see his abs through it. It's absurd. I apply a quick wing of eyeliner and mascara, and I'm ready to go.

As I get out of the bathroom, his eyes darken right away. His icy eyes are now the color of the abyss—hungry. And it's because of me. "Good enough?"

"You're fucking perfect." He sighs, scratching his throat. "So fucking perfect."

"Language, Mr. Lancaster."

He groans at the formal title, and then his lips are on mine. Not gentle anymore. Hungry and wanting everything. "Say it again, and I'm gonna fuck you until you can't walk anymore."

"You're saying it as if it's a bad thing."

"I'd make it hurt."

"Again, you're saying it as if it's a bad thing, Mr. Lancaster. It really isn't."

I swear I hear him growl. "Let's go. I don't want to be late."

He walks me toward the door, and after it's locked, we walk to the parking lot. His hand never leaves the small of my back. As we reach his car, his eyes widen, and he turns to see who's behind us.

"Flynn Lancaster," a woman's voice says, and I turn to look as well. "What a pleasure to see you."

"Monica Lazar. I wish I could say the pleasure is mine, but it really isn't," Flynn replies, tightening his grip on me. My eyes shoot in his direction, but he's fixated on the woman. His jaw is so tight I'm worried he might break his teeth.

"And you must be Talulla," the woman says to me. She's easily in her mid-thirties, with auburn hair, and her skin is so perfect it almost looks retouched. She's beautiful, confident, and a witch.

"Lazar, that's a—"

"Romanian name, yes. Your family and I go way back."

"Funny. I don't recall my father ever mentioning your name."

"Does Emil know what you've been up to?"

I raise an eyebrow at her as I cross my arms over my chest. "I don't think that's any of your concern."

"It is when you play with my toys."

"Excuse me?" I reply. As I try to make a move on her, Flynn's hand grabs me and holds me back. "And why are you stopping me?" I turn to him, making sure she can see how angry I am.

"Because I really don't want to clean up a murder scene tonight."

I sigh. "Fine," I say, and I hear her chuckle. I swear this witch clearly wants to die tonight.

"Monica, what the hell do you want?"

"I'm here visiting a friend. I truly had no idea I would have the fortune of seeing your pretty face around. Thought you were back in London."

"Then go on. Go see your friend. We have somewhere to be."

"So nice to meet you, Talulla. You look just like your dad. Don't worry, your secret is safe with me. But when Flynn's...dominant ways become too much for you, come look for me. I'll take care of him."

"You are a dead witc—" Flynn's hand covers my mouth before I can even finish my statement.

She laughs once again, and then she walks away. Only then do Flynn's shoulders relax, and he lets me go.

"Who the fuck is that?"

"That"—he points at the woman in the distance—"is a terrible mistake."

"Ex?"

"I don't even want to call her that. She likes to play with people's minds, and that is why I stopped you."

"What do you mean?"

"She makes you believe things that aren't real. She called me a toy because that's what I was to her. I didn't even know what was happening half of the time."

"What the—"

"Yeah, she doesn't love other supernatural creatures, especially men."

I can sense the topic is painful, so I let it go as he

opens the passenger door for me. Then he quickly gets to his side, and we drive off.

"I'm gonna have the Drusus coven look into her," I say as I pick up my phone.

"What?"

"You said it, Flynn. She doesn't like supernatural beings, and coincidentally enough, there is a potion going around killing them."

"It's too easy."

"I'm still gonna tell them," I reply, sending a quick text to Cassandra.

"You're angry."

"Yeah, well, I didn't really imagine meeting any of your exes."

"Let me make myself very clear about one thing," he says as he parks the car outside a venue. I didn't even realize we got to our destination because I was too focused on thinking about all the ways I could have strangled that woman. "I have no exes aside from my late wife."

"What?"

"You heard me."

"You're telling me you haven't been with anyone since your wife? Because, based on what the witch said, she clearly got to see you with no clothes on."

"I'm not saying I haven't had *encounters*."

"You can say sex, Flynn. I'm not expecting you to be a saint. I'm not either."

"Do not remind me of that." He sighs—or growls. It's truly a sound that mixes both. "What I'm trying to tell you is that since my wife, I haven't let myself fall for anyone. Monica tried. I thought I was feeling things, but it was all a lie. All her doing."

"You're telling me you haven't dated anyone until... now?"

"That is exactly what I am telling you."

Why me, then? Why this? I have so many questions, and I don't know if I am ready to hear the possible answers. "I don't even know what to say."

"Good, because it's time for the first surprise of the night."

"First? There's a second?"

"There is. You'll find out about it very soon, and if you're a good girl, you'll get a third one later."

God, I hope one of these is his cock because if he doesn't fuck me tonight, I might have to pull out a dildo and release the tension I've got going on right now.

He takes an envelope out of his blazer's pocket and says, "Here," and he gives it to me. It's two front-row tickets to tonight's Death Cab for Cutie concert. A concert I didn't even want to think about, because I knew that with everything happening, I couldn't possibly afford it.

"How did you know?"

"You wear their merch pretty often. It really wasn't a hard one."

"Okay, but how the hell did you know they were playing tonight?"

"I might be an old vampire, but I am capable of Googling."

"I can't believe it."

"You okay?" Flynn asks as another tear falls down my cheek. I never cry, and yet this man has picked up two tears in the last couple of hours.

"I'm surprised, that's all," I reply. "This is a dream, and I'm worried I'm going to wake up at any second."

His lips press against mine. "You're not dreaming. Now, time for another surprise."

"Already?"

"It's inside." His lips curl up. "Take off your panties."

"What?"

"You heard me."

"Flynn, no, I can't..."

"Yes, you absolutely can and will if you want a nice reward."

"What happens if I don't do it?"

"You get punished."

"See, when you say it like that, it doesn't seem like such a bad thing."

His hand grabs my throat and tightens slightly. "You dirty, dirty girl, of course you wanna get spanked."

"What's the reward?"

"A surprise."

"I don't think I like surprises anymore."

"That's a lie. Take off your panties, Talulla. Let me give you something you won't forget."

"Confident much?"

"Very."

I do as he asks. I slide off the lacy thong I'm wearing and place it in his open hand. Then, I make sure my skirt is in place. "Am I ever going to see those again?"

"Maybe."

"I'm on a tight budget. I can't lose underwear like that."

He shakes his head and then places the thong inside the pocket of his blazer. "Let's go, sweetheart. We've got a concert to watch."

I smile as he gets to my door and walks me to the entrance of the venue. We get to our spot, right at the front, and as I lean on the barricade, Flynn positions himself behind me, caging me in. People start filling up the space, and as the lights go dark, his hands, which until now were on either side of the barricade and keeping me in place, are now on my stomach, pressing my rear to his crotch, and right between my legs. "Flynn, someone will see us."

"No one will see anything. I'm going to make sure of it."

"But there are people around."

"You and all of them will be very busy watching a concert. I'm just making sure you get the experience you deserve."

"You are something else, Flynn Lancaster."

"I'm completely yours, Talulla Popescu." As he says that, his index finger flicks my clit, and I fight the urge to moan. "Shh, you don't want them to hear you now, do you?"

The band comes out, and as the singing begins, I get lost in a trance, listening to their music. Flynn's hand is just there, resting, and as I sing the words to the song, I rest my head on his shoulder and let myself go. That's when Flynn starts his predatory moves. His vanilla cologne is all I can smell in this room full of half-drunk and half-stoned people. His velvety fingers start circling my clit softly, getting coated in me.

His hand comes up at a reaching distance of my mouth before he whispers in my ear, "Open your mouth and lick."

I do as he says, and as I taste myself on him, I moan in ecstasy as the music continues. Then his fingers are back where they belong—right on my wet pussy. He moves with the music, following a painful, slow rhythm, and then he finally inserts two fingers inside. The initial stretch stings for only a moment before it becomes full pleasure.

"Flynn, oh my god."

"Having fun, little hunter?"

"You need..." I pant before continuing. "To find a new pet name. I really don't like that one."

"Babe? Darling? Love? I'll call you whatever you want me to, Talulla," he whispers as he continues to fuck me with his hand. Everyone around us is completely unaware of how close to orgasm I am.

"I'm so close."

"I can feel it, Talulla. Your cunt is trying to keep me inside the more I fuck it."

"I—" A wave of pleasure comes rushing, and as I climax, Flynn barely has the time to cover my mouth before I close my eyes and a moan escapes my lips. My entire body goes limp as I get down from the high of what just happened, but Flynn keeps me up, making sure I'm okay. I hold on to the barricade and try to regain a decent breath as we continue to watch the band play, as if he didn't just rock my world two minutes ago.

The show is incredible, and I feel like this state of serenity can't be topped by anything else right now. I'm watching my favorite band play, and the man holding on to me is worshipping every part of my being. I didn't think feeling all this was possible. It's not just lust or horniness or wanting affection. It's everything. I feel like I'm his whole world, and he's a satellite that has no choice but to gravitate around me to stay alive.

"Having a good time?" Flynn asks as he wraps his arms around me.

"The best night of my life."

He chuckles before leaving a kiss on my temple. "Well, I hope it will be just as good when I'm done fucking you later."

I look up at him, and I bring his face down to mine. I crush my lips on his, and I turn my body toward him, not caring about anything else anymore. Concert? Done.

People around us? Gone.

My father's disappointment? Forgotten.

This right here is all I can think about. It's only Flynn and me, and nothing else around us. I can't explain how, but in such a small amount of time, this man has seen me for who and what I am, and he's still here, wanting to spend time with me. "How about we turn that later into now? They're basically done playing anyway."

I feel his lips lifting into a smile as he continues to kiss me. "Your place or mine?"

I haven't been to his apartment yet, and I feel like his offering it as an option is a way of letting me in. "Yours."

He grabs my hand, and with that, we make our way out of the venue so quickly that I don't even realize we already are in the car, leaving the parking lot.

"Someone is in a rush," I jokingly say.

"I don't want you to consider every possible reason why you shouldn't be doing this."

"I'm not going to change my mind, Flynn."

"Good."

Fourteen

TALULLA

Flynn instantly cups my core as he parks his car, and at the touch, my hips start moving instinctively. We're in front of his building, and the way I feel right now is making me forget how wrong all this truly is. A vampire and a vampire hunter? This situation is so comical, yet here we are, incapable of keeping our hands off each other.

"So very greedy." He tightens his grip. My heart is beating faster than ever before. "Do you think I'll give you what you want so easily? So quickly?"

"Fine, whatever. I don't need this."

"Did you forget the part where I can smell your delicious desire? The part where just a few moments ago you were riding my hand as if it were the last thing you were going to do on this planet?"

My mouth shuts, and his lips curl up. "You want a minute to collect yourself? Take it, because as soon as you're in my bed, you're going to beg me to fuck you," he whispers in my ear before nibbling my lobe, forcing a moan out of me.

"Cocky much?"

"I will ruin you."

"Ruin me. Ruin every other man for me."

"There won't be any other man, Talulla." His words are a sweet caress that turns into a warning. "And when

I'm done with you, the moon won't be the satellite circling around you. I will be." Then he leaves a trail of soft kisses on my neck, making my back arch in return. He's barely touching me, and I'm already going insane.

"If you'll be my satellite," I start saying between heavy breaths, "I'll be your entire world."

He chuckles at my comeback. "My dear Talulla, you already are."

We reach a condo building that is unsurprisingly very close to campus.

A small laugh comes out of me. "Of course you've been this close the entire time."

"Well, I am definitely happy about the benefits of being adjacent to this institution."

"Oh yes, Bear Creek U has its charm. It's true."

His smirk is devilish before he crushes his lips on mine. "Are you sure you want this?" His tone is low and husky, the pure timbre of lust.

I look at his gray eyes, now a dark shade that resembles a deep abyss. "Positive."

Then we're out of the car and into the building. We remain in silence as we get into the elevator, and he hits the button for the sixth floor.

The light flashes. One. Two. Three. Four. Five. Six.

Finally.

He rests his hand on the small of my back as he guides me out of the elevator and to his living arrangements. A penthouse, of course. My eyes still widen because even if it's obvious how wealthy this vampire is, seeing it, touching it, and smelling it is different.

"You okay?"

"Yeah, I'm just—" *Nervous as fuck for some reason.* "You're filthy rich, aren't you?"

He chuckles. "I had time to save up." His lips rest on my temple. "I'm going to take care of you, Talulla. This is all I want."

Then we are inside his apartment, and all I can think of is how much I want to take care of him. As soon as the door is closed behind him, I drop to my knees and reach for his belt. Flynn's hand grabs my wrists and stops me, paralyzing me in place. My eyes widen as I remain in silence. Did I just blow it?

"Before I let your filthy mouth wrap around my cock, I need you to understand one thing," he starts saying, his grip firm, just like his body posture.

"What is it?" I manage to ask, with a voice low and full of heavy breaths.

"Here, I'm in charge."

"But—"

"No buts, Talulla. You follow my orders, and you get exactly what you want in return. It's that simple."

I raise an eyebrow at him, looking for a challenge. "Will you spank me if I don't?"

"Hmm." He wraps a hand around my throat and forces me to look up at him. The act is so arousing I can feel the wetness increasing right between my legs, and I know he can smell it. "You might get spanked in any case."

"I've been bad after all." Who am I? Who is this creature coming out of me, wanting to feel his delicious pain on my skin? He would make it feel so good.

"Pick a safe word, little hunter, and then you get to open that mouth of yours and let me fuck it."

Yup, I am definitely sitting in a puddle of my own desire.

A safe word. I never really thought about it. What do

people usually pick? Red? Is that too common? But what if—"*Rosu.*"

The corners of his mouth lift into a smile. "So fitting. Say it again."

"*Rosu,*" I repeat, the Romanian accent slipping in.

He inhales. "Fuck, you smell good." Then he releases my wrists and lets me get back to his pants. I unbuckle his belt, unbutton his trousers, and slowly pull the elastic of his boxers down, and what I see hidden is the most exquisite cock I've ever witnessed. Did I imagine the vampire to be...gifted? Yes, I did, but this? He's so big and girthy. I know it will be painful moving inside me. But when I adjust to it, fuck, it will feel so perfect. He must see my hesitation because the sentence that follows is exactly the little push I need.

"You can take it, little hunter. You can do anything."

With those words, I wrap my hands around his length, and then my mouth is on the head of it before going down, down to the base. It hits the back of my throat, and as I constrict around it, I come back up for air. I create a steady rhythm, and when he grabs my head to keep me in place, I know I'm doing exactly what he likes.

"I knew you'd feel good, but this is so much better than my imagination." His hips are now starting to move and meet my movements, creating a deeper and deeper thrust. "There, just like that. Good girl. You take me so well."

The praise sends me into a state of euphoria I've never felt before. I've had sex, and with supernatural creatures as well, but this? Everything I've had before can't even come close to this. What I feel goes beyond the simple act of pleasure. It's pure life. Moans come out of me as he continues with his dirty talk. One of my hands grabs his ass cheek while the other plays with his balls as I force him to get even deeper.

"Fuck." His movements get even faster and more desperate, and as he continues to throw praises and swear words, he coats my throat with his cum and lets me drink him until the last drop. His hand holds me firmly in place.

When I release his cock, he picks me up quickly and throws me on the bed, which makes me chuckle. His look is dark—predatory.

"That was astounding." His voice is husky as he starts pumping his cock. He's already hard again. Holy shit, I might be in trouble. "Take off your clothes and lie on your back."

I take my time slipping the miniskirt off, turning so that he can see my ass as I bend down and let the piece of fabric fall to the floor. Then the crop top comes off. I'm only in my lacy bra. Turning, I see Flynn taking off his T-shirt, showing off his absolutely perfect body. So pure and deadly at the same time. He's mouthwatering, and he only sees me. "You're a vision," he says in a low voice, the corners of his mouth lifted up.

"I could say the same thing about you," I manage to reply, unhooking my bra and letting it fall to the floor. Then I lie on the bed, just as he asked me to.

Flynn's eyes darken at the sight of me following his orders. I've never considered myself a submissive creature, but for some reason, here, like this, with him, it makes sense. Somewhere deep inside me, there's a voice that constantly repeats that he won't hurt me, that I can trust him, that what we are is completely right and sacred.

He gets on top of me, pinning me to the mattress with part of his weight, his hard length pressed against my belly. I can't help but stay silent as he reaches for something inside his nightstand, opening the drawer and picking out a tie. "Give me your wrists," he orders, and I happily oblige.

Shivers travel up and down my body as his velvety

fingers work their way around my wrists, securing them to the headboard. I could easily rip the fabric off and wiggle myself free—he knows it too—but I truly don't want to. I want Flynn to take every part of me and make them his. Because the reality is that I was feeling like a scared animal before I met him, but now? Now, I am ready to be tamed by the most dangerous predator that walks this earth—a vampire.

My vampire.

"Remember, you can stop this at any time." His eyes are on me, his serious expression doing something to me.

I nod. "I know."

His eyes fall to my breasts, my nipples now so hard they almost hurt. He cups them gently, and then, as he starts flicking one nipple with one hand, he brings his mouth to the other. I moan as he starts nibbling and sucking me.

"Your tits are perfect, you know that? So perfect."

I giggle as he continues to play with them. "They're pretty heavy, not gonna lie," I say between moans.

"So perfect." He goes from one boob to the other, giving equal attention to both. I'm already so close to coming just from this, from him sucking my nipples so hard the sting makes my pussy throb in pleasure. The heat between my legs now is so strong it could light its own fire. Right before I'm about to come, he stops his torturous game.

"No, no. Please come back."

"I have a better idea, little hunter." Then he's down between my legs. "Do you know how hard it is to be around you and smell your constant desire?"

"Are you going to act on your words or just stay there drooling over me?"

He shakes his head. "You need to be taught a lesson, Talulla." Then he does something that no one has ever done to me. His hand goes up in the air and comes down onto my skin. Hard. He slaps my folds, hitting my clit just right. The quick sting turns into a heating pleasure right after, and I can't help but moan at the action.

I jerk my hips up, trying to get him to do it again. "So greedy."

"Touch me, Flynn."

Another slap, and my moan is even louder. "Wrong request. Try again."

"Please touch me."

Slap. "You can do better than that, little hunter."

"Touch me, sir. Please touch me, eat me, fuck me."

He growls as I continue to beg. "There you go," he says before dipping his head between my legs. One hand presses on my lower belly while the other parts my opening, preparing me for his tongue.

He slides inside and starts licking and sucking while also keeping me in place. The way his tongue moves sends electric waves throughout my entire body, and then, when I think it can't get any better, he slides one finger inside as his mouth nibbles and sucks on my clit.

"Oh my god," I moan as my orgasm starts to build.

"No one has ever called me a god, but I'll take it," he grunts, his voice blowing right on my core as he continues to thrust in and out.

"Please don't stop," I say as my orgasm gets closer and closer.

Then, as I'm about to explode, he slides his finger out and gets off the bed.

"What the fuck?" I yell.

He chuckles as he brings his fingers to his mouth, licking my wetness clean. "I told you I'd punish you, didn't I?"

"Are you serious?" I groan, trying to get my hands free.

"Now, now, don't be a brat. I'll make you come when I want you to come."

"Flynn."

"You wanted this, Talulla. Now you accept the consequences."

My mouth closes shut as he gets back on the bed. "You wanted to get spanked if I remember correctly..."

I nod.

"Use your words."

"Yes, please."

"That's *my* girl." *His* girl. Such a small statement, but with a much deeper meaning because he's been saying what I've been to him this entire time. I never felt part of something, like I belonged to someone, but with Flynn, I truly can't see myself without him. We're like two magnets bound to be pulled together.

He flips me over, keeping my arms tied. I get on my knees, feeling the wetness trail down my legs.

"You are the most exquisite being on this planet. You know that, right?" he says, caressing my inner thighs and collecting my wetness. Then, his mouth is back on my pussy. From this position, it feels even more sensitive than before, and I end up rubbing my ass on his face as his hands squeeze my ass cheeks. He devours me like a madman, and this time, when my orgasm builds, he lets me get closer and closer to it.

Two fingers thrust into me, and as I start to come, he sucks and licks. Then he spanks me—hard—and the moan that comes out of me is so high-pitched I feel like I might be floating into another dimension. I've never come so hard in my entire life. But he doesn't stop. He continues to thrust and suck, and another orgasm builds, quicker than the last. And then again. *Smack*.

A spank on my ass, and I scream so loud I am sure everyone in the building woke up from it.

"I knew you'd be vocal, but fuck, Talulla, your sounds are my new favorite melody. Addicting."

"Fuck me, Flynn. Please put your cock inside me right now."

"Just because you asked so nicely."

He reaches for my tied hands and slowly unties the restraints, massaging my now-freed wrists.

I'm lying on my back again, and he's already positioned at my entrance. He's so big, and I know it will hit literally every nerve inside me.

"I wanna look at you when you come with my cock inside you."

"And I want to look at you as you come inside me."

Grabbing his length, he guides the head to my entrance, slowly pushing inside me with ease, and I gasp at the sudden fullness. His lips fall to mine as he continues to slide into me until his entire length is deep inside. So deep, I feel his balls pressed against my skin.

"If you want to stake me, do it now. Like this. This is exactly how I want to go."

I chuckle at his dramatic statement, but my laugh dies on my lips as his mouth attacks my own. I moan in approval, and I wrap my arms around his toned body. My hands grip his back. Flynn starts his torturous thrusts, slow and methodical, and then hard, hitting that spot inside me. Every. Single. Time.

"Faster," I demand as my nails dig into his skin.

I hear him hissing as his movements get faster and faster. A painful rhythm full of desire, the need to feel more and more with every movement. The crazy part about it? It actually does get better with every thrust. With every cuss, every moan.

I can feel my climax growing again, and by the look on his face, I know he's close too. "Fuck, Talulla, you feel so good."

"You too. So, so good."

"Are you gonna come again for me?"

"Yes," is all I manage to half moan and half whisper as I reach this new state of ecstasy that I truly thought was not possible. Is this what nirvana is? Because I'd like to remain here forever, please and thank you.

"Fuck," he shouts. "You're gripping my cock so hard."

"Come for me, Flynn."

His eyes widen as he hears my breathy words. "What did you just say?" His hand grabs my neck, and he tightens his grip.

"Please come for me. I need to feel you spill inside me."

His mouth falls open for just a moment, and then his lips are devouring mine as he empties himself inside me.

Marking me, claiming me, making sure I know I'm his and that he's mine.

We stay like this for a while, trying to regain our breathing, and then he finally pulls out of me. As we lie beside each other, he drags me close in a tight and possessive hold, one that I truly don't want to escape from.

"It's true," I say with heavy eyelids.

"What is?" I feel his lips brushing my forehead.

"You just ruined every other man for me."

"Good thing there won't be anyone else besides me, then."

Yes, because the reality is that after tonight, everything I knew has been wiped clean. I'm an empty canvas. A new night sky where he's the brightest star. I'm his world now, and he's my satellite.

The sound of the shower in the distance is what makes me open my eyes. The sunlight peeking through the window creates a golden atmosphere that contrasts with the modern furniture in my vampire's house.

I can't help but smile as I look down and see my naked body entangled in Flynn's sheets.

This is right. This feels so, so right.

I grab his pillow and sniff his intoxicating scent. It feels so sophisticated, like everything else around me.

"Are you awake, darling?" I hear him yell from the bathroom.

"Maybe," I reply, biting my bottom lip as I think back to what we did last night. If I close my eyes, I can picture his hands on my skin, the memory making me gasp and turning me on as if I had his fingers still inside me.

"Come join me."

Getting out of bed, I let the bedsheet fall, my nipples pebbling as the cold air of the morning reaches my skin.

Pacing to the bathroom, I take a peek inside. Flynn's head is currently under the showerhead, his eyes closed as he enjoys the steamy water traveling down his body. God, he's so perfect, even like this. Almost vulnerable, yet so deadly.

He turns to look at me, the steam blurring his features momentarily before he wipes away the condensation on the glass and continues to stare at me. "Are you just gonna watch me? I can do so many things in here for you."

Oh, he definitely can do many things, but I'm feeling naughty, and I want him to beg this time. "I think I'm gonna stay here. Maybe take care of myself all on my own."

His eyes narrow on mine. "Don't even think about it," he says as he stares at my hand tracing my clavicle, then slowly going down to my hard nipple and down, down to my belly. "Stop."

"Or what?" I challenge him with one eyebrow raised.

"Or I'm going to—"

A sound coming from his phone breaks the little magic we had going on. I instinctively look down at the phone on the counter, and as my eyes scroll through the words, my jaw tightens.

"What is it?" he asks, but I don't even pay attention to him turning off the water and stepping out of the shower. All I can think about is the message I just read.

> **Evanora**
> Your death potion will be ready next week.

Words aren't enough to describe what I'm feeling right now. My stomach drops, and then I can only react.

Because what happened between us was not real, and I should have known that. I should have known I was just prey. Nothing more. Just a game, and fuck, he played me so well.

"Talulla, let me explain," he says as he looks down at his phone and realizes what just happened.

I run outside the room and grab the first chair I find. Anger pouring out of every pore, I grip one leg and rip it off, ready to use it.

"Talulla," Flynn says, trying to get close.

I shove him away from me. "You used me."

"Never. I would never do that to you." His voice cracks with desperation. His eyebrows furrow, but he stops moving.

Those are the last words I hear him say before I charge at him. He remains immobile, knowing exactly what's coming next. Ready to welcome death like an old friend.

Tears stream down my face as I pierce his skin and push the broken piece of wood deep into his flesh.

But as his eyes widen in shock, I realize I purposely missed his heart. Blood spills down his chest.

He doesn't try to stop me when I grab my clothes and flee the apartment.

I rub my bloody hands on my skirt, the tears still coming down uncontrollably, my heart tortured and shattered into thousands of pieces at the thought of what I just did. Because despite everything, it seems so, so wrong.

Fifteen
FLYNN

I fall to my knees as soon as the door to my apartment closes. Talulla ran away from me. From her fears. From the knowledge of what she had done. Because, despite her feeling of betrayal, she still couldn't let herself do the one thing she was brought up to do—kill my kind. Kill me.

She couldn't kill *me*.

I wrap my hands around the broken piece of wood sticking from my chest and pull it out. There's no pain from the open wound, only despair. My body seems to be paralyzed as the smell of crimson makes my throat go mad.

She couldn't kill *me*.

My body clenches at the thought of her trauma—her constant fear of being abandoned—and who am I to change that? She might think I'm the killer behind the werewolves' deaths right now, but what will her reaction be when she finds out the potion is for me? That the potion is a cure to give me a chance to let my body die as a human once more.

How can I look her in the eyes and tell her why I came to Palo Alto in the first place? How can I tell her my intentions were always to give up this non-life, even if the potion didn't end up working? Yes, because the reality is that I came to California knowing that Evanora was here, but knowing that Emil Popescu was here as well.

I was ready to let him stake me if that was what it took to end me.

His own daughter changed everything.

His own daughter gave me a reason to wake up in the morning.

His own daughter just tried to kill me and couldn't.

But I do deserve infinite death. I remain a predator despite my decision to stop feeding from humans. I remain a killer who won't stop at anything if someone tries to touch what's mine.

And Talulla is mine. Even if she decides she doesn't want to be with me, she still will be mine. My world. Until *my* end.

As the wound finally closes, I get up and start cleaning up the blood on the floor. The mix of bleach and iron makes my nose flare.

I have to get to Talulla before the Drusus coven gives her the wrong information. Because even if she is upset with me, and rightfully so, I still have nothing to do with those damn dogs dying.

I dress quickly and make my way to her dorm, and before I even get a chance to knock on her door, Cassandra swings it open, her palm raised to my chest.

"Let me in, witch."

Her hand, still raised, creates an invisible barrier that prevents me from stepping inside.

"I need to talk to her."

"She doesn't want to see you." Her eyes narrow. "And you're trying to step into your own grave, Lancaster." Asmodeus walks beside her, ready to use his own powers if I step out of line. "You know what's going to happen next. I don't have to tell you."

I groan, my nostrils flaring. If they only let me explain what the fuck is going on, maybe they'll understand that this is truly not what it seems. "The potion is for me,

Cassandra, and it's not a death potion." I start, my shoulders falling in defeat. "I asked Evanora for a cure, a way to die on my own terms." My jaw clenches before I raise my voice once more. "Why am I explaining this to you? I need to talk to *her*."

"Give her some space, Flynn. You fucked up."

"The potion—Talulla made me change my mind. It's not what it looks like."

"What do you mean?" Asmodeus asks.

I sigh. They wouldn't understand why I was ready to let myself go. "I thought I was done living, and then Talulla walked in front of me. I have never felt anything until *her*."

"Those are pretty words. Talulla needs facts, Flynn." Cassandra's voice is firm. I can tell she believes me, but the reality is that even if I am not a killer, I still omitted to tell her friend something major, something that my beautiful hunter fears—losing someone she loves.

This is the moment when Talulla bursts out of the bathroom with a stake in her hand. God, she's so beautiful, even when she's ready to murder me. Just like earlier today, I won't move. I won't defend myself. I will accept everything she needs to give me. I will take her pain and make it my own.

"Time for round two, little hunter?" I tilt my head, not knowing if the sudden urge to humor her will even do me any good. "You know I won't escape my fate."

She's angry. I can sense her frustration and hurt, and it's something I will devote my life to never seeing again. Her father tried to create a being with no emotions, but the reality is that my girl can't stop feeling, and she shouldn't have to.

Talulla doesn't say a single thing. She just acts. I can tell she's not actually fighting to kill me. She just needs to get the anger out, so I let her do that. "Take it all out,

Talulla. It's okay," I say in a soft voice. "Give me your torment."

"You don't get to say a word," she spits back, and as she continues to punch and kick, I see how her friends are just there, witnessing this anger tantrum. Something I feel like I deserve, but most importantly, something she needs. My Talulla is terrified of letting herself feel anything because she's used to people disappointing her. She is used to never getting her way, and if this is what she needs to understand that I am not going anywhere, then so be it. Because even if she might think so right now, there's no way I'm walking away from her.

My phone rings, and I let it. I need to take care of this now, and everyone else can wait.

It rings again.

On the third call, I look at it and see Evanora's name flashing. "You might wanna get that," Talulla says, panting. Raising one eyebrow at her, I pick up my phone, and she walks away from me a second time. No stake in my chest this time, though.

"Evanora, I am busy," I growl, but she doesn't let me finish my sentence.

"I need to see you right now, Flynn." Her voice is concerned. My eyes widen as I sense her panic just by her tone.

The witch wouldn't have called so many times if it weren't important. "I'm on my way."

Cassandra tilts her head slightly. "Is she okay?"

I just look at her. "Let me go find out." I look toward the door to the bathroom, where I know Talulla is. "Take care of her."

Sixteen

TALULLA

As I hear Flynn's words to Evanora, I decide it's time to check on what is actually happening with him. If he's the reason four supernatural creatures died, then I need to get solid proof and call reinforcements.

I hear the front door close, and that's when I get out of the bathroom. "Cass, I think we should follow him."

"You could have killed him. Why didn't you?"

"He's hiding something, and I want to know what that is before I stake him for good."

"Do you think he's really behind all this? Because Evanora never would have agreed to it. I think he might have been—"

I sigh. I trust Cassandra, and she trusts her witch friend. "No, don't even finish that sentence. He's here for a reason, and I need to find out what that reason is."

She sighs. "Okay, fine. If this is what you need, let's go." Then she adds, "It might be good to hear what Evanora has to say as well. Might be about the case."

"Am I the only one who believes the bloodsucker?" Asmo asks. "No, because he seemed pretty convincing when he was—"

"Shut up," Cassandra and I reply in unison.

"You should be on my side, Asmo, not his," I add, my jaw clenched.

"Okay, well, while you two go stalk a vampire, I'm gonna go and find out more about Monica Lazar."

I almost forgot about the encounter from last night. I was too focused on being angry with Flynn that I let what could be the real killer slip out of my mind. "I can't stand her."

"I figured," Asmo says, trying to hide a laugh.

"Let's go." Cassandra walks to the center of my bedroom, and I follow. She grabs a few vials from her bag and holds them tight in one palm. I tilt my head to the side, and in confusion, I look at my friend. Asmodeus chuckles from behind me, and before I can say anything, Cassandra grabs my hand and we apparate to the beginning of a dirt road.

"Fuck. Why didn't you tell me we were gonna apparate? I would have made sure not to eat anything." I hold my stomach as I try to calm my breathing and not puke everywhere. Acid coats the walls of my mouth, and I know I got really close to emptying my insides. It burns my throat as I swallow some saliva to try to calm down.

"Drink this," she says, handing me a vial. "It's an invisibility potion. This way, we can sneak in without being seen."

"You are a genius." I grab the small container with a purplish liquid. My eyes brighten at the thought of not being seen.

"I know." She drinks her vial and immediately disappears.

"Oh god, where did you go?"

She snorts before replying, "Drink up, and you'll be able to see me."

I do as she says, and she appears again. "Okay, this is really cool."

"Let's go. We gotta be cautious. He might be able to hear footsteps." Cassandra's right. We might be invisible, but we also have to be extremely quiet, or he'll know we're there right away.

We walk up the dirt road, and as we approach the house, we take our time to get to the window framing the living room. Flynn and Evanora are talking, sitting at her table. He seems distressed, and Evanora looks *worried*. She constantly brings a cup of tea to her mouth, trembling more and more as they continue their conversation. We get even closer to try to catch some sound, and as we do so, my nose starts itching.

"Oh no," I whisper.

"What is it?" Cassandra asks in a high whisper.

"Calendula flowers," I reply, pointing to the plants framing the entire front porch.

Cassandra's eyes widen, and I cover my mouth and pinch my nose to try to cover my sneeze.

"Fuck, fuck, fuck." She tries to pull me away from the window, but it's useless. I'm too strong, and she knows it.

"I'm okay. Let's get closer. We need to hear."

We do just that. We basically end up with our ears pressed to the glass of the window.

"Flynn, you don't understand. I need to get in touch with Talulla Popescu. I've been trying to reach Cassandra, but she isn't returning my calls." Evanora's voice sounds rough, and as I look at her now, I can tell she hasn't slept in days. Her dark brown eyes are almost invisible from her heavy eyelids and the dark circles around them.

Cassandra's eyes widen. She picks up her phone and sees the missed calls just now. "Okay, I swear I would have called her back if I knew it involved you."

I shake my head, trying to contain a laugh.

"Why do you need to talk to Talulla?" Flynn's voice brings us back to the scene in front of us.

"I just...I need to make sure about something."

"Evanora, you know I can easily compel you. If there's

something concerning you, especially about Talulla, you have to tell me."

"I had a dream about *her.* It was odd, and then, when I did my tarot reading in the morning, I just...It was about her, and I need to make sure."

Flynn's head slightly turns to the side, his eyes moving toward the window—toward us. He can't see or sense us, but for some reason, his eyes are looking straight at me. His lips curl up into a smirk. "Why don't I call her right now and find out if she can come over here?" He then walks toward the front door, opens it, and starts shaking his head as we try to stay immobile. "Little hunter, I thought you were better at hiding." Flynn picks up his phone and dials my number. I have no time to silence my phone. He already knew I was here.

"How did you—" I say, my eyes open wide in shock.

He takes a deep inhale. "Did you really think I couldn't smell you?"

Then I sneeze. Fucking calendulas.

"Or hear you sneeze?" Flynn tilts his head. "You're allergic to this plant."

"No shit, Sherlock."

"What an odd thing."

"But the glamour—" Cassandra starts, but gets interrupted by a genuine laugh.

"Get in here, you two. Evanora has a question, and I really need to hear the answer."

"You're mad," I state as I get closer to him. "I'm the one who should be mad," I say, poking his chest with my invisible finger. He grabs my wrist, and even if I know I'm still invisible to him, he knows exactly where my body is.

"I'm not mad." He tsks. "A bit disappointed, a bit amused," he says before adding, "I wish I could see you right now, though. It's hard to read you when you're invisible."

"I'm sorry. No, why am I sorry? You're the one hiding shit."

"Just get inside, Talulla. I'm not in the mood to fight right now."

"You should have thought about that before sleeping with me then."

He brushes a lock of hair away from my face. "You know what? Yes, I am mad. At myself for giving you a reason to follow me and hide in the process. I'm mad because despite the fact that you staked me this morning without giving me a chance to explain, you still thought that the best way to do things was to hide from me. Do not hide from me—*ever*. You talk to me, you get angry with me, but don't fucking *hide*."

My mouth closes shut. "We were just worried..."

Evanora clears her throat. "Talulla Popescu, it's a pleasure to finally meet you in the flesh." In her hands are two vials of what I assume is the counter potion to the glamour I'm currently under.

Moving toward the witch, I not so accidentally brush my hand with Flynn's, and my heart skips a beat. "The pleasure is mine, Evanora." I take the little container and down the liquid in one gulp.

"Please sit."

I do as she says, and then she takes a seat on the opposite side of the table, shuffling a deck of cards. Then she hands me the deck. "What do you want me to do?"

"These are tarot cards."

"Okay?" I say, raising one eyebrow at her.

"I want you to shuffle them yourself and then pick two cards from whichever part of the deck you want."

I start mixing the cards. I take my time, then I put the deck down and pick a card from the top. I flip it, and it's a card with ten coins on it.

"The Ten of Pentacles," Cassandra whispers.

"Is that bad?" I ask, looking at everyone's expressions. They're all looking at my hands and at the table, but not at me. Just at the cards.

The one who orders me to pick another tarot card is not a witch this time, but Flynn. "Pick the second one, Talulla."

I turn to look at him, his hand massaging his chin nervously. His posture is still, and he's barely blinking. So I do as he says. I cut the deck in half and pick right from the middle.

A skeleton holding a scythe.

"Death," I say with wide eyes.

"Evanora, you have to tell me what's happening," Flynn demands.

"What does it mean?" I ask.

"I've been picking cards all day. Always the same two."

"What does the Ten of Pentacles card mean?" I repeat, hoping that someone will finally pay attention to me and not to the pieces of cardboard on the table that are apparently making everyone freak the fuck out.

Flynn looks at Cassandra, and I turn to see her eyes. She nods at him, and then he finally speaks. "The Ten of Pentacles represents riches, abundance."

"I don't think I'm following..."

"Your name..." He sighs. "Talulla means 'lady of abundance.'"

"So what? I'm not gonna die. Death could mean so many things, no?"

"Tal, like this? This is a warning," Cassandra says, squeezing my shoulder.

"Okay, it's a warning. It doesn't mean it's going to happen. Now we know, and I'm going to be extra careful."

"We need to find whoever is behind this so I can rip him to shreds."

"Or her," I say, trying to lighten the mood. "It could be a her too." Because if I had any possible doubt before, I know now for certain that Flynn is innocent and that what he said in my dorm earlier is the truth. If that's what it is, I don't know how I'm going to accept it.

Evanora takes Cassandra's hand. "Let's give them a minute." She nods, and they step into the other room.

The vampire I was calling mine just a few hours before stands tall and firm, his hands clenched into fists. Flynn's posture is so rigid that he almost resembles a statue. Perfectly immobile. No heartbeat, no blinking, no movement at all. He could be mistaken for a marble sculpture created by a Renaissance artist so long ago.

"I'm going to be okay, Flynn."

"Yes, I will make sure of it."

"I don't need to be saved. I know how to take care of myself."

His fingers gently grab my neck and pull me closer. "You're not leaving this earth, Talulla."

"I know." My eyes widen as his soften.

His forehead gently touches mine. "There's so much you need, no, *deserve* to see."

I grab his head in my hands, forcing him to look me in the eye. "I'm not going anywhere."

Then, he does something unexpected. He wraps his arms around me, and he nestles his head in the crook of my neck. A sudden wetness reaches my clavicle. "Flynn, I'm right here." I grab one of his hands and rest it on my chest. "Hear this? My heart is still beating."

"You can't die." His arms tighten. "You deserve so much."

"I've avoided death many times. This time won't be different. Besides, last time I checked, you were the one receiving cryptic texts about a death potion."

His face turns from soft to annoyed, and before he can even get a word out, my friend comes back into the room.

"She's right," Cassandra states as she looks at us from the kitchen. "She won't go easily, and we won't let her, am I right?"

Flynn's eyes are red and dark, and his jaw is locked. "Anyone who comes for her will be facing their Angel of Judgment."

"Now, can we go home and not be sad? I'm still alive, you know."

"How did you follow me without a vehicle?" Flynn asks, realizing only his car is in the driveway.

"Cassandra almost made me puke by apparating here."

"Ah." He smirks. "Dandy little power you have, detective witch."

"Do you have a nickname for everyone?"

"Only the people I like."

"But you call Asmodeus by his full name."

"I stand by my statement."

I giggle and then remember why I was—still am—mad at him, and my gloomy mood comes back. "Maybe I should call a cab." I catch my bottom lip between my teeth and bite hard, trying to calm my nerves.

"I'm not gonna let you drive back to campus with a stranger, Talulla." Flynn rolls his eyes before adding, "And stop torturing that poor lip. You've already spilled enough blood today."

His comeback feels like a stake to my chest. "Well, I don't want to drive with you."

He shakes his head and then opens the passenger door. "Even when you're angry at me, please accept the fact that I'll be there, making sure you're okay."

"This doesn't change anything," I say as I sit in the passenger seat.

Flynn opens the back seat door for Cassandra, but she just smiles at him and then winks at me. "You guys go. I'm going to talk to the rest of the coven to see if they have any new clues. Besides...another body just showed up," she adds, waving her phone to show she got a message from someone.

"Cass, don't you dare," I say as her form disappears out of thin air. "Fucking witch."

"Language," Flynn says as he takes his seat.

"I'm not talking to you."

"Interesting how two seconds ago you were letting me hear your heartbeat, and now you're ready to stake me for the third time today."

"Yeah, well, what can I say? I'm a little moody today."

"Sweetheart, let me explain, at least."

"You're here to kill someone."

"Yeah, well, maybe it's not as simple as that. Didn't you hear what I said to Cassandra and Asmodeus?"

"What's the potion Evanora is brewing for?"

He sighs, and I see his hands clenching so hard on the steering wheel that the veins pop out deliciously. "The potion is a cure."

"What?"

"It's for me, and—"

"No. You know what? I don't think I want to know anymore."

"Talulla, I've been walking this earth for way too long. I just wanted to go on my own terms."

"If you really want to die, I'll end your misery right now."

He chuckles. "And not so surprisingly, it would be my favorite way to go."

"Okay, so your big plan was to come here, get this arsenic cocktail, and fuck with my head in the process?"

"What? No, of course not."

"Then why did you even go out of your way to ask me out and be around me when you were going to leave me?"

His lips close shut. I took him by surprise. The next words that come out of his mouth are calculated, and I don't know if I can believe him. "You were not planned, Talulla. When I saw you, I just...I had to get to know you."

"Were you even gonna tell me, or were you just gonna disappear one day?"

"You're making it sound like I'm already gone. I'm not, and I won't leave until I'm sure you're safe."

"Yeah, well, I'm sorry, but this is a lot."

"Do you think I wanted this? Do you think I got on a plane on purpose to come here and fall for you? I just wanted to die in peace, but you showed up and brought me back to life." His voice sounds like a desperate lament. "Try to put yourself in my shoes, Talulla. I've been here for too long. I haven't felt anything for far too long."

He hasn't felt anything. He doesn't feel what I feel for him, because he can't. "I—"

"You make me feel things—beautiful things—but..."

"It's not enough."

He sighs once more. "I just told you that you brought me back to life, and you think you're not enough? *I'm* not enough, Talulla, and I'm being selfish because even if I know that I'm not enough, I still want to spend my last days with you."

I think I might puke if he continues to talk. "I need some time to think."

He just nods. "I understand." Then he crooks a smile. "Take all the time you need, little hunter."

I roll my eyes at the ridiculous pet name. "You really need to stop calling me that."

He parks the car, and in less than a second, he's out

and opening my door. "Can I at least walk you to your dorm?"

I look up at him as I exit the vehicle. It seems so innocent—protective—but for what? He's going to leave me anyway. What's the point of feeling what I'm feeling when there's a clock ticking, reminding me he will be gone?

"Yes," I say as I start walking toward my building. He slows his pace to stay beside me, never touching me, but it's as if I can feel his hands on my body. His finger touching me, his lips kissing my neck...I might go insane if I don't put some distance between us right now.

I see his lips lifting into a smile, probably feeling, or rather, smelling exactly the effect he has on me, even if I am mad at him. Even if I asked for space. Even if I know he wants to let himself die.

We reach my door, and the silence is now becoming awkward. Biting my lower lip, I say, "Well, good night then."

Flynn reaches for a strand of my hair that fell in front of my eyes and pushes it behind my ear. It's peculiar to see him this gentle when I know exactly how deadly he can be, and how strong and dominant he is. Yet, he always takes his time and never assumes or takes more than what I offer. "Anything you might need or—"

A text comes through, but I ignore it.

"Read it. It's okay," he says. "It might be about the case."

I do as he asks, but instead of Cassandra's name, I see Paolo's. "It's just the organizer telling me when I'm fighting next."

His jaw clenches. "And when are you fighting?"

"I asked for time, Flynn."

"And I'm going to keep my distance, but you can't blame me for wanting to make sure you're okay."

"I'm a vampire hunter. You should be worrying about the other guy."

He groans at my constant defiance. "You're so stubborn."

"And you're a little too demanding."

He chuckles at my comeback. "I wish I could punish you for that."

Heat rises between my legs because I know exactly how delicious that would feel. "Good night, Flynn."

"Fine. I'll ask the witch."

"Which one? My friend, the one brewing your death, or your ex?"

His right hand rests on his heart. "Ouch."

"I'm sorry. I don't even know why I said that."

"You're hurt."

Then I give in. "The fight is Friday night."

He nods. "Good night, Talulla." With that, he walks away. The vampire I called mine not many hours ago walks away without another fight because, despite the ocean of emotions we both feel, he still respects my wishes to be alone.

It's too bad I regret asking for space as soon as I close my door and crash onto my bed because I've been alone my entire life, even when surrounded by people.

But after spending time with Flynn, I know exactly what it means to be *with* someone, and it's something I don't think I'm ready to give up.

Seventeen

TALULLA

"Tal, wake up." A voice pierces my ear and then hands start shaking me. This has to be how I find out I died and went straight to hell.

I groan in protest as I open my eyes and realize it's still dark outside. "What the fuck, Cass?" I say, realizing the madwoman creating an earthquake by moving my mattress is my best friend. A friend who seriously needs to learn boundaries. "You know I've staked vampires for less, right?" I add, yawning repeatedly.

"You need to come with me now."

"What?" I rub the back of my hand over my eyes, trying to get them to focus on my surroundings.

Cassandra speaks again. "The body that was found earlier tonight...it's Scott."

With that statement, I'm out of bed in less than a second. "Same modus operandi?"

"Yes, and Kaden...he won't talk to anyone. He was barely able to talk to the police."

I don't even bother putting on socks. I grab the first T-shirt and pair of jeans I find and put them on. "Okay, let's go."

"Asmo is outside waiting. We can't apparate. I don't know where the police are searching."

I nod, and out of the dorm we go.

I look at my phone, pondering if I should text Flynn,

but this isn't any of his concern. He didn't know Scott, and he definitely doesn't care to comfort Kaden in his time of sorrow. The brightness of the screen dims as I let seconds go by. No need to worry him in the middle of the night. Not when I requested space that I know I need.

We get to the pack house and walk inside. The police are slowly leaving the premises, probably already with all the information they need to write their useless little report. Every single light is currently turned on in the rooms. A couple of people are slowly cleaning the mess that was made.

Stepping into every single room on the main floor, I try to find any sign of my friend, but he's nowhere.

I then run upstairs, straight to his bedroom, and as I see an empty bed, I feel the breeze coming from the window. It's open, and right outside, sitting on the roof, is Kaden. A sigh of relief rushes through me as I see his broad shoulders.

I silently make my way to him, making the least amount of noise, not knowing the kind of reaction he might have right now.

"Hey," I whisper, reaching for his hand. I squeeze it to let him know I'm here, but it's as if he can't even feel my skin on his. He's completely numb, staring apathetically into the distance.

"I didn't think you'd care to be here. Especially after finding out you're sleeping with your own enemy."

I hold his hand a little tighter, letting his thorny words pass right through me. "I'm here for you, Kaden. What I do in my free time isn't important right now."

"It is when you sleep with my brother's killer."

"Flynn is not behind this, K. He never was."

"Then who the fuck is it?"

"You know there's a witch involved. You're the one

who has omitted sharing important details with people who are only trying to help you."

"I don't need your help." Kaden's jaw clenches, and he rips his hand away from mine. Werewolves are known to be stubborn creatures, but this? This is another level.

"I'm talking about the Drusus coven. This is what they do. Why aren't you cooperating?"

He shakes his head and groans before speaking again. "Because every time I involve someone, they fucking die, Tal. That's why."

The thought of my tarot reading comes back to mind. Should I take a step back and reconsider my involvement when I know my life is also at risk? No, I can't. Not when my father decided to close his eyes and turn his back on this, knowing he could have prevented some of this, if not the entire situation. "Tell me then. Tell me what you think is happening."

He sighs and then starts getting up. "Let me show you something. It's easier that way."

I follow him back inside, and even if I know Cassandra and Asmodeus are outside the bedroom listening, I pretend it's just us.

Kaden grabs a file from his nightstand and hands it to me. "This is my father's murder case file."

"Murder case? I thought he had a car accident."

"That's what was told on the news and disclosed to the public, but I was able to get the report. There was something wrong with the car, and it was clearly hidden because half of the fucking thing is blacked out."

I look down at the pages and see exactly what he's talking about. "Every single detail and name is not here."

"Exactly."

"When did you get this?"

"A few days before Kyle, the first pack member who was murdered, died. I had my suspicions about my father's death, and as soon as I started digging, people started dying. This is why I haven't told anyone, and this is why Scott died tonight. I should have continued this on my own."

"You told him what you were working on a few days ago, didn't you?"

"I did, and now he's gone," he says, choking on his own words.

"That's why Flynn saw him with the witch."

"I asked him to go buy some protection potions, which clearly did nothing."

"We need to find the clear report."

"Good luck with that, Tal. I've been trying for weeks."

"Yeah, well, you didn't have Cassandra and me before."

"I still don't. You need to get them to stop poking around. *You* need to stop poking around."

"Why?" I ask, crossing my arms over my chest.

"Because I don't want to bury you as well." Kaden's hand brushes my cheek, and for a second, I let myself accept his gentle touch.

"Too late. You're not fighting alone anymore."

"Yes, I am."

"No," I say, my tone firm and final. There's no way I'm walking out of this now, not when we finally have some sort of a lead.

Cassandra and Asmodeus walk in, right on cue. "If you seriously think you're going to make her change her mind, you're a dumb werewolf."

Kaden growls at the sight of my friends. "I told you guys to leave."

"And we did. Now we're back." Asmodeus takes the file from my hands. "Okay, so Set and I are going to break into the police archives and look for the right report. Easy peasy lemon squeezy."

"No," the werewolf shouts. "You're not doing anything if you want to live."

"Meh. Living is kind of overrated these days," Asmo says, shrugging his shoulders.

"You know what? I don't care. Do whatever the fuck you want, but leave that file here."

I turn and face Cassandra and her blond best friend, and I ask, "Guys, can you give us a moment? I'll be right out."

They nod and leave the room once more.

"Kaden—"

"Go away, Tal."

I groan and grab his arm, forcing him to look at me. He has always towered over me, and right now, he seems even bigger than usual. His muscular frame takes up half of his room. "Whether you like it or not, we're friends."

His arms cross over his chest. "Are we?"

"We are friends, and I care about you."

"Then stop caring because I don't care about you."

"Well, ouch. Until a while ago, you wanted me to be your mate, and now I'm just a stranger to you?"

"You walked out of that club with a vampire boyfriend, not me, Talulla."

"Can't you just believe that I'm here because I care for you and because I cared for Scott?"

"Oh, come on. You just fucked around until you found your shiny new toy."

"Are you kidding me? You two were the ones fucking around every day, and now I'm the hoe? Are you even listening to your words?" The volume of my voice is rising, just like his.

"Does he buy you pretty things? Is that why you picked him?" I know he doesn't really mean the words he's saying, but they still hurt the same.

"Picked? Do you seriously think I wanted to fall for a

fucking vampire? You know exactly who I am. Stop making it about something that it isn't. Go to bed. I'll call you if we find anything new, and for the love of whatever god werewolves believe in, stop playing with fire." I am now full-on yelling at this point, to the point of panting as I finish talking.

"I can't step away."

"Then let us be with you if you plan something moronic."

"I—"

"Stop fighting. You're not alone in this, not anymore."

He growls. "Fine."

"Now I'm walking out that door, but know that the Drususes are going to find out who's behind this." I start making my way out of the bedroom.

"I can't believe I agreed to this."

Stopping next to the doorframe, I say, "Yeah, well, it's not my fault I got woken up in the middle of the night because a stubborn werewolf didn't want to cooperate."

"You always have to have the last word." He finally smiles, and for a split second, I see the Kaden I know and like, the exuberant guy who just wants to have fun any chance he gets.

"Always," I reply, winking at him.

I walk out of the house and find Cassandra and Asmodeus talking to someone. No, not just someone, but Flynn.

"How did you know I was here?" I ask, only paying attention to the vampire and completely ignoring the fact that my friends are a little too cool with him being around right now. "Did you follow me?"

"I called him," Cassandra says.

My head snaps in her direction, my eyes ready to pop out of my eye sockets. "Why?"

"Because she didn't know how your werewolf would react." Flynn's voice caresses my ear, and I hate that his accent and his presence do that, even when I'm mad at him.

"He's not *my* werewolf."

"Well, I certainly hope not," he says, scratching his jaw.

"You don't get to be jealous."

"I am my own person, Talulla. I get to be whatever I choose to be."

I groan as I try to defend myself when there's nothing to explain aside from the fact that someone is murdering innocent creatures. "His brother died."

"And this is why I haven't ripped out his throat yet. Happy?"

"So generous of you." I turn to look at my witch friends. "Now, can we go? I need to sleep."

"Yeah, yeah. Thank you for talking to Kaden, by the way. I know it must have been hard."

I eye Flynn before replying to Cassandra. "It's all good. He just needed to get some anger out."

My vampire snorts. "He's lucky he has the dead brother excuse because if it were another circumstance, I would have stepped in."

"No, you wouldn't have, because I asked you for time. Go home, Flynn."

"So impertinent."

"Yeah, well, that's what you get when your girl had a fucking day."

The corners of his lips lift into a smile. Yes, because I just called myself *his girl*, and he definitely heard it. "Good night once again," he says, without even giving me the time to say anything back. He won this one, didn't he?

I groan and then turn to look at my friends, who are now beaming at me. "You two stop smiling and get me to bed. You better have a phenomenal breakfast waiting for me when I wake up, or I'll be pissed."

"As you wish," Asmodeus replies, opening the back seat door for me.

If I thought my day had been rough, I think the night was the cherry on top.

Eighteen

TALULLA

The next couple of days are quiet and filled with classes and work. No Flynn. As much as I appreciate him keeping his distance, I do miss knowing he is around. Can I really blame him for his decision? Who am I to ask someone who has lived as long as he has to just call it quits? I could make him change his mind. I could give him a reason to stay. But would that be enough? Am I really that selfish to ask for me to be the one who goes first? Because that's what would happen if we stayed together, wouldn't it? I would die, and he would keep living. I would age, and he would stay exactly as he is now. Yet, I can't find a way to truly believe this is how it has to end.

I'm so angry he kept this from me. I'm so angry I found out the way I did. But more importantly, I'm angry at myself because I didn't give him the chance to explain himself. I just picked up my things and left. I staked him, and then I left. When I saw him outside Kaden's house, despite my anger, I still wanted to jump into his arms, and I didn't. I built a shield, and then he still let me have time. The one thing I've requested.

It's typical of me, really. It's the first time in forever I've started to feel something for someone, and I run far, far away. Because, let's be real for a second, how can I trust someone else when even my own father abandoned me? Isn't that my excuse? That's what I've been telling myself every single day. How can I let someone in when I was brought up to fight my battles completely alone? Brought up to follow orders, no questions asked. Orders that end with me or my prey dead. Is it too late? Evanora said the potion would be ready in a few days. Did he already take it? Is he already gone? No, he wouldn't leave without saying goodbye, would he? Not when so much has happened.

Asmodeus and Set have been trying to find a way to break into the police precinct since that night five days ago, and they keep failing. The full report is nowhere to be found, and I have a feeling a witch is behind this as well.

"Talulla, you seem oddly distracted these days. Is everything okay?" Mr. Wagner asks me.

It's Friday afternoon. Tonight, I'm fighting, and I have to leave soon to get ready. "I'm good. Just haven't slept much lately."

"Trouble in paradise?"

"What?"

Eric gets up and pours himself a cup of tea, then pours a second one. As he walks back toward the table, he says, "The vampire, I meant."

"Oh," I say. "He's not around right now, Professor."

"Is that why you're so distracted?" He hands me the cup.

"Thank you." I take a sip. "And...not really. It's more about those werewolves, actually."

"The guys from the house on Kirby Street?"

"Yeah."

"Didn't the police say they died from the flu?" Eric asks, sitting right beside me. It's weird being this close to him, but it's also comforting somehow. Knowing that I can now freely talk about my second life is nice.

"The Drusus coven has been working on the case. They're like our version of detectives, but with magic at their disposal."

Eric's eyes widen. "Wow, okay, that's a lot."

"I'm sorry, Professor Wagner. You didn't ask to get involved in this."

"Eric." He clears his throat and sips his tea. "You know you can call me Eric here, and don't apologize. You can tell me about anything."

"Eric, yes. Well, let's just say we thought vampires were behind it, but—"

He doesn't even let me finish my sentence. "Is this why Flynn Lancaster isn't around? Did you...stake him?"

I chuckle. "Well, I did, but not to kill him, but that's beside the point. Vampires are not behind those deaths. A witch is."

"A witch?"

"Yeah, which is very odd because a witch wouldn't risk going against our rules."

"You have rules?"

"Yeah. Basically, only certain kinds of supernatural beings are allowed to kill without consequences."

"I don't think I'm following."

"I'm a vampire hunter. I was trained to kill vampires because vampires typically don't follow our rules. We are the only supernatural creatures free to kill with no consequences because it's our job." I rub my palm on my nose, feeling it itch. "I know it seems odd, and it definitely doesn't prevent crimes, but a witch? Now, that is very odd."

"Is it?"

"A witch doesn't just decide one day to kill a bunch of werewolves, unless..."

"Unless?"

Eric's wife's research comes back to my mind. She

knew about werewolves, vampires, the Drususes, and even my family. I wonder if...

"Eric," I start, biting my bottom lip, knowing that the following question might be a little too much. "Did your wife ever mention a witch named Monica Lazar in her research?"

His posture completely changes, and I know for a fact that I fucked up. Bringing up his dead wife was definitely not a good idea. "I'm so sorry. Forget about—"

"Would it help the case?"

"I mean, maybe. I'm honestly just theorizing. I met her the other day, and she isn't super pleasant."

"Let me see if I can find it here." Eric gets up and paces to the bookshelf behind his desk. It's filled with history books and papers, lots and lots of papers. He crouches and digs out a small folder from the bottom left shelf. "I haven't heard the name before, but if she mentioned it, it has to be here."

We start going through every single page, and I chuckle at some notions and almost gasp in shock at how many things this woman found out. "This is actually impressive," I say as I continue to browse the pages. "That's a picture of my dad." I turn to face Eric. "It's a little creepy to see my family like this."

"Alina was very meticulous about her work. She put her heart and soul into everything she did." The corners of Eric's mouth lift up, his eyes lost, probably playing a memory of her in his mind. "Sometimes, we actually fought about that. Believe it or not, she worked more than me."

"You're the most hardworking person I've ever met. There's no way."

"I guess that's what happens when you lose the one thing that made you go home at night."

"You're going to find that again." My own words pierce me right through my chest because I do have a reason to go home now, and despite the clock ticking over us, I'd be an idiot to just let it go.

We get to the last page, and there is no mention of Monica. "Well, it was worth a try, I guess." I quickly check the time and realize it's late, and I have to go get ready for my fight. "Shoot, it's late. I have...work to go to."

"Talulla?"

"Yes?"

"If this witch is really behind it, be careful, okay?"

"Nothing will happen to me, Professor. I'm a tough cookie."

"Oh, I almost forgot to tell you that I'd like Cassandra and you to talk at the fundraiser next Thursday. It will be good for you to see how these things work for the future."

"Sure, sounds good." It sounds like an absolutely terrible idea. I feel my stomach doing backflips already. "Good night, professor."

"Eric."

"Right, Eric."

"Good night, Talulla."

Just like that, I'm out the door, stumbling toward my building. My heart is beating so fast it makes my chest hurt. The past sleepless nights are finally catching up with me, and at the worst possible time. I almost feel as if a train had hit me right in the face.

Opening the door to my dorm, I basically launch myself onto my bed, groaning at how tired I feel. My chest is getting heavy, and I suddenly cough to try to fill it with air again.

"Are you okay?" Cassandra asks as I twist my face off the mattress to face her. She's sitting at my desk, probably waiting for me.

"No, I'm not. I'm tired."

"You're not fighting tonight." Her tone is final and quite bossy. I don't like to be bossed around unless it's a six-three god of a vampire doing the bossing.

"Yes, I am."

"You look like you haven't slept in a week. You got here basically running, and you almost missed the bed as you wobbled over it."

"Well, I indeed haven't slept in days, and I got carried away with Eric's wife's research."

Cassandra's eyes widen as her jaw drops. "What?"

"Yeah. We were drinking tea, and we got to talking about Flynn and then about the case. We ended up reading her work to see if she had any idea who Monica Lazar was."

"You really don't like this witch."

"Well, she didn't really make a good case for herself."

"Did you see anything useful to the case in there? Did she even get anything right about us?"

"She did, actually. It was very detailed, and aside from a couple of funny theories she had, it really was well-done research. Nothing for the case, though."

"I don't know how I feel about a human knowing about us."

"I mean, Eric is harmless. He already knew before I started working for him."

"I guess you're right."

I rub my palms over my eyes, feeling my vision getting blurrier and blurrier. "Do you think you could give me something to help out? I won't ask again, but I think I need a little help tonight."

"I can brew up something quickly." Then she's off to the kitchenette, making something, and I just lie in my bed, thinking about how fucked up my life has become.

Twenty minutes later, Cass comes toward me with a

vial. “Here. This should help with the nerves and the few sleepless nights you had. A nice boost of energy.”

I take it and down it like a shot. Immediate relief travels from my mouth down to the tips of my toes. “Ah, thank you. I already feel better.”

“Good. Get your shit and let’s go.”

Asmodeus is waiting for us when we walk to the parking lot. “Ready?” he asks me with his usual smirk.

“Always ready to kick some man’s ass.”

“You scare me, you know that, right?”

“Aw, thank you.”

We get to the venue, and after I drop my stuff in the changing room, I take my time to stretch and warm up.

“Kid, are you ready?” Paolo asks, peeking through the door.

“Yeah, give me a minute,” I say, taking deep breaths.

The middle-aged man walks in and hands me a bottle of water. “You sure, kid?”

I accept the offering and take a big sip, the liquid traveling down my chest, feeling like burning lava. I look down at the bottle and realize it’s cold from the fridge, the condensation confirming it. Odd. “I’m all good. Ready to go,” I say, cracking my neck and getting up.

My head feels a bit heavy, but this fight is the exact distraction I need.

We make our way toward the ring. Paolo continues walking toward his station, and I get ready to step into action. The lights seem brighter than usual, and the audience is louder too. I turn to the left and see my friends sitting in the front row. Right beside them, my blond vampire sits as well. My heart skips a beat as his eyes find mine. Flynn’s stare is blank but attentive to me. He looks even more beautiful than usual, his pale skin almost looking like porcelain in the fluorescent lighting. I step into the ring, and as I look up at my opponent, I realize something really, really unfortunate.

The world starts spinning, and a ringing starts crushing my ears. The one opponent now almost looks like...two.

I'm not okay at all.

Nineteen

FLYNN

As Talulla steps into the ring, I notice her uncertain pace. Now, that's odd. Her hands shake for just a moment until she seems to regain control.

"Something is wrong," I say out loud, never taking my eyes off her.

"What do you mean?" the witch asks me.

The match starts, and I try to relax, leaning my back against the seat. Talulla throws a punch into her opponent's stomach, and he steps back a few steps. Good. Her walk is still a little wobbly, but as she shakes her head, she seems to regain her focus and is able to dodge the following moves. A punch and a kick. Good girl.

The loud cheering makes it hard to follow her heartbeat, but as I concentrate on her, I hear the irregular beats and frown. What the—

Crack.

The bastard was able to hit her in the face. Hard.

As she turns her face toward me, I see the fear in Talulla's eyes just before her back hits the mat. Her breathing is unsteady, and I almost miss her cry when she mouths, "Help."

I don't even think about the consequences of my actions. I run into the ring and put myself between her and her opponent. Then, Asmodeus and Cassandra are at the side of the ring as well.

"The fight is done," I say to the guy.

"We haven't even started," the opponent spits.

I crack my neck as I feel my thirst growing. My throat is itching for some crimson liquid, and right now, my anger is getting the best of me. "You don't want to fight with me, trust me," I say before turning to look at Talulla, now unconscious.

"You talk so tough. Why don't you take her place?" the guy says, and if he continues to talk, I might just give him what he wants. A slow, painful death.

"Flynn, don't fall for it," Cassandra says, her eyes focused on me. "He's not worth it." She's worried about the consequences of something so public, and I get it, but I wasn't born yesterday. I just want to get my little hunter out of here. Quickly.

The corners of my lips curl into a smirk. "Don't worry, I don't eat manure." Then I look at my beautiful Talulla, pick her up, and get her out of the ring.

"You can't just leave," Paolo says to us. "She signed up for this."

"Whatever she owes you, I'll triple it. You forget her name, face, and phone number, or I'll find you, rip your heart out, and make you eat it." I know he can see my fangs. I know my eyes are definitely not looking the way the eyes of a human do, but I don't care. I only care about the girl in my arms.

Paolo's face turns pale. Good. Let him fear me. "But isn't she a supernatural being? I thought—"

"What did you just say?" I ask, my voice resembling a growl.

"That's why the Caputos agreed to give her the loan. They knew she'd always win."

"Where can I find them?"

"Flynn, we have to go." Cassandra's voice brings me

back to reality. I didn't realize how close I'd gotten to Paolo's face and how close I was to biting him.

"Don't you even think about running away. I'm a predator, and I always get my prey," I say, licking my lips and making sure the moron understands who he is up against.

"I'll stay. You guys go. I'll take care of this," Asmodeus says, stepping into the ring. What the fuck is the warlock going to do? I don't have time to think about him. All I need to do is make sure Talulla is okay.

We get to my car and lay Talulla on the back seat, Cassandra sitting with her friend's head on her lap.

"What the fuck happened, Cassandra?"

"I don't know, but after she came back from classes and work, she felt weird and tired. I gave her a stress potion, and she seemed back to normal."

"A stress potion? What are you now, a drug dealer?"

"It was barely an herb infusion, and Talulla takes stress potions all the time."

"Did she take anything else?"

"I have no idea. It could have been anything. She could have drunk something before the match."

"A stress potion, really?"

"She hasn't slept for days, Flynn, and she refused to cancel the fight. I had to do something." Cassandra's jaw is clenched, just like mine.

Talulla hasn't slept because of me and the information she got about me. This could have been prevented, but I gave her space, and now she might die because of it.

I try not to focus on the latter information Cassandra shared with me and say, "Fix it."

"Stop ordering me to do shit and drive. I need to think." I look into the rearview mirror and see the witch at work, trying to examine Talulla's body, smelling it, and trying to get any sort of vision from her.

"If she doesn't wake up, I'm going to kill you."

The laugh that comes out of Cassandra resonates in my ears as if it's in my fucking mind. "If you think you're threatening, you're not." I really do not like it when witches play dirty.

I drive like a maniac, and as soon as we get back downtown, I decide to take her to my place. "I have better security here than she does and a small pantry of herbs."

"Fine. I'll give Asmo the address."

As I pick her up again, bridal style, I realize how hot her skin is. Too hot. "She's burning up as if she has a fever."

"That's because she does have a fever." Her quick, witty reply makes me roll my eyes. I'm all for sarcasm, usually. Not today, though.

"It's impossible, Cassandra. She's...Goddammit."

"What is it?"

"Call Evanora, call your mother, call whoever you need to call because if she dies, I'm not going to be very pleased."

Realization finally hits her, and her eyes widen. "I'm on it. Try to lower her temperature down. Your skin is cold. Hug her or something." Somehow, Talulla took the potion that has been killing supernatural creatures.

So I do just that. I lay us down on my bed, and I wrap my arms around her, my cheek resting against her forehead. She's so hot it almost feels like she's bringing me back to life.

"Flynn." Talulla's voice is so low it's barely a whisper.

"I'm right here, little hunter," I say, trying to get her even closer. But there's not enough skin contact, so I decide to move her to the mattress for a second as I quickly unbutton my shirt.

"Don't leave me." Her voice is so soft, so desperate, and I bring her back into my arms as fast as I can.

"Shh, it's okay. Sleep, sweetheart. I'm not going anywhere," I say, rocking her back and forth, trying to create a steady rhythm.

Talulla's eyes close again, her heartbeat slowing down even more.

This is not good at all.

Cassandra walks into the room, a bunch of vials in her hand, as she blabbers on the phone to someone. She puts the call on speaker as she sits beside us, checking Talulla's temperature. "Shit, shit, shit," she mutters.

"What are these?" I gesture to the vials she put on the nightstand.

"Temporary fixes," a voice on the other side of the line says. "You need to find out who made that potion." Sybil Drusus, Cassandra's mother and head of the Drusus coven, is on the line.

"How temporary?" I ask, my voice cracking.

Cassandra chews her lower lip nervously, trying to find the right words. "An hour, maybe even less."

I am going to lose my goddamn mind.

"Did you already talk to Evanora?" I turn to the witch currently forcing one of the vials' contents down Talulla's throat.

"Mr. Lancaster, Evanora Hart is not responsible for what has happened to Talulla."

"I did not say that."

"Cassie Bear?" Sybil ignores me.

"Yes, Mom?"

"Did you see anything?"

Her shoulders drop in defeat. "Not about this."

My eyes widen at the statement. "What does that mean?"

Cassandra looks up at me. "I have visions if I touch people. That's why I don't usually look very...friendly."

"Then *touch* her."

"I've been touching her since we got into the car, Flynn. I see nothing. I see you, I see me, I see all her fucking life, except for this."

"Then focus and tell me who the fuck did this to her."

"I'm trying," she yells, her breathing fastening. "Something is blocking it. It's as if she has a protective spell on her."

Then it hits me. "Protective spell, like something that blocks her mind?"

"Yeah."

Of course. I'm a fucking idiot. "Give me the phone, Cassie Bear," I say, my anger making me quite unlikable to anyone around me.

She narrows her eyes at me, but hands me my phone.

After a few seconds of searching for the name, I dial the number.

One ring.

Two.

"What a nice surprise," the woman on the other end of the line says.

"Name your price, Monica, whatever you want."

"Flynn, you're not a generous man, so please enlighten me on why I am getting this wonderful new side of you."

"You know why."

"Do I?"

"If she dies, there's no place you'll be able to hide. I'll be your own personal hell."

"Now, now, are you really in the position of threatening the only person who can give you exactly what you want?"

"How did you even do it?"

"This is not something I am going to share, pet. I am a businesswoman, after all. I only prepare the product and sell it. I don't use it."

"Just tell me what to do to save her." My voice is desperate at this point. I'm ready to beg if I have to. I'm ready to give up anything if it means saving her.

"I suppose you have a witch with you," Monica states.

"Yes," Cassandra says. "I'm Cassandra Drusus."

"Very nice." A wicked laugh follows Monica's words. "You are a fortunate man, Flynn, and you know I don't like it when men get this lucky."

I sigh. "Tell me what you want. It's yours."

"Alighieri's notes," she says, and pauses for a moment. "And you're escorting me to an event I have at the university on Thursday evening."

I shake my head and laugh at the request. With my answer, she will know exactly how much Talulla means to me, and I'm sure she'll find a way to use it against me.

"You have Dante Alighieri's notes?" Cassandra's jaw drops.

I ignore her and go back to the problem. "Deal. Send me the address, and they'll be there by morning."

"I'm shocked, Flynn. The most valuable thing you possess, and you're ready to part with it for a mortal?"

"You knew I would say yes. Now tell Cassandra what to do."

"And you know I don't like orders, pet."

"Please."

Monica's laugh is haunting. It makes my body quiver, which makes my anger grow even more. "Boil three leaves of sage, a root of ginger, one chicken foot, and one drop of her blood."

Cassandra is writing everything down, nodding every time Monica adds an ingredient to the list. "All this is boiled in milk, I suppose?"

"Clever witch. You're a Drusus, after all," Monica replies. "By morning, Flynn. If I don't see my pretty package, I'll be very displeased. Oh, and don't forget the fundraiser in three days." The line cuts, and Cassandra is already working in the kitchen.

Then I'm back holding Talulla in my arms. I caress her hair and skin and listen to the sounds she's making now that she's asleep. A low inhale and exhale. She seems so peaceful, yet so scared. The way she looked at me earlier and asked for help—she's never been in that situation in her life. A moment where she knew exactly that she couldn't do anything to save herself. She felt helpless and turned to me, and I was ready to abandon all this for my selfish, depressed mind that thought I was ready to give up. I can't give up. I can't leave her. We belong in the same life. Even if she decides we can't be together, we still belong to each other, like two magnets that can't stay apart.

Cassandra comes back with a new vial. "Hold her head up," she instructs.

I do as I am told, and then the liquid is poured down Talulla's throat.

A couple of minutes pass by, and her temperature slowly comes down. Her skin is almost back to its normal temperature. I could kiss this witch on the face, but instead, I grab her hand, taking her by surprise, and simply say, "Thank you."

Cassandra's eyes look down at my gesture. Then, with a wide look on her face, she stares up at me. The corners of her lips lift up, forming a genuine smile. "Now, this is a turn of events."

Tilting my head to the side, I ask, "What did you see?"

"A reason to use my passport more often." She winks at me. "I'm gonna go grab her some clothes and see where Asmo is. I'll leave you two alone for a bit."

I nod, and she walks out the door, making sure it's closed.

Finally, I feel small movements in my arms, and the

most beautiful blue eyes finally look up at mine again. For a short moment, I truly think my lungs fill with air. I almost feel my heart start beating again. Talulla is my life. A chance for a new beginning. One where we both are each other's salvation.

Twenty

TALULLA

Icy-gray eyes are staring at me. I'm in Flynn's arms. In Flynn's bedroom. And I am completely soaked in sweat. We both are. Yes, because I'm currently nestled on his naked chest.

"What happened?" I press my palm to my forehead, trying to see if I'm all in one piece.

"What happened is that someone drugged you, and now I feel quite murderous."

"Flynn." I've been awake for two seconds, and I'm already annoyed at his constant murder threats.

"Talulla, someone tried to hurt you, really badly. To the point where I had to do something I know I'll end up regretting really soon to make sure you'd be okay."

"I'm sorry."

"Sorry? Why are you sorry? Someone hurt you, Talulla. I just—"

"And you stopped it right away."

"I stopped the fight, yes, but you were already not okay. I should have been more careful. I could have given you space and still kept an eye on you, but I didn't. Not like I should have."

"You gave me space because I asked for it. This is not your fault."

"What if I hadn't been there tonight? Cassandra and

Asmodeus wouldn't have noticed as quickly that you were not okay. It would have been—"

"There's no point in wondering what could have happened. Now we know we need to be even more careful about who we keep around."

His arms tighten around my body. "I don't know what I would have done, Talulla."

"I'm right here." My hands cup his cheeks, forcing him to look at me. "Right here, in your arms. Lying on your extremely gorgeous naked chest. Isn't that a turn of events?"

He chuckles, and the sound of his laugh makes me feel high. "You are indeed in my arms." His hand brushes my hair, and I comfortably rest my head on his chest again. "And I can't believe you're already trying to get into my pants."

I snort. "Oh, shut up. You are clearly doing it on purpose."

"I'm doing nothing on purpose," he says, continuing to brush my hair, and I groan as I keep getting lost in the pools of his eyes.

"Have you looked at yourself? Literally any woman who walks past you can't help but look at you."

"Someone sounds a little jealous."

"Oh, please..."

"I ran to save you, Talulla. I wouldn't do this for many people."

I raise my head to look at him. "Flynn, I—"

"You need to rest."

"No, wait. I need to say something." I bite my lower lip, knowing what I'm about to say will change everything.

He tilts his head. "You're nervous. What is it? Are you feeling okay? I should have taken you to the hospi—"

"I don't need more time."

"You took five days."

"Yeah, well, that's all I needed, okay?"

He laughs. "And your verdict?"

"I am tired of pushing you away. So, so tired."

His eyes soften. "You had me the first time you laid eyes on me, Talulla." His lips brush my temple. "Don't ever make me stay away for so long again."

"The cure thing...It took me by surprise. I've already lost so much. I don't think I can handle more losses."

"You never let me finish telling you why I want to take that cure."

"To end your life as a human again."

"That might have been my initial reason, but that's not why I want it now."

"And what is?"

His velvety fingers push my chin up, forcing me to look at him before he replies, "You."

My head tilts slightly. "I don't think I'm following."

"I want to be able to live a human life with you, Talulla." The corners of Flynn's lips lift up. "I want you, and if there is no you, there is no me either."

I crush my lips on his, and as I sit up in his lap, I feel his length harden under me. It's exhilarating, feverish. A burning sensation flourishes under my skin with his touch. I feel alive as our breaths consume one another. A holy redemption.

"Talulla, we gotta stop." Flynn breaks the kiss, making me frown.

"Why?"

"Because."

"That's not a valid reason." I dip back into the kiss, his lips hungrily molding with my own.

His hand gently wraps around my neck, and my core throbs at the sensation I feel all over. "You just got drugged, and we haven't even talked about it. We need to make a plan."

"I need to forget about everything right now—my family, this case, school. I just need you."

"You're still too weak, sweetheart."

"Flynn, I know how I'm feeling," I shout, moving my hips and creating a delicious friction that makes him groan in response.

"Do you now?" His smirk is so sexy it pains me.

"Yes..."

"You don't need my dominance."

"As much as I like that part of you very, very much, that's not what I was thinking."

"You don't need that right now."

"We can do that tomorrow. I just need you."

"Then, take whatever you need, darling. It's yours. Anything you crave for me to do, I'll do it."

"I need you to let me do what I'm about to do."

"Use me, Talulla. Do as you please."

My shorts are off right after, and then I unbuckle his belt before unbuttoning his pants and slowly pushing them down just enough to have access to his now rock-solid length. His black boxer briefs are ready to tear, and my mouth waters just thinking about his cock in my mouth and then inside my core.

"You're going to let me fuck you, Flynn."

"That can be arranged, little hunter."

Then, as I push the boxers down, his length comes out—so thick, long, veiny, and delicious. Ready to be sucked.

I close my mouth around the head, and he stares at me as I continue to explore his twitching cock. I take him as deep as I can, and right when the head hits the back of my throat, I pull out, and a smirk appears on his face.

"Look at you. You can take it all with no problem," he says, his hand massaging my throat.

"I like a challenge," I reply, making him chuckle.

Flynn's hips move up against my mouth again, and I take the head between my teeth, biting down. His eyes roll back as I continue to take him in. His hand grips my hair so tightly that I feel it getting ripped.

"Please ride me, fuck me, and use me until you come all over me," he says, his voice barely a whisper.

"I thought I was the one giving orders tonight."

"And you are. I am your servant, Talulla. You can ask me to do anything for you."

That's all I need to hear before I lower myself down onto his thick length. The painful stretch quickly turns into pleasure as I get readjusted to the size of his cock.

"Divine, that's what you are," he whispers as I start to move my body.

"I can't imagine my life without you, Flynn."

"Good thing I don't plan to go anywhere without you, Talulla." He grabs the bottom of my sports bra, and I instinctively pull my arms up, letting him take the fabric off completely, loving the breeze caressing my tits.

"Oh god," I moan as I continue to take him, bouncing on him faster with each stroke. Our bodies are entangled so tightly that we mark each other's skin. Flynn's mouth closes on my nipple as he keeps me in his embrace, a hand firm on the back of my neck and his other arm around my waist. Then, as my moans get louder and louder, he pulls my hair, exposing my neck to him.

Dipping down, he licks my collarbone, creating a trail of shivers. "The things I want to do to you, Talulla. I don't know if you understand—"

"If they're your hands, I want them on me and in me, Flynn."

"Such a dirty mouth," he says, going back to my tits. The way he sucks and nibbles on my pebbled nipples is so deliciously painful I could come just with that, but mixed with his cock impaling me? There is nothing that can remotely compare.

This is when I shatter. Piece by piece, he breaks my walls down and lets himself in. The way he holds and marks me is a reminder of his decision and what he would do for me. We continue molding our bodies together like this, with no anger, no control, just our souls trying desperately to hang on to each other for as long as possible.

Twenty-One

TALULLA

I don't remember falling asleep, but when I open my eyes again, the rays of sunshine lazily peek through the big window in front of the bed—Flynn's bed. I shift my gaze to my right and find the space empty, and for just a moment, that same feeling of emptiness pierces my lungs. Then they fill with air again when I hear voices in the other room, and I decide to get out of bed. Putting on the first clothes I find piled on the chair at the end of the bed, I make my way to the living room.

"Good morning, sunshine." Cassandra's voice is the first one that reaches me. It's soft, yet there's a tone of excitement. She's happy to see me.

I rub the palm of my hand over my left eye as I reply, "Good morning, crew." I turn to look at my vampire, his stare penetrating, and I suddenly feel weak in the knees. How can he just look at me like that? "Good morning, fangs," I say, the corners of my lips lifting into a smile that he clearly adores by the way he's looking at me now. His gray eyes create a thunderstorm in my chest.

"Good morning, darling. How are you feeling?" he replies as he gets to my side.

"I'm good. I didn't realize I fell asleep after we... *talked.*"

He snorts. "You needed the sleep." That I certainly

did. I feel like I still need to recover, but I also feel as if a weight has been lifted off my shoulders.

"So how did you guys wake me up after I passed out? What happened?"

Asmodeus gets up from the couch to join us in the middle of the living room, and now that I can finally see his face, I spot a bruise on his right eye. "Asmo, what the fuck happened to you?" I ask, my eyes widening. The purple of his skin makes his irises look even darker than usual.

"So when Cassie and your vampire took you away, I stayed to settle some stuff and, well...cover for you in the ring."

My jaw drops at his nonchalant attitude. "You did what?"

"Hey, calm down. I won. It's all good. You didn't lose your reputation."

I slap his arm so hard I can tell the guy is in pain. "I don't give a shit about my reputation! You can't do stuff like that, Asmodeus. You could have gotten really hurt."

He shrugs. "You do it all the time."

"Yeah, and I'm fucking trained to get beat up." The volume of my voice is getting higher with each word.

"You're not gonna do that anymore." The voice I hear now is not Asmodeus's. It's Flynn's, and his tone is low, firm, and *final*.

I tilt my head slightly. "What is that supposed to mean?"

"It means exactly what I said. You're done fighting."

"Flynn, I can't just stop. I have a debt to pay off," I say, crossing my arms over my chest.

"It's been taken care of."

"You did what?"

"Paolo won't need your *services* anymore." Flynn's

tone is so casual I almost let it slide, as if it's okay for him to decide something so major for me.

I narrow my eyes at him. "You can't just do stuff like that without consulting me. This is a lot."

Cassandra and Asmodeus leave the room as Flynn takes my hands in his. The contact sends electric shocks throughout my entire body, from the tip of my nose to the point of my toes. "I'm sorry I didn't talk to you about this, but you were dying in my bed, and I couldn't bear even the thought of you going through anything like this again."

I groan at his softness because why can't he just let me be mad for a second? "It's so much money, Flynn."

He smiles as he brings my hands to his mouth and kisses both palms. Such a gentle gesture coming from this dominant being who needs to be in charge at every moment. "It's the bare minimum, Talulla. What I did is the bare minimum, and you deserve so much more than that."

I shake my head in disbelief. "I don't think any man I've dated ever went past the flowers on a first date. I didn't know helping me pay my school debt was on the list of things I should've been looking for."

Then, he lowers his face to me, his lips barely touching mine. "Don't ever mention another man dating you, touching you, or looking at you. I don't need to go into stalking mode and torture anyone else right now."

I raise one eyebrow. "Dramatic much?"

"Never again, Talulla."

For a split second, his eyes turn dark red, a shade of anger I haven't seen in him yet. He would do it. He would go through the list of every man I've dated, one by one, and make sure they wouldn't walk again just for touching me. That should be enough to scare me off, yet it exhilarates me. But a pit in my stomach still keeps me grounded, a constant voice reminding me that what we have can't be real, because why would someone go through all this just for me? Why would he, a powerful vampire, decide to go through all this, knowing that I could stake him at any moment, and for good this time?

"How did you cure me? Was I given something? Because I don't remember taking any—"

"You were sick, as in you had the flu—a crazy flu. Someone gave you whatever was given to the werewolves."

"Okay, well, thank you, Cass," I say as she and Asmo walk back into the room, knowing she definitely gave me something to save me.

"Don't thank me yet. I had to cooperate with your new best friend," she says, playing with a strand of her silky black hair.

"Cassandra," Flynn growls.

"What? Were you really going to pretend you didn't have to call Monica Lazar?" she asks, resting her elbows on the table. "Because I certainly can't do that."

"Excuse me?" I ask, my voice clearly hinting at my sudden state of rage.

"After I called my mother, Evanora, and basically every witch I know, Flynn put two and two together and realized who brewed the lethal potion."

"So we know it's her. We finally have our killer."

"She might have procured the weapon, but she did not use it," Flynn spits out.

"Are you seriously protecting her right now?"

"I'm not protecting her. I'm just telling you that she doesn't do things randomly. Someone must have paid her a lot of money for it."

"Did you have to pay her to save me?"

He sighs. "Yes."

My eyes widen. "How much did she ask you?"

"It's not really how much. It's more what she asked me to give up, and I did it gladly."

"Flynn, spill it."

"It's not important. What's important is that you're here."

"She asked him to give up some of Dante's stuff he has, and—"

"Cassandra, I liked you more when you didn't feel this comfortable around me," he says, growling at her but staring at me, analyzing me.

"Dante's notes? Are you fucking serious right now?"

"You need to work on your language."

I narrow my eyes at his words before replying, "That's the most precious thing you own, Flynn. Why would you do that? I can't believe you gave up something so valuable."

"Your life is way more precious than those notes, Talulla. I'd do it again if I was asked to."

"You...I can't even begin to comprehend what you did."

"And I can't seem to understand why you're so surprised by my actions."

"You basically threw away millions of dollars."

Flynn shrugs his shoulders. "To save you."

"And what did she ask for afterward? Neil Armstrong's flagpole?" I ask, my arms now in the air.

Flynn laughs at my question. "The pole is still safe on the moon. Dante's notes were the most she asked for, and I am afraid of the repercussions this event might have with your father."

"Why?"

"Because she now knows how much you mean to me, Talulla, and she is an opportunist."

"I can't believe you went out with her. She literally looks like a snake."

He chuckles, shaking his head. "Please don't remind me of my stupidity."

I join in his laughter. "Okay, well, I need to go see if I still have a job."

"It's Saturday."

"Yes, and I have a presentation to prepare for next week."

"Can I take you out for dinner later?"

"Can't we just stay in?"

"Whatever you prefer. I just want to see you."

I nod. "Sure, I'd like that."

"Wait, I'll come with you. I have a meeting for my dissertation in half an hour," Cassandra says, getting up.

Asmodeus follows her. "I guess I'm meeting Set all alone," he says in a dramatic voice.

"What are you doing with Set Drusus?" Flynn asks, his fingers scratching his jaw.

"We're going to analyze Scott's body. Set might have... borrowed it."

Then I hear Flynn laugh. A true laugh. A full-body laugh. "Of course he did. Good old Set, always ready to go over the limit." I don't think I could love a sound as much as this one. Pure serenity and tranquility are what Flynn's laugh radiates.

And then I do what I know my vampire will absolutely hate because he might be the love of my life, but he still needs to be taught a lesson—at least this once. "Fangs, you should join them."

"Wait, what?" Asmodeus and Flynn say in unison.

"Aw, look at you two, already finishing each other's sentences."

I can see Flynn's nostrils flare. "Talulla, you're gonna pay for this."

"You can punish me all you want later." I wink at him, grabbing my stuff.

"Actually, that's a really good idea," Cassandra says to Asmo, barely brushing his arm. The closeness is already enough for him to relax. "The analysis of the body, not whatever you two weirdos do in bed."

Asmodeus's eyes roll. "Fine, but don't sink your teeth into anyone while we're out."

Twenty-Two

FLYNN

Do I want to spend my free time with Asmodeus Gratiadei? No, I truly don't. But Set Drusus is someone I haven't seen in a while and someone I don't particularly despise either. If he can help find who is behind these deaths, then it will be a faster solution to finding out who tried to hurt Talulla. I can't believe she forced me into this situation.

I could ask Monica, probably bargain something else for it, but the reality is that she is too loyal to her customers, and she would never give out the name, just like she would never let me compel her to tell me the name. After what I'll have to endure, maybe it's better if I never mention her name again, even if she did save Talulla.

I decide to drive. Asmo, in the passenger seat, remains silent after giving me the address.

"We're making a stop along the way," I state, gripping the steering wheel so tight I feel the piece of leather-covered plastic mold between my fingers.

"Please don't make me clean blood so early in the morning. I'm wearing new sneakers."

"We're not going to kill anyone right now...if they behave, of course."

Asmodeus rolls his eyes. "I knew I should've driven."

"Hey, you can apparate out of here anytime you want. I didn't really ask to be in your presence, but here we are."

"Listen, I know you don't particularly like me, because I am of the male species and Talulla likes me—"

I snort. "That's not entirely true."

"Oh?"

"I haven't been given a reason yet to like you. My judgment could change."

He laughs at my words. "You're an asshole."

"I know."

"Fine, let's go play with Paolo."

"Thank you."

We park right outside the warehouse, the place that only a few hours ago almost became the burial of my soul. I was ready to rip everyone's head off. I was ready to give all of them a reason to end me because seeing Talulla unconscious in my arms gave me the only reason why I would want to die. Living a life where she isn't breathing is not something I desire.

"Flynn," Asmodeus starts, pressing his hand on my chest to stop me. "We question him, and we leave."

"I'm not going to eat him for breakfast, if that's what you're worried about."

"You wanted to last night."

"Last night, I was a little upset." I scratch my throat. "And don't boss me around. I don't like being told what to do."

"So no sudden urge to change your ways?"

Is he really worried about me biting into some innocent's neck? "No, I'm not going to bite anyone." I roll my eyes. "See, this is why it's hard for me to like you. You have no faith in me."

"You're a vampire."

"An old one who knows how to control himself," I reply. "God, you're unbearable."

"Fine, I'm sorry. Let's get this over with so we can go admire a dead body in my basement."

I knock on the large metal door, and not even a minute later, Paolo opens it, not really surprised to see us in front of him.

"Good morning, sunshine," I say, smiling nice and wide and making my fangs visible.

One of his eyebrows lifts up. "Is she okay?"

I shake my head. "You don't get to ask how she's doing," I reply, my voice turning into a growl. Asmodeus grabs my arm, and I swear if he touches me again, I might rip his hand off. "Take your fingers off me," I say, turning to look at the wizard beside me.

He ignores me and goes back to looking at Paolo. "We have a couple of questions."

Paolo nods and lets us walk in, then he closes the door behind us and locks it. "How do you know about Talulla?"

"I didn't. One of my superiors saw her and told me to accept her request."

"One of the Caputos?"

"Yes," he says, shifting his weight from one foot to another. "They've dealt with other supernatural beings in the past. I think they just saw the easy money."

"What happened last night?"

"You tell me. She seemed tired when she walked in, but after I talked to her, she was okay."

"Did you give her anything?"

"What? No, only a water bottle."

This is when I grab him by the throat and push him against the closest wall. "You call a water bottle nothing?"

"It was in the fridge. A brand-new water bottle."

Asmodeus cracks his neck. "Do you still have this bottle of water?"

"If it's still here, it's in the changing room."

"Great," I start, moving toward the back. "Pray the

bottle is still there because if it isn't, I might have to play my favorite game."

Paolo's eyes widen when he sees the tip of my tongue pressed against a fang, crimson liquid dripping onto my bottom lip.

"He's just messing with you. He's truly harmless," Asmodeus says, squeezing the human's shoulders. "Just don't disappoint him, though. I really don't want to clean up another mess."

Well played. Maybe I don't despise being in his presence too much.

"The bottle is there. I know it is. No one came in to clean yet."

That I can tell. The smell of sweat and dried-up cheap beer is still everywhere. The plastic cups are mostly contained in big, black garbage bags, but the ambiance is still the same as last night.

I enter the changing room, and the faint scent of fresh strawberries hits me. Even after so many hours, her essence still lingers here. I close my eyes for a moment, remembering that Talulla is okay and at school. She's back to normal and with me. Mine once again.

Looking around the space, I see the bench where she leaves her bag, the big gym bathroom with showers right in the corner—where I've been dreaming to fuck her—and then, to the far-left corner, on the floor, a bottle of water stands. "Bingo," I say to myself, making my way to it.

I march toward Asmodeus, handing him the water bottle. "So? Can you tell me anything?"

"Yeah, that we need to go home and test it."

"Can't you just tell me if there's a potion in this?"

"It clearly was made to look invisible to the eye," he starts. Then, after smelling the contents, he adds, "And to have no smell, so no, I can't tell you without testing it."

This means I don't have a reason to kill Paolo yet. My nostrils flare at the thought of having to let him go. "Fine. Let's go meet Set." My teeth grind.

"Hey, it's okay. You can play with his organs another day." Asmodeus pats my back, and I snort at his choice of words because Paolo is terrified at this point.

"It's your lucky day," I tell him. "But if I see you anywhere close to her again, I might change my mind."

"I never wanted to hurt her."

"Good, don't start now," I say, following Asmodeus toward the exit. "And tell your wannabe criminal friends that if they mess with someone close to me again, they won't get the same treatment. I will rip them to shreds without giving them a chance to explain their actions."

Paolo simply nods. "Understood."

We get on the road once again, and after a few minutes of silence, I notice Asmodeus looking outside the window, deep in thought.

"Are you ever going to act on your feelings, or are you planning to suppress them for much longer?" I don't even know why I even bother asking. It's something I actually don't care about, but Cassandra has been decent with me, and he's been somewhat bearable to be around this morning.

The wizard's jaw tightens. "I don't think my personal life is any of your concern."

"Ah, I see. A bit of a touchy subject."

"Not that it's any of your business, but Cassandra needs time to heal, and she won't let herself go until she finds out what happened to her father."

"You might have to wait a long time for that."

"She's worth the wait. I'm sure you can somewhat relate to that," he replies, taking me by surprise. Because I do in fact understand that. He has seen how agitated I get when the topic of Talulla's safety is on the table.

"Well, I certainly hope you won't have to wait as long as I had to."

He turns his face toward me. "Can I ask you something?"

"I guess."

"Before Talulla, why did you want to take the cure?"

"Because I decided that it wasn't worth the wait anymore."

"Okay, but it's a cure. You wanted to be human again. Why?"

"When I got turned, I wasn't given a choice. I had to endure the loss of all my loved ones, knowing that I would remain the same. Yet, I was becoming a shell of a creature." My hands grip the steering wheel tightly as I continue my story. "I wanted to take the cure to feel something again. To feel real pain, real sadness, real everything before letting myself go. I haven't felt any kind of emotions—human emotions—since I left for war."

"Okay, but you were still human when you enrolled. What makes you believe you'll feel what you need to feel by taking the cure?"

"Hope never dies, Asmodeus."

"And what about now?"

The corners of my mouth lift up as I continue to look at the road. "You know why I want it now."

We turn into a subdivision of Palo Alto, a well-kept suburban area. The road is perfectly pristine. The trees are well-groomed, and the houses are more like mansions than anything else. "I didn't expect the Drusus coven to have a place so out in the open."

"We like to blend in. It helps make us look normal."

I laugh at that statement. "Sure."

After parking the car in the driveway, we make our way to the big wooden entrance doors. Asmodeus doesn't even have to put the key in the lock before it slowly swings open.

Set Drusus awaits right behind it.

"Flynn Lancaster," he says, his lips curled into a smirk. "Can't believe it took you this long to come visit." His sandy blond hair is up in a bun, and his dark eyes are the complete opposite of Cassandra's. They look like the definition of yin and yang. Sun and moon. She, with her black hair and light eyes, and he, with his blond hair and almost black eyes.

"I've been busy these days," I reply, smirking right back at him.

"So I've been told." Set raises an eyebrow at me. "Talulla Popescu. Quite ironic, isn't it?"

"I guess I'm a bit of a masochist."

He chuckles. "Just a little...but it makes sense, somehow."

I tilt my head slightly to the side. "How?"

"You're both people who were forced into a life you didn't ask for."

"Doesn't it bother you?" Yes, because in our world, there are unspoken rules, and what Talulla and I have been doing isn't really seen as normal.

"Why would it? You're both adults. Just because your heart doesn't beat doesn't mean I will stop you from falling in love. Talulla needs to be cared for. She never really had that."

"That's all I want to do."

"Then we're all okay with it. I mean, Cassie and Asmo have been okay with it since you showed up."

"Thank you."

"Sure." He nods. "Okay, let's look at this corpse now. I already had to use a potion to stop the decomposition."

Twenty-Three

FLYNN

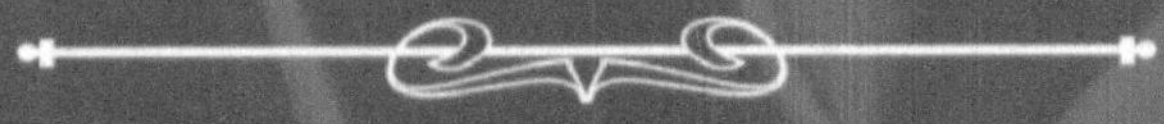

If I had known I'd be poking a half-putrefied body today, I'd have worn different clothes.

After Set informed us of the state of the dead werewolf, we came down to the basement immediately. The Drususes definitely have all they need to do pretty much anything down here. You'd imagine a witch's basement as decaying and scary. This is filled with modern technology and furniture. There is a second kitchen, and instead of an island, there's a big metal table illuminated with fluorescent lights. Scott's body lies on it.

"Fuck, he smells terrible," I state, walking a few steps backward, my senses running wild.

Asmodeus is quick to reply. "I mean, he is dead."

"Why wasn't he kept in a freezer?"

"Oh, he was," Set says, rubbing his forearm against his nose. "And I've used I don't know how many potions to stop the process."

"Strange."

"Did you guys know him?"

"No, I think only Talulla did," Asmodeus remarks, slipping the latex gloves off and throwing them into the garbage.

"Someone is clearly trying to cover their tracks." Someone like Monica, and even if I understand why she wants to keep herself out of the equation, we all know she's right at the center of it. "Didn't he go and buy some protection potions?"

"It could be a reaction from the mix of ingredients in his body." Set is close to Scott once again. It's truly remarkable to see him so impassive to the stench filling the basement.

"Did it happen with the other bodies as well?"

"Can't really say. We didn't have a chance to get our hands on those ones before the pack did."

"And what does Bear Creek U say about this?"

"That it's truly a tragedy, but that it's clearly contained to the frat house, which is the pack house."

"Too bad we know it isn't."

"Why would Talulla be involved in this, though?" Set asks, raising the question we all have.

I sigh. "I'm going to regret asking this, but was she involved with any of them?" I question Asmodeus.

"I don't know for certain about any of the dead ones, but I mean, I know she did go out with a couple of werewolves."

"A couple?" My nostrils flare. I did ask. It's my fault. "That dog she was dancing with that time at the club?"

"I don't think I should be telling you any of this."

It's too bad that now my brain can only think about that. "That night?"

"God, no. She was too busy trying to find excuses not to like you. Don't worry, she literally only has eyes for you."

"This still doesn't explain why she was given the potion as well."

"So if there are no current ties between the pack and the Popescus, it has to be something else. Maybe someone is seeking revenge, and they saw Talulla that night and thought she was part of it."

"That could be it," I say as I move around the body,

smelling and touching it. The rigid frame is turning squishier and easier to break the more we examine it. There's only one thing left to do now. "Any luck with the police report?"

Set shakes his head. They were trying to do this the legal way. I don't know why when they literally stole a dead body without thinking about it twice.

"I guess it's time to pay a visit to the police archives."

"We need a plan for that," Asmodeus says.

"You pretty wizards think about brewing that invisibility potion Cassandra and Talulla used to stalk me."

"And then what?" Set questions, his smirk never leaving his face, because it's clear he knows exactly what I'm thinking about.

"Then you let me do what I'm good at."

We take the potion and then apparate inside the police station. I grab the first police officer I see, and with his head in my hands, I start doing my part. "Do you have access to the archives?"

"No. You need a written request from the captain, and then you need clearance from the officers at the archives' door."

"And how do we go down to the archives?"

"You take the elevator right there." The compelled officer points to our left. "You go down to P3, and when you come out, the door will be on your left. Two officers are always on duty to make sure no one without permission goes in."

"Will they know where a specific file is?"

"They can tell you the general area. Everything is in chronological order, so if you know the dates, you'll be able to find what you're looking for fairly quickly."

"Flynn, we have to go. The potion is not gonna last much longer," Asmodeus whispers in my ear. The police officer blinks a few times, realizing something weird is going on.

"Forget everything I asked, and even if you remember it, who's going to believe you? No one is in front of you." The man blinks a few times, and then he's on his way again.

"We can't take the elevator. It would look like air is moving."

"Then let's apparate to P3," Set says, grabbing both our arms and doing just that. "We have about six minutes left. Let's make them count."

We run into the police officers who guard the door, compel them, and walk right inside without anyone suspecting anything at all, just like we planned.

"When did the alpha die?" I ask the wizards, hoping they will know the exact date.

"Three years ago."

"That's all you know?"

"It's okay, dude. Let's find the boxes from 2021, and then I'll do my tracker juju." Asmodeus claps his hands and then rubs them.

"Did you seriously just say *juju*?" I ask, trying to contain my laughter.

"Yeah, I can say it. I'm allowed. I'm a fucking wizard."

The officers point us toward the 2021 section, and you'd think it would be smaller, knowing humans were going through a pandemic, but nope, it's massive.

"Asmo, you might want to do your thing now. We have less than two minutes left." Set is looking at his watch nervously.

"I'm looking," he replies, feeling all the boxes and carefully scanning all the documents.

"One minute."

Then the blond wizard stops in front of a section, looks down, and giggles. "Here it is." Opening it, he sees the file, grabs it, and carefully puts the box back exactly how he found it.

"Thirty seconds."

Asmodeus jogs toward us. One of my hands is holding Set's arm, the other ready to catch his friend.

"And we're out of here." We hold on to each other and make our theatrical disappearance just in time.

We're back at the Drususes' now, and with the alpha's report in our hands.

"Where do you keep the whiskey?" I ask Set, pacing toward the kitchen.

"Bottom drawer on your left."

I get the bottle and three glasses. We all need a sip right now. Set and Asmodeus both sit at the island.

I pour the drinks and then say, "Well?"

"Wanna do the honors?" Asmodeus replies, sliding the folder across the countertop.

Grabbing it, I open it and start flipping through the pages. "What the fuck?"

Set and Asmodeus are at my side right away. Yes, because this might say that it's Dalton Reyes's file, but most of the pages are ripped out, and if there's any sort of wording, every possible name or connection has been blacked out.

"Someone got there before us."

We continue to look through everything, and despite the fact that there's no written information that can guide us in the right direction, I notice something in the pictures of the crashed car.

"There's a bag," I point out.

"Okay, so he had a bag in the car."

"No, look," I say, making Set look closer. "It's a purse."

"Dalton wasn't alone in the car."

Twenty-Four

TALULLA

I didn't think I'd be able to talk to my mom when I called her, but here I am, waiting for her to show up at my dorm with a dress for the fundraiser I have tonight. An event I haven't told Flynn about. I was going to do it yesterday, but he, Asmo, and Set apparently stayed out all night, and I didn't want to add to it.

Is it really that big of a deal? I am attending an event for my department with the professor I assist. It's truly just work. It shouldn't matter.

A knock on my door makes me jolt. My mother is here. I run to the door, my hands shaking, hoping she's alone.

"Hi, sweetheart." Her soft voice calms me down right away. She walks in and hugs me, her touch making my eyes water. I missed her, and I know she missed me too.

"Hi, Mom," I manage to reply, locking my arms around her and holding her tight.

After a few minutes of sobs and embraces, she wipes my tears with her thumb. "Now, this is a happy occasion, and there will be many more. Here," she says, handing me an envelope. "I'm going to bring you more as soon as I can. Cash is the one thing your dad can't trace."

"Mom, you didn't have—"

"Just because I married into a family of hunters

doesn't mean you need to be forced into one as well. My child, take this, and I will bring you more as soon as I can. Please don't get into any trouble."

"I'm just trying to finish school."

"I know you are," she says, her smile growing bigger and bigger. "And I am so proud of your achievements."

"Thank you."

"Here, I brought you the dress you wanted." My mom finally hands me the bag containing the one fancy dress I own and don't hate. A bright red dress with thin straps and a dangerously low V neckline. "I do think the décolleté is a little much."

"That's the point. Maybe it'll convince the investors to donate more money."

"And you're going with your professor to this event?"

"I am, yes."

"Is he—"

"No, Mom, I am not dating my superior. I'm actually...I'm seeing someone, but it's new, and I don't want to jinx it." *Or tell you it's a vampire and give you a heart attack.*

"Does he treat you well?"

"Very."

The corners of her lips lift into a bright smile. "Then I hope to meet him soon."

"Me too." *Not really. Again, you might actually die on the spot as soon as you see him.*

"I'd better go now. I told your father I was going to run some errands."

"I'm sorry, Mom."

"For what?"

"For making you lie to him, for having to be in the midd—"

"Don't you dare apologize for something you didn't

do. Now, get all pretty and have fun. Talulla, do not ever think that this situation is your fault. I am your mother. It's my job to protect you and love you."

"Love you too, Mom." With that, I'm alone again in my dorm room.

I haven't heard from Flynn or anyone else yet today, so I use this moment of solitude to take a bath.

I light a couple of lavender candles, put some music in the background, and start filling the tub with scorching hot water. The hotter the better.

I don't realize I've drifted off until I hear the door to my dorm open and then close. I don't even have to turn to know who's now resting against the doorframe of my bathroom.

As I step out of the bathtub, I grab my robe and start drying myself. I pretend not to see him and go on with my day. Then, as I tie the bathrobe, I turn to look at him. His eyes are as dark as petrol. He's looking at me as if I am his favorite cake. I swear, if I continue to stare at him, drool might start dripping from his fangs.

"Can I help you with anything?" I ask as I continue to dry myself, pretending his stare isn't doing anything to me. Spoiler alert: it's totally turning me on. I'm ready to drop this robe and let him eat me alive.

"No, I am quite content with the view already."

"I'm sure."

"Could be even better if the robe suddenly fell to the floor, though."

"I am certain that would please you very much." I grab my panties, and as I bend down to step into them, I hear him sigh. "Yes?" I question, raising my eyebrow at him.

"What do I have to do to get you to follow my orders?"

"I'm sure there are many girls who would do just that."

He gets behind me in less than a second. "There's only you, Talulla."

There it is—the absurd amount of devotion this vampire can't seem to stop showing me. "How can you just want *me*?"

"Just *you*?" He chuckles before turning toward the bathtub still filled with water. After he points at it, he turns his head toward me. "I'd even drink your bathwater. That's how obsessed I am with you, Talulla."

My eyes widen as I look at him, then at the bathtub, and then back at him. "Please don't do that. I know you're already dead, but I'm sure soap doesn't taste good."

"It would."

"What?"

"You were soaking in that water. It would taste like you. And god, I would do anything to just drink anything with your taste in it."

"Okay, fine. That's obsessive enough."

"I told you. It's only you, sweetheart, no one else. Not anymore. Not ever." Then he moves toward the sink, grabs the glass I leave there at night, goes to the bathtub, and scoops some water into it.

"You don't have to prove anything, Flynn. I get it. You like me. It's fine."

"Like you?" He shakes his head and downs the water in one go. "I crave you like I crave air. You are the most addictive drug, and you're *mine*."

I gasp as he grabs me by my ass and brings me closer to him. "Yours, Flynn," I say back to him.

Then his lips are on mine, and I melt at his touch, his scent, and how his tongue moves in unison with my own. I could now die a happy woman, knowing that I've been touched this way by this man.

"So how did it go with Set and Asmodeus?"

"Good. We haven't really found anything new yet, but we did make a little visit to the police archives. It's not surprising, but the report has been altered," he starts, following me out of the bathroom and pausing in alert. "Your mother was here."

"Yes, she came by a while ago. What do you mean 'altered'?"

"Can I ask how it went?"

"What?" I tilt my head slightly. "Oh, she just dropped something off for me. She also gave me an envelope full of cash."

"And you're okay?"

"I'm okay. I mean, yeah, I'll be okay. It was nice seeing her. So you were saying about the police report?"

"Pages were ripped, things were clearly missing, and every possible useful notion was blacked out. Set is trying to find a way to recover some of those words, but nothing yet."

"So someone is clearly trying to cover their tracks."

"Exactly, and we now think there were two people in the car, not just Dalton." He turns to look at my bed, and the corners of his lips lift up. "Planning to wear a gown for me?"

I snort. "I'm sorry to disappoint you, but that's for a fundraiser for my department. It's pretty fancy, so I asked my mom to bring me something. Just a university thing, nothing crazy."

"And when is this fundraiser?" His jaw clenches. Is he *nervous*?

I shrug my shoulders. "Tonight."

"You're not going."

"Flynn, you might order me around in bed, but this is my job. I'm not just gonna stay home because you told me to."

"And I would never ask you to do that except for this specific event."

"Why?" I ask, raising one eyebrow at him.

He sighs. "I didn't want you to get worked up about this, but—"

"But what, Flynn? Why can't I go to my own department's fundraiser?"

"Because I am going."

"Wait, what? You can't. You absolutely can't come tonight."

Fuck. Fuck. Fuck.

He crosses his arms over his chest. "And why can't I go now?"

"Because." *Because I am going with my professor, and you'll get quite pissed about it. That's why.*

"Talulla, are you escorting someone to this event?"

"You're making it sound like something that it isn't."

His eyes narrow on mine. "You're not going with Eric fucking Wagner."

I clear my throat, trying to find the force to keep fighting for something I truly didn't even want to do in the first place, but now have to. "I have to."

"I can't believe I'm hearing this."

"And why are you even going to this damn thing? It's just a Bear Creek event."

His jaw closes shut. He doesn't want to tell me. That's how bad this is. Why is he so worried to tell me? Because I know exactly why and who he's going with.

Monica Lazar.

"No."

"It was one of her conditions for the potion recipe."

I shake my head. "Absolutely fucking not."

"Talulla, I made a deal, and I have to fulfill my end of the bargain."

"You gave her the thing you valued the most, and now this?"

"You are the most valuable thing in my life, Talulla."

"Sweet talking won't get you anywhere right now, Flynn. I'm pissed."

"Yeah, well, I'm pretty upset as well."

"Why?"

"Because another man is going to spend time with you right in front of my fucking eyes."

"She's good, that's for sure. Fucking snake."

"Don't let her mess with your head."

"What game is she playing? She's clearly involved in those deaths. Why would she care about this event?"

"Probably because she knew you were going, something not even I knew."

"I was going to tell you. It has been planned for months. I didn't want you to get worked up over it. It's really just to get research money," I say, biting my bottom lip. "Cassandra will be there too."

His hand rests on my cheek, and I look up at him. If he had been angry before, that emotion had turned into something much softer, almost *gentle.* "If we want this to work, we need to tell each other things, even if they might hurt the other person."

"I'm sorry. I really didn't think it was a big deal...until you happened."

"I know." He kisses my forehead. "But if he touches you too much, I might break his hands."

"But you should've told me as well."

"Yes, I should have, and I'm so sorry my unfortunate past is forcing you to spend time in the vicinity of that woman."

"Can you promise me something?"

His thumb brushes my lower lip, forcing me to stop biting it. "Anything."

"Promise me to leave that place with me tonight."

His lips brush mine. "I'm bringing you out of there over my shoulder if I have to."

"And are you going to punish me?"

His eyes darken, and his hand grips my throat. "You did force me into spending time with Asmodeus. You definitely need to be taught a lesson."

Twenty-Five

FLYNN

Leaving Talulla's dorm to go and get ready to spend time with a witch I despise was harder than I thought it would be, but here I am, pulling out a damn tuxedo from my closet. Monica has planned this for a specific reason, and I truly can't understand why.

Knowing how broken Monica is almost makes me understand her mischievous ways, but there was no need to interfere with my lover's life. Not when Talulla has been under the torturous spell of a man for her entire life as well. They are so similar yet so completely different. Monica feeds on her anger and grudges, but Talulla—my Talulla—walks all over them and conquers them. She embraces her fears and accepts them as they are.

I look at myself in the mirror as I button my black silk shirt. I can already imagine Talulla's fingers caressing the fabric, and just the thought of her hands on my chest makes my throat constrict. The effect she has on me is just like her touch—ethereal yet deadly.

My daydreaming gets interrupted by a knock on my door, and I growl, knowing it's my unfortunate company for the night awaiting.

I told her I'd pick her up, but she insisted on coming here, where I live, probably just to piss me off even more, and yet I still owe her everything for giving me the cure to save Talulla.

"Good evening, Monica. You look well," I say, opening the door, my temples suddenly feeling unsafe.

"You always look the part, Flynn. I'm glad I don't have to force you out of this penthouse." She walks in, goes straight to the couch, and sits down. Her dark green satin gown complements her features, and her amber skin looks brilliant under the fabric that envelops all her curves. Her dark auburn hair is curled to perfection, and her hazel eyes pop with the earthy-toned eyeshadow she picked. I can't even lie about it. She also knows how to look the part.

"Are we ready to go?"

She eyes me, her head tilting a little before her lips curl into a smirk. "I was hoping for a drink before we take off."

I roll my eyes but make my way to my bar. "Gin martini is still your drink?"

Her smirk grows even wider. "You never disappoint me, pet."

"I'm not going to fall for it a second time, Monica. We're here because of a deal we made. I'm spending time with you because I gave you my word I would, not for any other reason."

"What is it you see in her?"

I take my time to shake her drink, pour it into a glass, and hand it to her. "Everything, Monica. I see everything in her."

"You're talking as if she were your mate."

"Would it be so crazy if she were?"

"She's a vampire hunter, Flynn. A human vampire hunter."

"Life can be quite ironic, can't it? Me, an old vampire, who ends up with a vampire hunter."

"You know what I think it is, Flynn? I think this is your way of playing with Emil's head. What better way to piss off the most famous vampire hunter in history than to fuck his daughter?"

This is when my hands end up around her neck, and not in a pleasurable way this time. "What I do with Talulla is none of your concern. Now, finish your drink, and let's go. This conversation was not part of the agreement."

"Fine, you moody vampire."

I growl as I open my fridge, needing to drink some blood before I break my non-neck diet and suck her dry. I grab my bottle and pour myself a glass, downing it so quickly I almost spill it on my blazer.

We reach the parking lot, and I almost automatically walk to open her door, but thankfully, I stop myself at the last second. "You're an independent woman. You can open your own door." Then I march to the driver's side.

"Your manners have definitely changed."

"They didn't. I did."

"Oh no, you're still exactly the same scared soul who just needs to feel something."

"I do feel something, Monica, and it's not for you."

She rolls her eyes. "We get it. You're obsessed with the Popescu prodigy."

"Yes, I am," I reply, my smile so bright it angers her even more. Good.

The fundraiser is being held in the main building at Bear Creek, and the Victorian-style architecture is giving me a little bit of nostalgia. I've been traveling around for a while, and I wouldn't mind going back to London at some point, but right now, my priorities are elsewhere.

I offer my arm to the witch, and we walk inside. I can pick my hunter's scent almost immediately, but she's nowhere to be found, and the thought of knowing she's close but not visible makes me feel on edge.

"Nervous?" Monica asks, and I ignore her, trying to

keep my senses on high alert for any possible problem. "Well, maybe you'll start speaking after the first few key speakers. I'm very intrigued by these young minds working so hard to discover frivolous things we tried to keep hidden."

"If this is your way of insulting my partner, it's not working."

"Partner? Is that what you call her?" She chuckles, continuing to annoy me.

"I'm done discussing my private life with you. Now, can we please go sit down and get this over with?"

"Fine, party pooper."

We take a seat at a table. Cocktails are being served, and I think I've never been happier to down any kind of alcohol being presented to me.

"Are you trying to get drunk?"

"Yes," I reply quickly, paying attention only to the stage. I recognize Cassandra's figure in the distance, a piece of paper in her hands, and then I look a little more to my right and finally see her. My mouth opens slightly as I stare at my only reason for existence. Talulla is also holding a piece of paper, and she's pressing her hand to her forehead and checking her temperature. She's nervous, and I can't go to her, not when Monica is around, ready to find an excuse to bring her down.

The lights dim, and as the waiters start bringing the appetizers, the first speaker starts talking. It's Ms. Sinopoli, the woman working on Da Vinci's life, who now has my sketches locked in her lab.

Then Eric talks, and as he does, he calls Cassandra and Talulla on stage to add something about human evolution. I'm not really paying attention to what the moron is saying, because my eyes are on my girl. Talulla completely transforms and turns into this creature who could talk about her interests for hours and hours without getting tired, and I'd listen to every single word she has to say about how civilizations are similar to one another yet so different, and how history repeats itself because we tend to always try to forget what happened in the past. She goes on and on, and I am mesmerized by how confident this side of her is.

She's confident in every aspect of her life, but it's clear how her traumas have made her doubt herself and everything around her. But this, this right here, is what she was born to do, and I will do anything in my power to let her have it. I almost wish her father could see her, could see how this side of her should be her entire life.

And that dress. That fucking dress is all I'm going to be working on later. Her full breasts are holding on for dear life as the deep V neckline of her gown shows her golden skin. This princess-style red dress makes her look both regal and sexy as hell. A queen in disguise. I've decided that red is her color, and she deserves to have hundreds of these gowns.

"Are you done?" Monica asks, breaking my hypnosis.

"You're still here. What a shame," I reply, grabbing my glass of whiskey and sipping it as I continue to listen. Cassandra has now taken over, and it's really interesting to see two walking weapons like them light up so much about something like history. Deadly for our world, but here, they're two women convincing us that their passion can actually help make a difference in the world.

Fuck, sign me up. Take all my money if this is how they feel by using it.

After all that, we finish whatever food they were serving us. Monica is staying silent, but her constant smirk makes me think she has something planned, and I really don't like it.

"What is it, Monica?" I finally ask, unable to control myself.

"Nothing, Flynn. Just enjoying this evening with an old friend."

"We're not friends, Monica."

"Oh, shush. Now, come on, come with me. I want to go say hi to your lovely lady."

"No."

"If you don't want to come with me, then I'll go by myself." She stands up, and I grab her hand so quickly she almost gasps. Not in surprise—she's never truly surprised—but maybe because of the contact of my skin on hers.

We make our way closer to the stage where Eric and Talulla are standing, talking to some other people, and as we approach them, my eyes lock with my favorite blue ones. The corners of my lips lift up as she looks at me, and she smiles back for just a moment, because then her eyes look at who is beside me.

Monica's grip tightens, and her hand rests on my chest as she greets Talulla. "You really do have a death wish," I whisper to her, grabbing her wrist and ripping it off my chest.

"Talulla, what a coincidence to see you here," she says before resting her hand on my chest once more. "Isn't it, Flynn? Such a wonderful coincidence."

I rip her hand off once more before looking at my beautiful hunter. "Yes, such a wonderful coincidence." I wink at her. "Always a pleasure to see you, Miss Popescu. Your speech with Miss Drusus was very compelling," I say, kissing her hand.

Then Monica turns to Eric, who is now holding my Talulla by the fucking waist. "And you are?" Monica's tone is higher, and her narrowed eyes on Eric definitely don't go unnoticed. What game is she playing? She clearly wanted to meet Mr. Wagner for a reason, but what is the reason?

"Eric Wagner," he says, extending his hand to shake hers. "Pleasure to meet you."

I snort.

His eyes turn toward me, and I take the hand he's offering. "Mr. Lancaster, I didn't expect to see you tonight."

"What can I say, Mr. Wagner? I'm a man full of surprises and money to throw out the window."

"Well, I'm glad I didn't ask you to give a motivational speech to my students earlier. They'd like to think your money will be well spent."

"I know I have invested my money wisely, Mr. Wagner. I'm not regretting one single penny," I reply, turning my eyes to my Talulla.

Then my senses go on high alert because someone we weren't expecting just walked into the room, and Talulla has no idea how complicated things are about to get.

I turn to look at Monica. "You did not." And she laughs in response.

"What's happening?" Talulla asks, probably hearing my change of tone.

"Eric, please take Talulla away from us." My voice sounds almost like I'm begging, and Eric is confused at my request.

"What? Why?" Talulla asks.

"Because your father is here."

Talulla's jaw drops open. "Fuck, fuck, fuck." The glass of red wine she was holding is now on the floor, her red dress stained. I quickly get to her and force her to move away so that I can deal with this situation.

Monica grabs Talulla's wrist before they even get a chance to leave. "I think you should say hi to your father now. Be a good *copil.*"

"Monica, let her go," I growl, my fangs definitely showing.

"You don't scare me, Flynn. I can make you fall to your knees in a second."

"You might be able to do that to him, but I will stake you like a fucking vampire if you don't let go of my arm."

"So dramatic." She finally drops Talulla's arm.

"Says the one creating the fucking drama," I shout back.

But it's too late because Emil is coming right for us.

"This is going to be so much fun." Monica's smile is so big and psychotic, I want to rip her head off right here, in public.

Emil Popescu has his eyes on me and a devilish smirk on his face. "My dear Monica, I thought you had better taste in escorts," he says, kissing her cheeks.

"Always a pleasure to see you, Emil," I say, my teeth almost shattering because of how hard my jaw remains clenched.

"Hi, Dad," Talulla says from beside him. He truly pretended not to see his fucking daughter.

"*Copil,*" he starts, then looks at who's beside her. "And who are you spending your time with these days?" Her eyes find mine for a split second before she turns to Eric.

"This is Professor Eric Wagner. I work for him, Dad."

"Mr. Popescu, it's a pleasure to finally meet you. Your daughter is quite remarkable."

"That she is," he simply replies, shaking his hand politely.

"Wait, so you two knew each other before?" Eric asks, eyeing Talulla and me.

Fucking moron who talks too much. "I don't know what you're talking about," I simply reply, trying to remain calm and drinking my whiskey.

"If Talulla knew Flynn Lancaster, she would have definitely called me. Wouldn't you have, *copil*?"

She's staring at me. "Of course I would have, Dad."

Then Emil turns to look at Eric once again, his disdain palpable. "Is this how you got to stay enrolled? By sleeping with your professor?"

"Dad..."

I don't even realize I'm now standing between them, my rage getting the best of me. "You might want to be careful with the words you use, Emil. You know I like to get my hands bloody." This is exactly when Emil realizes something is terribly wrong. Monica just won her little game.

Talulla's hand rests on my back, trying to soothe me and calm me down, but I am one second away from letting my control slip and ripping her father's throat out. "Flynn, it's okay," she whispers, and my shoulders relax, her voice sounding like the best melody I've ever heard. If I had any doubts about how much I felt for her before, I certainly don't have any right now. I already saw her as my world, but this? This is more. I am ready to go against everything and everyone for her, even her own blood.

"Talulla, do you have something you want to tell me?"

"Dad, you're making everyone very uncomfortable with your Romanian ways."

I almost miss Cassandra quickly grabbing Eric's arm. "Mr. Wagner, can I ask you something real quick?" she says, her eyes widening for just a moment as her hand touches his skin. She saw something, but I have no time to think about that when Emil Popescu is about to make a scene. Eric gladly follows her.

"Especially the vampire who's had his eyes on you the entire night." Emil snorts. "Excuse us," he says, grabbing his daughter's elbow and walking away with her. I try to follow them, but obviously Monica stops me.

"Let me go."

"Do you want to die, Flynn? No. Because it's three against one, and you know the Popescus are on a different level."

"You played the wrong game, Monica," I say, my breath getting heavier and heavier.

"I just made the meet-the-dad date happen a little faster. You'll thank me later."

"I'm going to kill you later."

"Always so extra." She rolls her eyes at me. She fucking rolls her eyes at me after the stunt she just pulled. "You had better self-control with me."

"You can play with my head all you want, but you do not fucking touch her," I spit out. Cassandra and Eric both look in our direction, their eyes wide open. Good, let them all be frightened by me. I don't care.

"I might be your enemy every other day, but today, I am playing as your friend," she cryptically says, still digging her nails into my skin.

"Let. Me. Go."

She does, and I walk toward my woman, who's shaking as she tries to keep control of her emotions now that her father knows exactly what's happening here. I keep adjacent to the conversation, ready to step in if and when necessary.

"Imagine my shock when I found out four werewolves died at the hands of a vampire, and then you end up being in the vicinity of Flynn Lancaster."

"What is it with everyone knowing who he is?" Oh, Talulla, always trying to keep the conversation light.

"Why have you not taken care of him? That is the real question."

"Because he didn't give me any reason to do that."

"He is a vampire, Talulla. I raised you to kill his kind. You did kill his kind until, for some reason, you decided this is what you truly want. Which I know it isn't." Emil's voice is a raised whisper. He's trying not to gain too much attention, but his emotions are getting the best of him.

"He isn't behind those deaths, and honestly, no vampire is, but why am I telling you this? Why are you here? I thought you disowned me."

"Monica called me to let me know something had happened to you. I just wanted to make sure you were okay."

She snorts. "She's the reason I almost died, Dad."

"I find that hard to believe."

"Then you'll find it hard to believe that the person who saved me was Flynn Lancaster."

This is my cue to walk in.

"Get away from us, abomination."

"Don't call him that."

"Why?"

"Because."

It's time to try to say something right about now. "As your daughter already explained to you, I'm not here to create any problems."

"But you did create a big one, Flynn. You befriended my daughter and somehow were still able to compel her."

Talulla's jaw drops open. "He didn't compel me to do shit. I chose to be here, and I chose to spend time with him, but that is none of your business."

"You are my daughter."

"It stopped being your business when you tried to force me into something I don't want."

"You have a talent, Talulla. I just want you to use it."

"I don't want it."

"*Copil.*"

"No, this is over, Dad. I found a way to financially support myself as you forced me to do, and now I am out of the business."

"And what about the werewolves?"

"I've been helping the Drusus coven this entire time. You're the one who didn't move a finger and actually made it easier for the murderer to continue with their killing spree."

"You cannot be serious."

"I am."

"You are going to get tired of this, and then what are you going to do?"

Talulla's laugh is automatic after her father finishes his question. "Definitely not come back home."

"So you're just gonna cut me and your mother out?"

"I have no problem with Mom. You're the asshole who constantly tries to bring me down when things don't go your way."

Then Emil turns his eyes toward me. "I am going to kill you for what you have done to her."

Before I even get to say anything, his daughter replies, "Threaten him once more, and you won't like what comes out of me." Her fists are clenched, and I can sense the smell of iron coming from her palms, her nails digging in so harshly to the point of laceration.

I rest my hand on the small of her back and whisper to her, "Come on, let's go."

"You are not going anywhere." Emil's tone is firm, its coldness almost making me, a vampire, shiver.

I don't even have the time to reply, because Talulla's hand grips something latched onto her thigh, and she says, "You're going to let us walk out of here, or I'm going to kill you the same way you taught me to." She has a stake under her dress. I can see the shape of it as she continues to hold it through the fabric. Blood is dripping from her hands.

Her father's jaw clenches just like his fists. "This is not

over," Emil says as I walk Talulla toward the exit, not even worrying about everything else around us.

"It is, Emil. You come for us again, and I'll make sure it's the last thing you do," I say, rubbing my hand on Talulla's back, trying to show her I'm right here and that I'm not going anywhere. Because I am not. I'm staying right here with her, as if she were a bright light and I were a moth desperately trying to be in her proximity as much as possible.

Twenty-Six

TALULLA

I don't even know when we arrive at Flynn's building, but as soon as we get to his place, he walks me to his bathroom and pulls out an emergency kit.

"Sit," he says, his voice so soft I barely hear it. But I do as he says.

"What are you doing?" I ask him, still in a dazed state. I feel as if my entire body is completely numb. No sensation, just nothing.

"Your hands," he starts. "Give me your hands."

I do as he asks, and as he gently touches my fingers, I relax and slowly open my fists. "Fuck, I didn't realize I cut myself."

"I know," he says, kissing my forehead before looking down again.

I try to get my palms away, feeling like this might be too hard for him, but he stops me. "I'm okay, Talulla. If my self-control wasn't as good as it was, I would have bitten you the first time I saw you."

Tilting my head to the side, I say, "I didn't have blood on me that time."

"You did."

My expression is blank. "What?"

"Your lip was cut. Actually, you do that a lot."

"Oh," I say before adding, "I'm sorry."

"And why are you sorry?"

"For what happened tonight..."

"That was not your fault, Tal. That was Monica and your moron of a father. I'm sorry you had to be there for it."

He has never called me Tal, but it sounds so nice coming from his lips. "I'm used to it," I reply, shrugging my shoulders.

"Used to your father verbally abusing you?"

"I—"

"Do not find excuses for his actions. I know that deep down, he might do it to protect you, but he could have found another way to show his affection. I shouldn't have given him the chance to say a word."

I snort at the irony of things. "Trust me, there's no affection. He always saw me as a weapon, nothing more, and when things don't go his way—"

"Did he do other things to you?"

"I—can we talk about other things? I'm not living under his roof anymore."

"No, and you never will again. I won't allow it."

"I know."

He grabs both of my bloody palms, the blood now almost dried, then lowers his head down, and for a split second, I wonder what he's going to do. My heart quickens, but not from fear, from something completely different. It's anticipation, as if this is something that's supposed to happen.

His lips softly brush my cuts, a gentle caress that transforms into warm kisses. I stop breathing as he continues to press his mouth to my skin, not to harm me but to comfort me. Then he guides my hands under the faucet, and he washes my hands with such tenderness I truly question if the creature beside me is capable of what my father always taught me to believe. Because even if I know his true nature, I'm certain he didn't choose this life, just like I didn't choose mine. But we still remain here, present and ready to fight for a different outcome.

He goes to grab a Band-Aid, and I cup his cheeks. "Thank you," I say, bringing his face to mine as I get on my tippy toes. His arms wrap around me, and we both melt into the embrace. Our tongues become entangled with one another, and every possible worry shatters into a thousand pieces because, despite everything, we are here.

"I'd do anything for you, Tal. Anything."

Tal again. That's the second time he's called me that. It feels so intimate, so familiar. The corners of my lips lift into a smile. "Anything?"

"Anything."

"Would you even punish me for making you spend an entire day with Asmodeus?"

He shakes his head, his mouth curving into a smile. "You don't need that right now, darling. You—"

"I need to forget about what happened tonight because if I think about it, my anger will get the best of me."

"You were incredible."

"What?"

"Your speech...it was remarkable."

"Oh," I start, feeling my cheeks warm up. "That was nothing."

"That was everything, Talulla. That was what you were born to do."

My eyes widen at his affirmation. "Thank you."

"Can I ask what you love about your studies?"

"Human evolution, how we evolved as a species...I love how cyclical we always end up being."

"Humans are creatures of habit, it's true."

"My specialization is in ancient civilizations. That's what I'm working on right now, and, well, I love analyzing human artifacts and remains. It's what made me get a minor in anthropology."

"You are quite a fascinating creature, Talulla Popescu."

"Why? 'Cause I like bones?" I cock an eyebrow.

"Because you light up every time you get the chance to learn something new and every time you get to talk about what you love. It's a synonym of intelligence, and you, my dear, are an extremely intelligent being. It's what I admire the most about you."

"Interesting."

"What is?" he asks as he starts to play with a lock of my hair, the gesture making me close my eyes in relaxation.

"My entire life, I was brought up believing everything I liked was basically useless and that my love for books was getting in the way of my training."

He shakes his head, his jaw tightening as he lets the words settle in. "I think you did quite well for yourself. You are passionate about your interests, and you are truly a deadly weapon, little hunter. I find that combination very attractive."

"You gotta stop saying things like that."

"Why?"

"Because I'll start believing you."

"You should always believe me, Talulla." Then his head dips, and his lips brush mine. "What is your dream?"

"What?"

"Your dream life—dream job. What do you want to do after you're done here?" Flynn's mouth caresses my temple and then starts a trail of kisses from my ear down to the hollow of my neck.

I gasp as he continues his slow reverence of my skin.

"Work at a museum, I guess. I'd love to work in the archives of a museum and maybe curate exhibitions too. The dream is the Natural History Museum in London, but there are literally never openings, and I need to save up for that."

The smile he gives me is heart-stopping. His eyes radiate brilliance, the gray in them almost shining. "Interesting pick."

"You're more of a British Museum guy?"

He shrugs his shoulders slightly. "I donated a lot of pieces to the British Museum. They do adore me."

His little cocky statement makes me chuckle. "Of course they do."

"You would absolutely love London, my dear, and if I can help you get there, I will do anything in my power to do so."

"Not even you can materialize a job opening right at the perfect time, but thank you."

"What about right now? What can I do for you now?"

I tilt my head slightly. "You already did so much, Flynn. So, so much." Then, I brush my lips against his once more. "But I wasn't joking when I asked for my punishment."

"I can't—"

"Then let me rephrase it this way...fuck me until I forget my own name because right now, I really don't want to think about anything else except you coming inside me."

His eyes darken, and he throws me onto his bed before I even finish my sentence. "You have such a dirty mouth sometimes."

"Sometimes?"

"Such a brat."

"Are you gonna do anything about it?"

"Get up," he demands, and I do as he says. Before

anything else happens, he turns me around and bends me down over the bed, my face against the mattress. "As much as I like this dress on you, I do prefer you without it." Then I hear him working on the zipper, and the sudden air feels cold on my back. My nipples harden fast as his hands caress my spine and stop right at the base of my back. Yes, because Flynn just realized I'm not wearing underwear or a bra, and I don't know if he's happy or upset about it.

"You planned this."

"Actually, if I recall correctly, someone you might know took my pretty pair of panties hostage."

"So you thought not wearing any around *him* would be a good idea?"

I turn my head a little to look at his expression. Dark, penetrating my soul. "I had a pretty good idea of who was taking me home tonight, Flynn. You promised."

"But—"

"No buts, mister. Just rip the rest of the dress off and fuck me already. I'm growing tired."

He does just that. He keeps his eyes on me as he tears the rest of the fabric off. Piece by piece, he gashes it to shreds. "I'm gonna have to put a collar on you if this is how you walk around other men."

"Try and see what happens if you do that," I spit back, getting him worked up just like we both want. "There's a clip to unhook the garter right on the inner thigh, by the way..."

"Oh, I'm not taking the stake off. It's staying right there." I gasp at his words and firm movements. "It's hot as fuck," he adds before I'm bent down once more.

I hear his belt buckle clinking, and then his belt is off and around my wrists. He ties them behind my back, and I stay like that, bent down, with wetness now dripping down my thighs.

His hand gently rubs my bundle of nerves, and I can hear him groan as he takes his fingers to his mouth and sucks my essence off them. "You are so wet already. It's insane."

"Imagine what would happen if you actually did something."

He chuckles before he does indeed do something. "You are truly my perfect match." That's all he says before pressing my face down into the mattress. Before I know it, his free hand lands on my ass. Hard. My cry of pleasure dies in my mouth as he keeps me pressed down.

"Is this what you wanted, darling?" Another spank, another faded moan. "Because I'll be your servant until the end of time." Another spank, but this time he lets me come up for air, and I can't contain the sounds I make as he continues to bring his hand down on my ass. The initial sting of pain turns into an even deeper bliss as he continues to mark me.

"More," I ask as his torturous motions continue.

"More?"

"I need more of you, Flynn. I need all of you."

"You'll always have all of me, Talulla."

He drops to his knees, and before I can even look down to see what he's doing, his tongue flicks at my entrance and then moves up and up to my ass. I clench as his tongue continues to play with both holes. He helps me onto the bed. I'm still at the edge of it, but now I'm on my knees, and my ass is up and more exposed for him. His hands caress the places he turned red, and then down they go.

"Oh my god," I pant as his fingers find my clit and his tongue dives inside my pussy—a gentle dance of movements that makes my legs quiver. "I'm gonna come, Flynn. I—oh my god, that's so good."

But then he's off me just as I'm about to explode.

Because that's what he does. He tortures and tortures until I can't take it anymore, and then he gives me the best release I could ever imagine. "Really?" I groan as I hear him chuckle. His pants come right off.

"You know I'm always going to give you what you want. Be patient."

"Yeah, well, I'm not in the mood for patience."

"Then you might be really disappointed."

"Flynn," I whine, and his chuckle turns into a sweet laugh.

"All right, all right," he says before positioning the head of his length at my entrance. "Be a good girl and take all of me now," he says as he pushes inside me in one quick motion, the sudden fullness making me gasp. I try to turn to look at him, but his hand is quickly on the back of my head, pushing me down to the mattress once more. "The way your body reacts to me is so delightful. Unique. Nothing and no one will ever compare to you, my darling." He continues his praises as his thrusts get harder and deeper every time. My moans reach him, even if my face is stuffed onto the bed, and my eyes roll back as he hits that perfect spot and continues with his methodical movements. He drives me insane, and he can tell I'm close to coming again. As I start to feel the orgasm erupt, he slides out of me and laughs at my groan of annoyance.

"That was so mean," I whine as I hear him opening a bottle of something. I remain in place but turn my face to look at him. He's pouring himself a glass of blood, and on the nightstand, he has a vibrator. "What are you doing?" I ask, eyeing him curiously.

"This is clearly for me," he says, raising the cup to his mouth and drinking slowly. His Adam's apple is going up and down, and my mouth opens in admiration. Every single movement this vampire makes is pure sex, and he's here, with me, giving me exactly what I want. When he's done with his drink, he looks at me, his lips curled into a smirk. "This though," he says, now grabbing the vibrator. "This is for you."

"I'm pretty sure I don't need a vibrator to come, Flynn. You were doing all right on your own."

"I know I was, but I'm not gonna stop thrusting until I come inside you, and this will help with the duration of your orgasm."

"What?"

"You heard me. When I get back inside you, I'm not gonna hold back, and this will help enhance your *experience*."

"I never want you to hold back."

"Good." He props himself at my opening once more. "Remember your safe word, darling."

"I don't need to use it."

"I know, but you need to know you have an escape from me."

Then he slides back inside hard, and before I can say anything, his hand wraps around my neck and he brings my back to his chest. With his free hand, he positions the vibrator right on my clit, and when I close my eyes to let him know he has the perfect spot, he starts tightening his grip on my throat and resumes his game.

I roll my eyes as the orgasm builds up once more. This time, so much faster and more intensely than the one before. I explode as he continues to thrust into me, his hand still choking me, making it almost impossible to even scream from the pleasure I'm experiencing.

I've never felt anything so fiercely with anyone else or even on my own, and before I move on from the ecstasy of the first orgasm, a second one arrives, even stronger than the one before. I feel my vision start to blur as he continues groaning and moving.

"Fuck, Tal, you take me so well," he says, releasing my

throat slightly, and I moan as the constant pleasure continues. I feel my tied arms plop to the side as the third orgasm arrives, and he isn't stopping his rhythm for anything. He continues to drive his dick deep inside me, harder with each thrust, and I can't help but sound like a cat in heat with the noises I'm making.

"Flynn, oh my god," I say as his grip around my neck tightens once again.

"You're being such a good girl, darling. I wonder what would happen if you came for me again."

Then I feel it, his cock twitching inside me, letting me know he's close to his release. My pussy clenches around him once more, and this time, as he drives his length in and out of me, I hear him growl as he empties himself inside me, taking me over the edge one last time with him. I pour myself out as well, a wave of pleasure that feels like an earthquake coming from within me. A rhapsody of contentment. Joy.

He releases my throat, but only after whispering something in my ear. "This right here is my favorite shade of red on you, my darling." A tingle starts at the back of my neck, traveling down my spine.

I feel his hands on mine as he unbinds me, silky skin caressing my own. "Look at you, making a beautiful mess on the bed."

Then I see it. Yes, because besides his cum slowly coming out of me, there's much more on the sheets. "Did I..." My hand covers my mouth. "I'm so sorry. That has never happened before." This is so embarrassing. I can't even close my eyes. I'm in legit shock.

Flynn is on top of me in a split second. "Don't you dare apologize for enjoying yourself," he says, his lips less than an inch from mine. "Your pleasure is all I care about."

"But—"

"No buts, Talulla. This is probably the hottest thing I've ever witnessed in my very, very long life."

"Okay, but now it's—"

"Next time, you're gonna do that on my face." His lips crush against mine, and I melt, my arms wrapping around his neck and our bodies molding into one once more. Because the truth is that we can never be done with each other. The kind of pull we have is so strong and constant that nothing can stop us from being connected like this.

I don't even know when we stop our declarations of love, but at some point, we end up in his bathtub, my eyelids heavy, my body sore, and my mental state pure serenity.

"I don't think anything can top this," I say, closing my eyes as Flynn rubs a sponge on my skin. My back is pressed against his chest.

I feel his lips on my temple. "I plan on giving you this every day."

"Promise?"

"I promise, Talulla. I am your servant."

"I thought I was yours. Didn't you say you wanted to tame me?"

"I did, but the reality is that I think you tamed me."

With that, my eyes close for a few minutes. I reopen them in bed, which now has clean sheets. My lips never stop smiling. "Can I ask you a silly question?"

"Your questions are never silly."

"Do you believe in mates? Like fated mates, soulmates?"

"Like the werewolves have?"

I bite my lower lip. "Yeah," I say, before shaking my head a little. "I know it's stupid."

"Not stupid at all." Then he's lying beside me,

bringing my head to his naked chest. "I choose to believe you're mine if that gives you reassurance."

"Yeah?"

"Yes, because what kind of masochistic creature would fall for his mortal enemy if it wasn't fate, destiny, or whatever force you believe in?" He chuckles. "The day I walked onto Bear Creek's campus, even before I saw you, I knew my life would be changed forever."

"You did?"

"I had this gut feeling, some sort of pull toward it. I just knew I had to go on with whatever I was doing. At the time, I thought it was my brain telling me I was right for wanting to end my life, for finding a way to go on my terms—as a human. But then...your eyes met mine, and deep down, I already knew the pull was toward you and nothing else."

My eyes widen at the thought of being the reason he decided not to give up on his life. "I felt it too. I still do."

"Then, even if the werewolves might say we're crazy, why can't we believe we're fated just like they can be?"

"I always found it unfair how they have that one person and no other being does."

"I'm surprised you're even questioning it."

"Why?"

"Because doesn't every civilization, every religion, every creature kind of have their own way of defining a union?"

"I never thought of it that way."

"Then think of it this way, darling," he starts, his lips brushing my forehead. "It's you and me for as long as you want me."

"But I'll always want you."

"Then it's you and me, always."

"And forever," I add, my hand caressing his cheek and jaw.

"Always and forever." He kisses my knuckles as I close my eyes once more, knowing that what we shared tonight is the acceptance of a life together.

My eyes open wide as my phone and his buzz at the same time.

Picking up mine, I see seven missed calls from Cassandra and various texts.

The last one reads:

Cassandra
I saw something tonight that I don't know how to interpret. Just tell me you're still with Flynn.

Me
Still with Flynn. Staying at his place tonight. Are you okay?

Cassandra
Yes. We'll talk tomorrow.

"Cassandra had a vision of some sort," I say, keeping my eyes on my phone. "She seems okay, but wants to talk to us tomorrow." I finally turn to look at him, and his face is blank and focused on his phone. He's paying no attention to what I just said. "Are you okay?" I ask, gently touching his arm.

"Yes, I—it's Evanora."

"Is she okay?"

"Yes."

"Then what is it?"

"She says the cure will be ready tomorrow at noon."

My stomach drops, and my jaw clenches. "And what do you want to do?"

His eyes finally meet mine. "I want you to come with me if you are okay with that."

"Of course I'll come with you."

The corners of his lips lift into a smile, his eyes brightening. “Thank you.”

“You don’t have to thank me. I wouldn’t let you go through this alone.” This is how we fall asleep, in each other’s embrace, knowing we are finally not alone and that we won’t be ever again.

Twenty-Seven

FLYNN

The drive to Evanora's is quiet, but it feels right. Talulla's hand is on top of mine, caressing my knuckles as I hold her thigh.

If my heart had a pulse, I know it would be beating fast right now as we approach the witch's driveway. Maybe by the end of this visit, I will have a pulse, and I will have Talulla falling asleep on my chest as she listens to my heartbeat. But what if we haven't avoided the biggest obstacle, and she's still in danger? Would this still be worth it?

We called Cassandra to meet us there to see what was bugging her, but mostly because I wanted Talulla to have a friend close by in case things didn't go as planned.

"Ready to go inside?" I ask, interlocking my fingers with hers.

"Are you?" she replies.

I nod. I get out of the car and jog to her door, opening it for her, a small gesture she still seems to find quite unnecessary.

We're greeted at the door by my lover's best friend, and I relax at the knowledge of her presence.

"Everything is ready in the living room," she says, gesturing for us to come inside.

"You wanna tell us what's up?" Talulla asks, still holding my hands in hers.

"After. This is more important right now."

Evanora has some tea on her coffee table and a vial with a greenish-blue liquid inside. It's almost fluorescent.

I don't know why, but I assumed it would be a different color, perhaps red. This looks like liquid sour candy or something like that, almost as bright as absinthe. Hopefully, it tastes like it too.

"Flynn, Talulla," Evanora starts. "It's so nice to see you both."

"It's nice to see you too," Talulla replies, her teeth torturing her lower lip. I press my hand on the small of her back, letting her know I'm still right beside her, and I can see her shoulders relax.

"Is there anything I need to know before I do this?" I ask, keeping my hand on my companion's back, caressing her.

"As I already mentioned when you asked me to prepare it for you, it might not work at all. It probably won't."

"Anything else? Could it have any side effects?" This time, Talulla is asking the question.

"I can't be one hundred percent sure, but no, there shouldn't be any sort of side effects."

With that, she sits down and rubs her hand on her forehead.

"Would it be too much if I asked for some privacy?"

"Of course not. Take the time you need," Evanora replies, leaving the room with Cassandra.

"Wait. Can Cass stay?" Talulla asks, her body trembling as she tries to get the words out, and I nod.

"She's right here," I say as her friend sits beside her, still keeping a bit of distance between us.

TALULLA

"What if it doesn't work? Or if it kills you? You can't—" My hands shake at the thought of possibly losing him.

"Talulla, I'm not going to die if I take this. Evanora would never give me something that would kill me."

"She isn't even sure of it—"

"I'm not going to leave you. You won't be alone." He lowers himself in front of me so he's at eye level with me. His soft, velvety fingers caress my cheeks.

"Flynn, I..." I feel my eyes filling with salty water and my lips trembling because I can't even get the words out.

"I know, and I don't want to leave you."

"Then don't risk it."

"You're my entire world, Talulla. If I have even the smallest chance to live a human life with you, I have to risk it." That's when he finally does it.

He grabs the vial, opens it, and then brings it to his mouth. My hands are clenched into fists as I try to force myself not to grab the little glass container and throw it far, far away.

Cassandra's eyes are wide as she stares at me and my reaction. I'm immobilized and rigid as a statue as I watch Flynn's Adam's apple go up and down.

We don't move for a moment that seems to last forever before Flynn finally breaks the silence. Evanora joins us, remaining in silence just like Cassandra.

The quietness of the room continues to envelop us as we patiently wait for something to happen. I can almost hear the chirping of the birds outside and the sound of the leaves as the wind caresses them, creating a beautiful, melancholic melody in my ears.

"Well, I don't feel anything different," Flynn says with his lips in a thin line.

I stand, and as I get to him, I start touching his hair.

Then, I pat him down to make sure he's still in one piece. "Open your mouth," I order, and he obeys with dark eyes fixed on me.

He raises an eyebrow as I continue to touch him. "I am usually the one giving orders."

"Well, not now." I carry on with my meticulous checkup.

I grab his jaw with my hand and bring his face down to my eye level. I examine his teeth and fangs, noticing no difference. I even press my fingers on them to make sure they're still working. That's when he grabs my hands before I puncture myself. His arms wrap around me, and I finally let myself melt into his embrace. He's still here, alive, and a vampire.

I take a deep breath and exhale as his skin touches mine. Electric shocks start to trail from my fingertips up to my arms and then down to my chest.

He's here. He's still here, *alive* with me.

"You're okay," I whisper, nestling my head against his chest. His vanilla cologne calms me down.

"I'm not human." His voice is a soft whisper.

I grab his head in my hands and force him to look at me. His gray eyes look particularly shiny right now. "It doesn't matter. You're still here," I declare, the corners of my lips lifting into a smile.

"Talu—"

"I don't give a shit if you're human, a vampire, or a fucking unicorn. I just need you, Flynn, no matter which version."

His eyes soften. "And you have me. You'll have me for as long as you want me, and even after that, you'll still have me. I'm yours, Talulla Popescu. Forever yours."

"Good. Now that this is settled, we can go back to our normal scheduled events." I turn to look at Cassandra. "What's up with you?"

"Well, you switched up moods real quick," Cassandra says, plopping into the loveseat closest to the fireplace. "What did you see?"

"When I grabbed Mr. Wagner's arm last night...I saw something weird."

"Okay?"

"It was Eric and his wife, and then I saw his wife with Dalton Reyes, Kaden's father."

"Cassandra, this makes no sense," I state, because what would these three have in common?

"I think they knew each other."

"Elaborate." It's Flynn who's talking now. I turn to look at him. He's focused on Cassandra, listening to every word she says.

"I think something happened between Eric, his wife, and Kaden's father."

My vampire rests a hand on the small of my back before he starts his theory. "We did assume that Reyes wasn't alone in the car the night he died."

"Alina and Dalton died at separate times," I say, not even sure about my words anymore.

"Are you sure?"

"Eric's wife has been dead for a while. Dalton died after."

"You weren't working for him when she died—" I stop Cassandra before she can finish her sentence.

"No, but we were both in his class when he took time off. It was before Dalton's death." There's no way he has something to do with this. Not when he did so much for me. "I know what you're thinking, but he is not involved in this. He even tried to help us."

"How?"

"If he really had anything to do with any of this, why would he let me read his wife's research? It makes absolutely no sense."

Flynn clears his throat. "Okay, so maybe we should talk to Kaden again and see if he knows who could have been with his father that night."

I nod. "Yes, good idea."

A phone call makes me jerk in surprise.

"It's Set," Cassandra says, pressing the accept button and then putting him on speaker. "We can all hear you."

"Good, because I know how we're going to get the full report for Dalton's accident," Set states, making us all close our mouths.

"Oh?"

"Yes," he adds before chuckling a little. "And Talulla is not going to like it one bit."

Twenty-Eight

TALULLA

"Absolutely not," I say, crossing my arms over my chest. "There's no way I'm calling my father after the stunt he pulled last night."

"Tal, you know he knows a lot of people..." I can't believe Cassandra is truly entertaining this. I know why Set would. He's rational, but he also wasn't at the fundraiser. After their father passed away, Cass became colder, but this? This is absolutely out of character, even for her.

We drove to the Drususes' house right after Set's phone call, and now we're all sitting in their living room like a happy family. Too bad for me that they're all banding together against me. Flynn hasn't taken a side, but I can tell he's clearly thinking about it. Because in actuality it is a good idea. My father could find out what happened to the report and find the full one. He knows really powerful people. He has to in the kind of business we're all part of.

"Yeah, so what?"

Flynn answers before one of the witches can even say another word. "Asmo and I could go meet Paolo again and see if he can ask the Caputos."

"What do you mean *again*?" I turn to face my vampire. "Do you have something you need to tell me?"

Flynn tilts his head. "We just asked him a few questions a couple of days ago."

"And you didn't tell me. Why?"

"Because there was nothing to say."

"Flynn."

"Why are you angry?"

"Because you terrorized an innocent man and didn't tell me about it."

He snorts. "Oh, I didn't scare him that much."

"He behaved, it's true," Asmodeus says.

"I couldn't make a scene. Asmodeus was wearing new shoes and whined about how he didn't want to get them dirty."

"You're nerve-racking." I groan. "Why would the Caputos know anything about this?"

"They're the ones who told Paolo to accept your request to fight."

"What?"

"When you were unconscious, he was shocked because he knew you weren't exactly human."

"And you all waited this long to tell me? Are you for real?" I raise my voice, waving my hands in the air, frustration building inside me and creating a knot in my stomach.

"Tal, you were dying, and we were trying to save you. It's not like we wanted to keep this a secret," Cassandra replies, taking Flynn's side.

"So you knew as well."

"I..." She sighs. "Yes, I did."

"Unbelievable," I spit back. "You almost made me think Eric was somehow behind this when there's literally a mobster family involved. Why aren't we on their asses?"

"That reminds me...Set, any progress on that bottle of water?" Flynn asks the other Drusus, completely brushing off my question. Asshole.

"Nothing. But if Monica Lazar is the one procuring the potions, she absolutely knows how to cover her tracks. She also knows we're keeping an eye on her."

"What if we speak to Kaden before I call the person who wants my boyfriend dead?"

The corners of Flynn's mouth lift up, but he says nothing. His hand moves up and down the small of my back, making my toes curl in my shoes.

"It could help us find out who the other person in the car was. What if she made it out alive, and that's why she isn't in the report?"

"She would still be in the report even if she survived. They altered it to cover someone."

"Okay," Flynn starts. "Talulla and I are going to talk to the dog, and you little detectives can call Emil."

"What?" the three witches say in unison.

"You heard me," my vampire says, his smirk getting bigger and bigger.

"But—" Set tries to protest.

"You're not going to force Talulla to talk to him." His tone is cold, protective, and absolutely final. He's showing me he's on my side and won't force me to do anything I don't want to do. But the thing is, I know it's a good idea, and I know it will give us the answers we need much faster.

I sigh in defeat. "Flynn, it's okay..."

"No, it's not."

"He won't listen if they call. I have to do it," I reply, looking at his icy-gray eyes that are trying to figure out my state of mind.

"Flynn, you know better than anyone else here that Emil can get that report." This time, it's Cassandra talking.

"I know he can. That's why I told *you* to call and not Tal."

I exhale as they continue to argue about who should call whom. "I'm gonna do it now and get it over with." I pick up the phone and dial my father's number.

Ring.

Ring.

Ring.

"*Copil,*" my father says, his tone distant and formal as usual.

I clear my throat. "Hi, Dad," I say, my voice low, hesitation starting to show as I torture my lower lip. Flynn's hand is on the small of my back in an instant. "We might have a lead on who is behind the murders on campus."

"And you are calling me. Why?"

"Because we need to find a police report," I reply, shifting my weight from one foot to another.

"You are capable of breaking into a police station on your own."

"We did...I mean, Set, Asmodeus, and..."

"And?"

"That's beside the point. The report was altered."

"You are giving me a headache."

"It's for the case, Dad, not for me." Because even if Emil Popescu is trying to teach me some sort of lesson, I know he can't bring himself to let this go if he has a way to get some glory out of it.

I hear him huff on the other side of the phone for a little longer, and I am ready to hang up, but then he surprises me. "Name."

"Dalton Reyes."

"The old alpha?" he asks, his voice rising slightly, showing some interest in the case.

"Yes."

"Is that all?"

I bring my thumbnail to my mouth, nibbling it. "And Alina Wagner."

Everyone in the room looks at me with wide eyes. "I will reach out when I have them."

Click.

"Why did you ask for Wagner's wife's report?" Cassandra asks, her eyebrow raised.

"So that we can all stop accusing a man who just wants to mourn his late wife in peace."

We reach the pack house in silence. I've been looking out the window while Flynn drives. It's rainy, and even if the temperature in California doesn't really get cold, the fall colors are showing. The weather isn't helping my mood. My conversation with my mother's sperm donor didn't either.

"Are you okay?" Flynn asks as he parks the car in the driveway.

I nod. "Yeah."

His lips brush my temple. "That was a lot to ask of you."

"It was a smart move. I wouldn't have suggested it, but I know it was smart. My father...he knows a lot of powerful people."

"He does."

"I don't think I can face him again."

"You won't have to."

"You can't promise me that. He'll always attempt to get his perfect weapon back."

"Talulla, look at me," Flynn says, holding my face in his hands and forcing me to look at him. "You're not alone in this. I'm not going anywhere, and I'll make sure to always protect you."

"You don't have to protect—"

"It's not that I have to, sweetheart." He kisses the tip

of my nose. "I want to protect you."

"I want to do the same for you."

The corners of his mouth lift up. "And you do. Every single day, you keep me alive just by being beside me."

"You're so extra."

He brings a hand to his chest as if I just stabbed him. "I'm just stating facts. Now, let's go. I don't like the dog stench here."

"Are you going to be nice?"

A slight furrow appears between his brows as he stares pointedly at me. "I'm always nice."

"Flynn."

"I'll behave with the dog," he says, exhaling heavily.

"Maybe don't call him that."

"That's what he is."

"A dog who can rip you to shreds."

This makes him laugh. "He can certainly try."

"You're unbelievable."

"Thank you, little hunter. I needed a compliment coming from you."

I shake my head and chuckle as I open the car door, but he's at the passenger side in an instant, obviously, because I can't even open my own damn door anymore. "I'm capable of opening my own door."

"And I still love opening it for you. Isn't that fascinating?"

I roll my eyes as we get to the entrance, and then I knock three times.

Kaden opens the door, his jaw clenched as his eyes move from me to the vampire beside me. "What do you want?" He has dark circles under his eyes. It's clear he hasn't slept in days.

"We have some developments to talk to you about."

Kaden's eyes widen for a second, and then he lets us in. The house is a total mess, with clothes on the floor and dirty plates everywhere, but I don't comment on the state of the place because I know it just reflects his mental state right now. It's not good, which means he is also on edge. Werewolves are probably the moodiest supernatural creatures I know, and we have to be very careful about how we talk because he will be in offensive mode about anything.

"So?" Kaden says, his posture rigid.

"There was someone in the car with your father the night of the accident. Do you know who it could be?" Flynn asks, handing him the picture from the report that shows the purse.

"I…The police never said someone was with him." He sighs. "They said he was alone. Why would they do that?"

"That's because it's not even in the report."

"You got the report and didn't tell me?" The hostility is starting. If we keep calm, everything will be fine.

"We got part of it, and we're telling you right now."

"Talulla."

"We're working on getting the real report. This is why we're here now."

"Fine," Kaden spits. "My dad…he met someone before he passed away."

My eyes widen at the realization. Kaden's father was deeply in love with his late wife, and I'm happy he found a way to move on, but for a wolf…that's so unusual. "He was dating again?"

"He was very vague about it, but…Tal, he said he had found his mate, and you know what happens in those circumstances."

Nothing else matters. They become the center of your entire world. "You do everything in your power to protect them."

"Yes. He didn't even want us to meet her until he was certain she was safe."

"So you have no idea who this person is?"

"No clue."

"Why didn't you tell me about her before?"

"Because I didn't know she could be involved, and she never cared to contact me or Scott after my father's death."

I turn to look at Flynn. His chin rests in his hand, and I can tell he's thinking about something. "Why would the police cover up something like this? It makes no sense."

"And are the Caputos involved at this point?"

"The Caputos?" Kaden asks.

"Yeah, they knew I was a hunter when...It's a long story that you don't need to know."

"Talulla, what is happening?" Kaden asks, grabbing my arm.

Flynn intervenes way too quickly. "Do not do that again."

"Or what, bloodsucker?" Oh boy, here we go.

"Or I'll rip your arm off." This is exactly what I was trying to avoid.

"Okay, both of you, stop. No one is ripping any arms off."

"He's the one instigating," the werewolf says, pointing at my vampire.

"Kaden, shut the hell up."

Flynn chuckles. "Yeah, what she said."

"You too, buddy. You're both acting like toddlers."

Flynn's nostrils flare at my quick comeback, but he remains silent. Thank God. "Any idea of who this mate could be?" I ask Kaden.

"No idea, but I know she was definitely living in Palo Alto."

"You never thought of following your dad?"

"Why would I have? I had no reason to doubt him, and he needed time. I didn't want to push him to make me meet anyone."

"You weren't even a bit curious?"

"Of course I was, but aside from her smell, I know nothing."

"Her smell?"

"Yeah, my father always had a distinctive smell after spending time with her. You have one too, and it's all over your vampire."

"I do?"

"Strawberries and roses," Flynn and Kaden say in unison.

"Okay, well, let's pretend that didn't creep me out. What did your father smell like when he was with her?"

"Wildflowers and...like a library?"

"A library?"

"Yeah, like old books."

"Well, that doesn't really tell us anything."

But Flynn's eyes are wide now. He has someone in mind. "Let's go," he tells me before adding, "We just need to wait for your father to give us the report, and we will have our confirmation."

"You're not going to tell me who you're thinking of?"

He shakes his head. "Not without being sure about it."

"Flynn..."

"I...You're not gonna like it."

I groan. "If my father doesn't get back to us before tomorrow evening, you're telling me either way."

My vampire agrees, his stare softening as his eyes meet mine.

Kaden's eyes roll. "Okay, well, you two can leave if you're done questioning me."

"Jealous, dog?"

"Flynn."

"Get the fuck out, bloodsucker."

Flynn smirks at him. "Always a pleasure talking to you, Kaden Reyes."

"Whatever," he says before turning to me. "Keep me posted, Tal."

"I will," I say, approaching the entrance before going in for a hug. Flynn growls from behind me, but I don't give a shit. Kaden is my friend, and Flynn needs to learn to deal with these things.

"I can't believe you're actually with one of them." There it is. The friendship moment is completely ruined.

"I can't believe she lowered her standards that one singular night."

As I said, toddlers. Two freaking adults acting like toddlers.

"Oh, believe me, she enjoyed every second of it. I can literally still hear her moa—"

My head snaps back in Kaden's direction. "Do you want to get punched in the face?"

The wolf shrugs his shoulders. "I'm not scared of him."

"You should be scared of me," I say, pushing him back inside his house. "This pissed-off version of you better fuck off soon because if you continue like this, you're gonna get hurt."

"Are you seriously defending him?"

"You don't talk about my fucking body or whatever happened between us, you asshole."

"It wouldn't have happened if he weren't here."

I raise one eyebrow as I cross my arms over my chest. "Get used to it, K. He's staying."

"Yeah, yeah, whatever. As long as he doesn't start killing people..."

"He won't."

"Unless they ask for it," Flynn adds, and I roll my eyes at his threat.

"Flynn..."

"If someone threatens you, what do you want me to do? Sit and watch?"

"I—"

"I told you I will always protect you. He's lucky he can still play the grief card, but next time, he won't be that lucky."

"Let's go. I'm tired of you two filling the room with testosterone."

We get to the car, and as soon as we're inside, Flynn breaks the silence.

"I'm gonna have to punish you for calling me a toddler. You know that, right?"

"I should be the one punishing you for falling for his taunts."

"Oh, I know he just wanted to piss me off. He still likes you and can't comprehend what you could possibly see in me."

"There was no need to play the alphahole."

"I'm sorry."

"I—" I stop in my tracks. My mouth shut. "You're apologizing?"

"You had a long day and were forced to talk to your father, and then your *friend* and I just added to it. So yes, I'm apologizing."

My eyes widen at his acknowledgment. I think I was expecting him to brush it off and for me to have to live with the anger for a while, but he apologized. "Thank you."

"What can I do to make it up to you?"

"I'm okay, fangs."

"Anything you want."

"You can take me home, give me some food, and put me to bed. I've got a long school day tomorrow."

"Yeah?"

I nod. "I have a meeting for my dissertation. I have to present what I want to work on for the remainder of the year."

"You're nervous."

"A little. It's a big decision for me," I say, my eyes lowering, staring at my shoes.

"You'll rule the world, little hunter. You can do anything."

"Yeah, fine, you can also go down on me."

He chuckles and then pulls out of the driveway. "You can sit on my face all night if you want."

"Now, that's an interesting proposition."

Twenty-Nine

FLYNN

The morning light peeks through the curtains, creating a golden glow around the small body nestled against mine. Talulla's grip around me tightens as she moves her head slightly. Her skin feels like the finest silk.

I turn to look at the alarm. It's seven in the morning, and she's going to wake up in the next ten minutes to get ready for school.

She looks so innocent and angelic like this—asleep, with nothing else bothering her. Her frame is fully relaxed against mine. I haven't had this constant need to protect someone in a very long time—maybe ever—but if this is how it feels, I want to do it for as long as I live.

"Are you done staring?" my hunter says, not raising her eyes to look at me. Talulla keeps her face against my chest, her eyes closing once again.

"Never," I reply, brushing my lips to her forehead.

"You'll get bored quickly."

"Of you? I don't think anything that outrageous is humanly possible."

She groans, covering herself in the sheets. "I don't want to get up."

"The faster you get up, the faster you're gonna get to school, and the faster you'll be back in my arms."

"Are you using a child method to get me out of bed?"

"Is it working?"

I see her crinkle her nose. "A little."

"I'll take you out to dinner to celebrate and then continue said celebration between your legs."

"It's not really a dinner celebration kind of thing."

"I'm making it a reason to celebrate your achievements."

"I haven't even started my dissertation. It's a little premature, don't you think?"

"It's a push toward a bigger goal, which will require a very big celebration."

She chuckles. "What are you going to do all this time without me?"

I shrug my shoulders as she slightly raises her head to look at me. "Wait for you to come back."

"Oh, please."

I laugh and then add, "I have to run a couple of errands, and then I'm meeting Dean Jefferson to finalize some paperwork."

"Still about Da Vinci's things?"

"Something like that." I do have to sign some last-minute papers for the pieces I'm donating, but I've also asked for a meeting with Jefferson for another reason, one that Talulla would prohibit me from doing if she knew what I had in mind.

I feel her stretch beside me. "Okay, time to get this over with."

"You're going to impress them all, sweetheart."

"I really hope so. I'm pretty proud of my idea. I just need a few of them to like it enough so that I can work on it."

"And they will." I grab her hand and pull her to me once again.

Her mouth slightly opens as her eyes get lost in mine. "Thank you," she whispers as I crush my mouth to hers. I can't get enough of her plump lips, her sweet taste, and her essence.

"Time to start the day."

We both get out of bed, and as she gets ready, I make my way to the kitchen to prepare some coffee. Weirdly enough, even if it doesn't do anything to me, coffee is one of those things I like to indulge in, even as a dead creature.

I pour two cups just as Talulla joins me. "Here," I say, handing her the beverage.

"Just what I needed," she says, drinking it fast. "I gotta go now, though."

"Wait." I run to the coat hanger, pulling a key out of my pocket. "This is for you."

Her eyes widen as I drop the key into her palm. "Is this what I think it is?"

Tilting my head to the side, I say, "It's whatever you want it to be."

"Flynn."

"Don't take it so seriously. I know you have your dorm and want your space, but if you ever want to come here, even if I'm out, I just wanted you to know that you can."

"So you're not asking me to move in after a month?"

The corners of my mouth lift up. "As much as I'd want that—and believe me, I do—you're never going to agree to it unless you're sure about it. So no, I'm not asking you to move in, but you still get that key."

She narrows her eyes at me just as a grin appears on her face. "That's a compromise I'm willing to accept."

"Good."

Talulla's eyebrow rises. "Wonderful."

"Marvelous."

"You're not gonna let me have the last word, are you?"

"You can have whatever you want, little hunter. It's yours."

She rolls her eyes. "You're so extra." Then she adds my key to her keychain with her lips raised in a smile.

I want her to feel at home with me. I want her to be able to come to this space that I call mine and make it her own, just like she did with my soul.

After Talulla left, I ended up at the blood bank for a much-needed refill, and now that I am satiated and full, I can go see Jefferson without wanting to eat him the whole time.

I amble through the main building. It's a busy day. Students walk past me without paying attention as I stroll toward the administration office for my meeting.

"Mr. Lancaster," the receptionist says. "Dean Jefferson is waiting for you."

"Perfect, I'll go in, then."

I make my way to the back and knock on the large wooden door.

"Come in."

I take a seat in the ugly-ass pea-colored chair and pretend I still don't think it's offensive to the sight.

"Dean Jefferson, it's a pleasure to see you again." God, he smells awful. He wears this crazy, earthy cologne. It smells like artificial pine trees. It's honestly one of the worst scents I've ever had the displeasure of smelling, and I have smelled a lot of shit throughout the years. Like, literal shit.

"The pleasure is mine, Mr. Lancaster, especially after seeing the large donation you made to the history department after their fundraiser."

"I know my money is in good hands."

"You said you wanted to talk to me about a student?"

"Yes," I start, signing off on some paperwork presented to me. "Talulla Popescu."

"Ah, yes. Miss Popescu is quite remarkable. She and Miss Drusus have a bright future ahead of them."

"They absolutely do, and this is why I wanted to make sure that happens."

Dean Jefferson tilts his head slightly. His toupee almost remains immobile as he does. Did he cover it in gel? It looks like Lego hair. "I don't think I'm following."

"I would like to help her out with her tuition, maybe make it a scholarship."

"Her fall tuition has been paid. She doesn't need more money."

"I would like to replace that payment and then also pay for her final semester."

"That is almost fifty grand."

"Would that cover her rooming expenses? I'd like to add that to the list as well."

"Mr. Lancaster, that is an enormous sum of money."

"It's money well spent."

"Are you sure about this? The total cost after her scholarships is still over sixty grand."

"As long as she gets her twenty-five grand back, I am willing to pay that amount right now."

"May I ask why?"

None of your fucking business, but I guess it is an odd request, so I can give him something. "I got to know Miss Popescu, and I can tell how passionate and hardworking she is."

"You've already donated $100,000 to her department."

"I did, and now I want to make sure she can have her last year fully taken care of."

He shrugs. "I mean, it is your money. I don't see why this can't be arranged."

Wonderful. I didn't even need to use my compulsion on him. "Thank you, Mr. Jefferson. I know I'm doing the right thing."

"Talulla will be very happy."

I take out my checkbook and sign one. I don't even bother putting a number on it. "Here. Whatever it is, just fill it in, and please, have her money deposited back into her account by tomorrow morning."

"Will do."

I feel my phone buzz as I get up and shake his hand. "It was nice seeing you again."

"Goodbye, Mr. Lancaster."

I exit the room and basically flee from Jefferson's premises, his smell almost giving me a headache.

I sit down on a bench, the one where Talulla was sitting the first day I saw her, and finally take out my phone.

"Flynn, what are you doing here? Talulla is busy all day."

I look up and see Cassandra holding something like ten massive books in her hands. "Do you need a hand?"

She shakes her head. "I'm good." Then, shifting her weight from one hip to the other, she reconsiders. "Okay, fine, grab a couple of these. I need to drop them off at Sinopoli's office."

"Okay, let's go."

Walking back inside, Cassandra keeps a safe distance, not wanting to accidentally touch me and see something she doesn't want to see. "Are you spying on her? Because she would never do anything to upset—"

"I had a meeting with the dean. I was ready to go home and think about what to cook for dinner before you showed up."

"So you're not stalking her."

I chuckle at her persistence. "No. I know she has an

important meeting today, and I'm not here to possibly ruin it."

"Oh, okay, then."

I raise one eyebrow at her as I drop the books on the counter. "Disappointed?"

"What? No, I just...It's hard to read you sometimes."

"You as well."

My phone buzzes again. This time, I pick it up, and the messages I see ruin my entire mood for the day.

> **Evanora**
> Flynn, you need to come here right away.

> **Evanora**
> Please, Flynn, there's not much time. The house is on fire.

I look up at Cassandra, my eyes widening in shock.

"What is it?"

"We need to go to Evanora's right now." I show her the texts.

"Fuck, fuck, fuck." She grabs my hand, not worrying about the contact anymore, and pushes through the people, looking for a safe place to escape. "This will have to do," she says, pulling us inside the men's bathroom.

I send a quick text to Talulla, letting her know where I am and telling her to take my car and come to Evanora's if I'm not back before she is.

Then we apparate out of the campus bathroom right in front of a house in flames. I run to the door and swing it open, smoke obfuscating my vision for a moment.

"Flynn, you can't come inside," Evanora says in a brittle voice. "You need to find her."

"What?" I ask, and then notice what she's doing. She's

sitting at the table, shuffling cards. "Come on, Evanora. Let's go. I got your texts."

My friend shakes her head. "I can't leave the house, and Cassandra won't be able to get me out either. No one can. Monica failed as well."

"I don't think I'm following."

"If you get inside, you're not getting out, Flynn. I didn't send you those texts."

"It's a trap," I whisper to myself.

"The cards," she says, raising two tarot cards to show me. "They haven't changed."

My eyes widen as I realize what she wants to show me. The Ten of Pentacles and Death. Talulla is still in danger.

"Who did this?"

"Just know she tried to find a solution this time. She really did, but humans...They can be even more ruthless than supernatural creatures."

"What does that mean, Evanora?"

Then I hear branches cracking. I inhale and smell them—two men trying to run away.

And I am not in the mood to let them go.

"You deserve this epic love. You deserve it all. You're worthy of her."

My eyes widen. "Evanora."

"It was an honor being your friend, Flynn Lancaster."

"No! There has to be something—"

"Goodbye." Those are the last words she says before the flames take over. She doesn't scream. She just sits, waiting for the inevitable to happen, and I am left here, outside, incapable of saving my friend.

Cassandra finally joins me, tears streaming down her face as she watches the scene, feeling just as useless as I do.

Then the sound of leaves crushing brings me back to the situation at hand. I turn to look at the witch. "Call

Kaden. Call Asmodeus as well. Set. Everyone you can think of."

"What's happening, Flynn?"

"They took Talulla."

I turn to my right and look at the forest. The trees move in unison with the wind, creating a melancholic melody of sounds. Two men are trying to hide. I inhale, trying to figure out which direction they're walking in...or rather, running in.

"Gotcha," I say with a smirk on my face and an insatiable thirst growing in my throat, making it burn as much as the fire behind me.

"Flynn—" Cassandra has no time to finish her statement because I start running at vampire speed as soon as I locate the bastards.

I get to the two men in an instant. "Trying to sneak out?" I say, making them jolt in surprise. "You can't outrun the Angel of Judgment."

They turn to look at me, their eyes widening, and then they try to run away from me.

Morons.

Do they really think they can outdo me? I literally just told them they can't escape. I'm not in the mood for little games.

"Where is she?" I yell as I let them think they have the upper hand.

"You're supposed to be dead," one of them replies, still trying to meander as far away from me as possible.

"Yeah, well, sorry to disappoint. I am pretty hard to exterminate." I reach for one, my hand grabbing the back of his head, ripping chunks of hair out. "How do you want to die?"

"Screw you."

"So the painful way," I reply, tightening my grip on the nape of his neck. "Ever seen a human heart before?"

"Wha—"

The man chokes on his words as my hand rips into his chest. The warm flesh and blood coat my hand and arm as I continue to push inside him.

The fucker starts to lose consciousness, but I am not done. I grab his chin with my other hand and force him to look me in the eye. "You're going to keep your eyes open, and you're going to die as you look at your own heart stopping in my hands."

Closing my hand around three ribs, I pull, ripping the bones from his skeleton. I need to create an opening so that I can get the heart out, nice and slow.

Crack.

The sound of the bones detaching from the spine is music to my ears. Blood pours out, and just as the man is ready to fall to the ground, I grab the still-beating muscle, carefully get it out, and bring it to his eye level.

The walking corpse's eyes widen as I bring the heart to my mouth and sink my fangs right into it, my rage getting the best of me, and the thirst for revenge making me more dramatic than necessary. My gums hit the warm flesh, coating my mouth in crimson. It's almost impossible to resist the urge to drink his blood and drain him, but even the thought of it makes me want to vomit because he's not even worth the effort.

I bite down and tear the muscle, blood spraying all over my face and his.

Then his eyes finally close for good, and he plops to the ground.

I spit out any blood and residual pieces of the organ, and then throw the rest of the heart with the body's remains.

"Jesus, dude," Asmodeus says from behind me. "Remind me to never piss you off."

"Nice of you to join us," I say before adding, "Clean this up. The other one is still running."

"Copy that."

I run, reaching the second pawn, and before I end his miserable, useless life, I ask, "Who did this?"

"The Caputos don't like to have favors owed."

"Elaborate."

"What's the point? You're going to kill me anyway."

"It's true, but I am calmer now. I could give you a faster death."

"They cover their tracks so nothing's left behind."

"Why Talulla?"

"She got too close."

My nostrils flare at his words. Grabbing his chin and forcing him to look at me, I ask, "Where is she now?"

"I don't know."

Useless piece of shit. I grab his head between my hands and quickly snap his neck.

Crack.

He's gone in seconds, not having time to think about anything more creative.

Cassandra and Asmodeus are already working on making the second body disappear when we hear sirens in the distance.

"The fire department is finally coming."

"Too bad it's too late," I say, my voice cold as I am reminded of my friend dying in her house, still trying to help me until her last breath.

There's no time to spend mourning when my Talulla is in danger.

"Do we have any idea where she could be?"

"She was supposed to be on campus all day. Her meeting was going to take hours," Cassandra states.

My phone vibrates in my pocket, and a sense of relief fills my lungs.

"Little hunter, please tell me you're okay," I say as soon as I press accept.

Then the unexpected happens. "I did not know we had pet names for each other."

"How did you get this number?"

"I dropped off the police reports at the Drususes' house. Now, take care of the problem. It's Wagner, but you knew that already, didn't you?" The voice on the other side of the phone is from my mortal enemy, Emil Popescu.

"Why did you call me?"

I hear him chuckle on the other side of the line. "Because I want you to know I can find you wherever you go, Lancaster."

Thirty
TALULLA

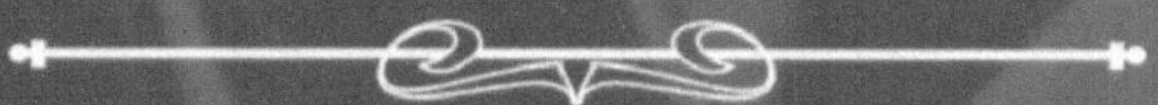

A round of applause makes me realize I got to the end of my presentation, and they liked it. I turn to look at Eric and see his eyes focused on me as he joins in on the applause.

"You definitely know what you're talking about, Miss Popescu," Ms. Sinopoli says, giving me a confidence boost. "I can't wait to see what you'll achieve."

"Thank you, Ms. Sinopoli."

She collects her curly hair and clips it up. "Now go and impress us all."

I nod and start making my way out of the classroom, followed by my mentor, Eric Wagner.

"The entire department was astonished, Talulla. Well done."

"Thank you, Professor." The corners of my lips lift up as we march through the hallways of Bear Creek. This is it. My way of finding an alternative for my future. This is all I've worked for, despite what my father wanted me to do. I did all this.

"I think you deserve a drink," Eric says as we step into his office.

"You keep alcohol in here?"

He chuckles and then shakes his head. "Not when my apartment is three floors up," he says, pointing at the ceiling.

"Professor—"

"Eric."

"Right, Eric. I gotta meet up with—"

"Your vampire. Yeah, yeah. This is just a quick drink, Talulla. Then you can go off to do what people your age do. I'm proud of you. I just wanted to say that." He's looking at me with his chin raised. Eric is truly proud of me.

"It wouldn't have happened without your guidance."

He chuckles. "Well, that is certainly high praise. Shall we?" he says, gesturing to the door.

"Yes." I nod. "Let's go."

We make our way up the stairs and to the door of his apartment, like we've done many times before, and for some reason, this time feels different. Today, it feels good. Despite a murderer being on the loose, I feel like I have a purpose again.

"It's going to be a busy year. You can't get distracted," Eric says, opening the door.

"I won't."

"You know, I really didn't expect him to show up at the fundraiser with the witch who tried to kill you the other night."

"It's a long, funny story," I say, dropping my bag on his couch and laughing at how unfunny the situation really is. He passes me a glass filled with amber liquid, and as I take a seat, I focus on the crystal tumbler in my hands before taking a quick sip. Monica introduced herself to him that night. "How do you know about that?"

My eyes widen as the glass drops from my trembling hands. "You," I say as my vision blurs, forcing me to blink uncontrollably.

"There you go, little hunter," Eric says. "Isn't that what *he* calls you?"

"How did you do it?"

"See, the first time was really easy. You just drank the tea and had no idea. It definitely helped cover my tracks when the Caputos' pawn gave you a bottle of water later that night. Poor Paolo. He was unaware of it all."

"Flynn is going to kill you."

"See, he would have if he were still alive, but," he says, looking down at his watch. "By now, he's probably ashes inside a witch's house." He shrugs his shoulders. "It's sad I had to kill Evanora Hart in the process. She absolutely had nothing to do with all this...until she told you that you were in danger."

"Why the werewolves? What did they do to you?"

This is when Eric hands me a folder. "Imagine my surprise when my brother called me to let me know someone broke into the federal archives to steal two very specific reports."

The potion seems to be acting faster this time, my bones aching as I force myself to open the file and read the report.

First on the scene: Officer Wagner.

"Your brother...he was there the day of the accident."

"Oh, yes, he was. I was as well."

Then I continue reading.

Two bodies were found dead. Dalton Reyes, 46. Alina Wagner, 31.

"Oh my god," I whisper to myself. "She was—"

"His mate," he spits. "Can you believe it?"

"Eric, you don't have to do this."

"Trust me, I didn't want to get to this point, but you had to keep snooping around."

"You were hurt."

He snorts. "Hurt? That's the understatement of the century." He walks into his kitchen to grab a knife. "They wanted to be my friends."

"She told you."

"Alina just had to continue with her stupid research, and in the process, she met this fucking wolf." He grips the knife's handle so tightly his knuckles turn white.

"Dalton."

"They came over here, sat me down, and told me how they couldn't resist their bond."

"Oh my god," I say, covering my mouth with my palm.

"Yes, *oh my god.* My wife cheated on me with a fucking werewolf."

"And you killed them."

The corners of his lips curl up. "I did."

"How?"

"Let's just say I had some magical help."

"Monica."

"Yes, she really is a good businesswoman. What's even funnier is that she absolutely doesn't want to know what happens with what she sells."

"She couldn't out herself. It would have made her a target."

"Yes, your weird, unspoken rules are truly flawed."

That's why she wanted Flynn to go to the event so badly. It was her twisted way of hinting at Eric. Hinting that my father could help. "I can't believe it."

"Yeah, well, you don't have to. You'll be dead in less than twenty-four hours anyway."

"How did you cover it up?"

He takes a chair and sits right in front of me. I start to feel sweat dripping down my forehead, and I lean my back against the couch. "My brother was owed a favor. You see, he might have been a little corrupted."

"He was helping the Caputos."

"Ding ding ding! See, you can be smart, but then you go and dumbly accept any drink presented to you."

"They helped cover the scene."

"They did. They cleaned it up so quickly that it was easy to alter the reports afterward."

"Oh my god."

"And you...we could have been so much together, but you had to stick your nose where it didn't belong, and for what? A werewolf who screwed you once? A vampire who will outlive you?"

I take this moment to jump on him, but my body betrays me as I do because the reality is that with this potion in my system, I can't even get up and stand straight. Which translates to me miserably falling to the ground and Eric laughing at my useless attempt.

"Fuck."

"You had to fall for one of them as well."

"I am one of them, Eric."

"Yeah, I guess that's why I won't be that sad after you slowly pass away."

I groan, trying to sit up straight. "The Drusus coven will come for you. My father will come for you."

"Your father? I don't think so, but yes, your precious witch friends will certainly try, but I am prepared." He shows me a vial filled with a purple liquid. "This glamour will cover my tracks."

"Did you buy every single potion Monica Lazar has ever made?"

"I had life insurance money to spend."

"I'm going to kill you."

Eric laughs as he gets up and brings the vial to his lips. "You're cute when you threaten lives. I see what the vampire sees in you."

That's when I hear the door swing open, and when I turn toward it, I see Flynn covered in blood at the entrance. Beside him are Kaden, Asmodeus, and Cassandra.

"You should be dead," Eric says, the knife in his hand pointed right at my chest.

"Yeah, well, I'm not that easy to kill. Ask Tal, she failed twice."

"I didn't fail," I say, trying not to roll my eyes as I continue to slowly die.

"Semantics, darling."

"You can't come inside, Lancaster. None of you can."

Cassandra looks down at the floor and notices two stones. I see them too as I try to keep my breathing steady. "You gotta move the stones," I yell before Eric punches me in the stomach, almost making me puke from how strong the hit was.

I hear Kaden and Flynn growling as I try to recompose myself. They're two predators ready to attack, and this time, they have all the right to do just that.

Eric Wagner killed multiple people, including Kaden's dad.

"We can't move them from here," Cassandra says, attempting to touch the crystals. Which means I have to do it from the inside.

"Don't you even think about it," Eric says, grabbing me by the neck and pushing me onto the couch.

"I can't wait to rip your head off, Eric." Flynn's voice is almost a bark.

"You will have to stay there and witness the love of your life dying in front of your eyes because the agony you'd go through trying to come in here is too much, even for an old vampire like you."

My eyes widen at the words he just used because the truth is that I know nothing is worse for Flynn than the prospect of me dying, and if going through any kind of pain means he can get in here, he will do it. "Flynn, don't you dare," I say, my tone bossy as I look at his eyes turning a deep shade of red.

Flynn chuckles before turning to the alpha and patting his shoulder. "Kaden, buddy, I'm sorry. I'll be the only one having all the fun," my vampire says before stepping inside the apartment, with no sign of pain on his face. "But I'll make sure to avenge your daddy as well."

"How did you step inside? You should be dying from the pain."

"See, that's the thing, Eric. I am very old, and I learned how to deal with torture, especially when a dumb human is trying to kill my girl for the second time."

"You can't touch me, Flynn," Eric says, showing his wrist. "I'm protected, remember?"

My vampire laughs. "It's true. I can't use compulsion on you, and I can't really touch that bracelet made of silver and all that, but you're forgetting something."

"And what's that?"

"Sweetheart," Flynn says, looking at me. "What is it that you like to call me?"

I tilt my head to the side, not really understanding where he's going with this. "Extra?"

He runs toward Eric at vampire speed and grabs him by the throat with one hand. The other one tightens around his left forearm—the arm with the bracelet. The knife falls to the ground. "Yes, exactly. I'm a little extra." That's when he twists Eric's arm and pulls. The sound of the flesh and bone ripping makes my stomach flip, and bile comes right up. "Here, problem solved. No bracelet to stop me now." Flynn drops half of his arm to the side, his smirk never leaving his face.

Eric drops to his knees in agony. Blood splatters onto the white rug in his living room.

"Let's try this again, shall we?" Flynn says, gripping my professor's chin and forcing him to look into his eyes. "You're not going to fight what is about to happen to you."

"I won't fight."

"Flynn, no. It's not worth it," I say, my breath getting heavier and heavier.

But it's too late. My vampire's teeth are at Eric's throat in the blink of an eye.

"Flynn..." I whisper as I continue to look at the scene, paralyzed on the couch.

His bite gets deeper and deeper, and that's when I realize he's not drinking Eric's blood. He's slowly ripping his neck apart, trying to detach the head from the rest of the body. Just like he said he would. His fangs meticulously work through the flesh. Even when he loses control, Flynn still doesn't let himself drink from a living creature —well, half-living. Let's just say Eric is basically dead now.

He grips Eric's hair and pulls.

Crack.

The rest of the body falls to the ground with a huge thud. I should be disgusted and afraid, but the reality is that I am in adoration of the being in front of me.

"You're mates," Kaden says, still from the doorframe. "That's how you could withstand the pain. You are her mate."

"I didn't know vampires and hunters had mates," Cassandra adds, her eyes still focused on Flynn's hand holding Eric's head.

Mates. We joked about it, and yet it feels like the only plausible explanation, even for me.

"Mates," I repeat out loud, this time with wide eyes, and then turn to look at my vampire's face. Deadly, murderous, and still incredibly beautiful. "It's okay, Flynn. You can let the head go," I whisper as he pants, almost in need of catching his breath. I try to get up, but it's useless. The potion has already taken too much from me, and I fall back onto the couch.

Icy-gray eyes look into mine, the red in them having

almost disappeared, but Flynn still keeps his distance. His mouth is completely covered in blood. All of him is. Then he walks to the door and kicks one of the crystals with his boot, making it possible for the rest of the crew to walk in. But they don't. No, because the person who steps into Eric's apartment is someone I truly did not think I'd see again.

Emil Popescu, my father, is here.

Shit.

Kaden is at Flynn's side in a second, almost as if he's protecting what he witnessed, as if the knowledge of our mating bond is too sacred, even for him. "Mr. Popescu, you can't touch Flynn. He just saved your daughter's life and ended the life of a killer."

"Wolf, do you really think I kicked the crystal because I wanted you to come and rescue me? I smelled him." Flynn groans as he looks at his hands covered in red. I know he's judging himself, waiting for his moment to end after what he did to Eric.

Emil laughs as he steps onto the murder scene. "I am not here to execute anyone, alpha. Let me give this antidote to my child."

My father's slow pace makes me more nervous than anything. "Here, drink this." He throws me a vial before turning to look at the crimson-colored face of my lover. "And you, clean this mess. It is your lucky day. Next time, I will have a stake in your heart." Then he walks toward the door again.

"Wait," I say, trying to gain his attention.

"*Copil.*"

"How did you know?"

He sighs before saying, "After Set helped me deal with the rest of the Caputos, our mutual friend had a change of heart."

"Monica?"

"Get some rest, *copil*."

"I don't understand."

My father snorts. "I am just making sure you still have the choice to come back."

"Is this what it's all about? Me now owing you a favor?"

"One day, you will understand he is just using you."

"I'm not," Flynn growls, finally dropping the damn head beside the rest of Eric's body.

"And that is my cue." Emil Popescu walks away from us. From an apartment covered in blood. From his daughter and from the vampire who just killed a human right in front of all of us.

"Asmo, do your thing here," Flynn says as he walks to me. "How do you feel, sweetheart?"

"I'm okay," I say, grabbing his hands in mine. The feel of his skin on my own is all I need to take a deep breath, filling my lungs completely. "I'm alive. And you just did something completely reckless by walking in here without knowing if you'd survive."

He laughs at my scolding. "I told you I'd always protect you."

"You could have died, Flynn."

"You can be mad at me for as long as you want, little hunter. Just as long as you're alive to do so."

"God, you really need to find a better pet name," I say, chuckling before I wrap my arms around his neck and pull him to me. My lips crush against his without even thinking about the blood staining his face, the smell of iron mixing with his vanilla-scented cologne.

"Okay, well, I need a drink now," Cassandra says from behind us. I break the kiss and see my friends pouring cleaning potions around the apartment and doing spells to make the body disappear.

"Next time, can you please limit the body-ripping

part?" Asmodeus says, making a disgusted face as he holds Eric's arm.

"Sorry, I got a little carried away." Flynn laughs before helping me get up.

"So this is it?"

"This is it." The person talking now is Set, walking inside the apartment with a glorious smile on his face.

"What took you so long?" Cassandra says, slapping her brother's chest.

"I was busy dealing with the rest of the problem and also making quite the case with Daddy Popescu."

"What?" My jaw drops open.

"I just talked very nicely about Flynn. You're welcome, by the way. Now, can we eat? I'm hungry. All this murdering made me grow quite an appetite."

"Let's go to my apartment. I need a shower," Flynn says, his hand resting on the small of my back.

"Yeah, I do too," I say, looking down at my appearance.

"We can definitely make that happen, little hunter."

I shake my head. "My day started so well, and now...I don't even know what the fuck I'm going to do tomorrow."

"You're going to get your pretty books and continue to go to your pretty classes."

"But I don't have a job anymore. I can't—"

"I'm sure Ms. Sinopoli will be more than happy to step in."

"Flynn, I'm serious."

The corners of his mouth lift up. "And I am as well. Now, let's go. It's time for a celebration."

We apparate all together inside Flynn's apartment as if nothing had happened, and yet my entire life just changed forever. We order food and get cleaned up as we wait for dinner to arrive.

My body still feels weak, but seeing all of us here together makes me feel like I'm part of something.

Kaden sits right beside Set, and on the other side, Cassandra and Asmodeus are arguing about something to the point of throwing fries at each other.

"You okay?" Flynn asks, brushing his hand against mine under the table.

"Is it weird that I feel *happy*?"

"Not at all."

"I should be sad that Eric died despite everything. I should feel something, but I just feel...happy."

"You are feeling something, darling, and no one can tell you what that is supposed to be."

My phone vibrates, and I look at who's calling. The administration office? Why would they be calling me at this time of night?

"Hello?" I say after accepting the phone call.

"Miss Popescu, I just wanted to let you know the payment went through, and you should be seeing the money back in your bank account by morning."

"What?"

"Good night, Miss Popescu. You have quite the admirer."

I turn to look at Flynn, his face blank. "What did you do?"

"I made sure you could finish your last year at this wonderful institution you seem to love so much."

"Flynn, it's too much."

His hands interlock with mine. "I'm just investing my money very wisely, darling."

"I don't even know what to say."

"'Thank you, Flynn. I'll give you the best blowjob of your life.' You could say something like that," he replies, making me laugh.

"Guys, you're in public." Cassandra throws a fry at us. "Gross, so gross."

"Sorry, not sorry," Flynn says before his face turns grim.

"Hey, what is it?"

He gets up and grabs a wineglass. "Before I kick you all out of my house, I'd like to make a toast."

"Wow, very subtle."

"To Evanora, the first person who ever believed in me for some unknown reason, a great witch, and an even greater friend."

"To Evanora," we all repeat in unison.

The doorbell rings, and I go to open the door to see who it is, but no one is at the door. Flynn follows me and then looks down. "Well, this is odd."

"A package?"

He picks it up and opens it.

"Are those what I think they are?" I ask, my mouth open in surprise.

"Dante Alighieri's notes." He chuckles. "Fucking witch."

"I guess she really did have a change of heart."

"For now, at least," Flynn adds, looking at me. "I'm just glad I get to see your face again."

"And I'm glad to see yours."

"I'm sorry for...earlier."

The corners of my lips lift up. "You were quite extra."

My vampire chuckles as his arms wrap around my waist. "I'm going to be whatever you want me to be, Talulla." His vanilla and tobacco scent makes me dizzy. Or maybe it's fate doing all the work because after all we've been through, we're finally here, together, and I don't plan on changing a single thing about it. This is exactly where I'm supposed to be—with the people around the table and Flynn.

"Mine. I just want you to be mine," I say as my lips cover his own and our tongues dance with one another.

"Always, little hunter." I know he's going to do everything in his power to keep his promise because he's my home now, and I'm his.

Two broken anchors that were able to bring each other out of the abyss, filling their hearts.

Two souls now molded into one.

Epilogue

TALULLA

Six Months Later

Flynn
Your dinner is getting cold.

Me
You've been cold for a while, fangs, and you're still my favorite meal.

Flynn
Flattery will get you nowhere.

Me
I beg to differ.

Flynn
Still have lots of work?

Me
I'm much closer than you think.

Flynn
Not close enough.

Me
Aw, miss me?

Flynn
Always, little hunter.

The corners of my lips lift into a smile as I open the door to Flynn's building. Slowly, I make my way to the elevator and press number six. As soon as the doors open, I spot a very impatient vampire standing outside. *My* vampire. All *mine*.

"You sure text a lot for an old grandpa," I say, tiptoeing for a quick kiss. It's too bad it's never quick when Flynn Lancaster is the one you're kissing. His arms wrap around my waist, and I get lost in his vanilla and spice scent. His velvety fingers keep me as close as possible.

"I gotta catch up with the younger generation, you know?" he says, interlocking his fingers with mine as we make our way back to his apartment. I've been spending most of my nights here since the moment he gave me a key —well, six months ago now.

"Are you gonna start sending me memes?" I drop my bag in his—our—bedroom and pull my hair up in a ponytail.

"Never," Flynn says as he walks back to the kitchen. The aroma of tomato sauce and the new basil plant on the counter give away his menu for the night. He's been taking care of me in ways I didn't expect. The cold-hearted predator who can't stand being around people too much is here, giving me every kind of attention that is humanly possible, and there are days when I ask myself how I got so lucky.

"Hi," I finally say, my voice barely a soft breath as I hug him from behind. My hands rest on his hard chest as he stirs the sauce and makes sure the pasta doesn't overcook.

"Hi, darling." One of his hands rests on top of mine, the soft touch sending electricity down my spine.

"Whatever you're making smells amazing." It really does. This man could be making the simplest thing, and it'd turn into a Michelin-star-level meal. Every. Single. Time.

"Just a quick homemade tomato sauce and pasta. Sorry, it's nothing quite elaborate tonight. I was trying to acquire a Monet."

"You're apologizing because you cooked me dinner," I state. It's not a question.

"A simple dinner, and yes, I am."

"Flynn, do you realize just the fact that you went out of your way, even when you were busy working, is more than amazing in my eyes?"

"You deserve sophistication every single day."

"How are you even real?" Because what man does this every single day for their partner? Heat grows between my legs as I continue to stare at him working around the kitchen, his black silk button-up shirt neatly contained in his dark trousers. The sleeves are rolled up to make sure he doesn't stain the fabric. Flynn's head slightly turns to the side, his grin impossible to hide as he inhales my scent.

"If this sight turns you on this much, I might have to cook for you every night."

"I think you've realized by now that there is basically nothing you can do that isn't a turn-on."

I hear him chuckle as he shakes his head. "Go change. Food will be ready soon."

"Yes, sir."

He drops the wooden spoon in the pot and quickly turns to face me. A hand grabbing my throat makes me gasp. "Say it again." His other hand cups one of my breasts, his fingers toying with my nipple, the fabric of my T-shirt adding to the friction.

"Sir," I whisper, my entire body ready for him to do literally anything.

"Fuck, you follow orders so prettily."

"Only when it's you requesting things."

"Only me, Talulla." He undoes my belt, and before I know it, my jeans are off. "Here, let me help you get changed."

"I'm capable of taking off my clothes."

"You can do anything, but I want to strip you and have you ready for what I have planned later."

"Oh?"

"Take everything off."

I cross my arms over my chest. "Eating dinner naked while you're fully dressed seems very unfair."

"It won't be when I have my sweet dessert."

"Which is?"

"Your pussy riding my face."

I gasp at his quick comeback. "What if I want to do something for you instead?"

"You can choke on my cock anytime you want, darling. Now, be a good girl and take your shirt off."

I'm now down to a red lacy bra with a matching thong. Flynn's eyes darken at the sight of my bare body. "Seeing something you like?" I say, turning around and showing off my ass to him.

"Every single inch of your body is a work of art. You're absolutely exquisite, Talulla." His tongue caresses my neck. "And red is my favorite color on you."

The timer for the pasta goes off, and we both jolt at the high-pitched sound. "Your pasta is overcooking."

"It will be perfect. Here, take this," he says, handing me an open bottle of red wine. "Now, please go sit down and stop distracting me."

"Distracting you? You're the one who stripped me naked."

"Semantics."

I roll my eyes as I make my way to the set table and pour two glasses of wine. Then I get to the fridge and grab a bottle of blood, only to be stopped as I try to walk back to the dining room. "Can I help you?" I ask Flynn, raising an eyebrow at him as he keeps his grip firm on my wrist.

"You don't have to do that."

"You drink blood around me all the time, but I can't take the bottle to the table where you'll be drinking it?"

He sighs and lets go of my arm. "I don't expect you to do that."

"Just like I don't expect you to cook dinner for me."

He tilts his head to the side. "But I want to cook dinner for you."

"And I want to pour you a glass of blood."

"Fine."

"Can we eat now?"

The corners of his lips tilt up, and fuck, he's gorgeous when he smiles. "Absolutely."

We sit down and start eating. As I take a bite of the pasta he prepared, a moan escapes my mouth. It's perfect —a freaking mouthwatering, perfect plate of pasta.

"This is so good."

"Glad you like it," he says as he takes a bite for himself, his fangs appearing as I watch him sip from his glass of blood.

We continue to eat in silence, and as I truly look at Flynn, I notice his posture is different. He's tense, as if something is bothering him.

I put my fork down. "What's up with you?"

"Nothing. Why?" he says, continuing to avoid my stare.

"Spill it."

This is when his icy-gray eyes finally look back at me. "Talulla, you know I don't like insolence."

"And you know I don't like it when you avoid telling me things."

He rolls his eyes but smiles at my comeback. "Oh, I

will tell you what I'm thinking. I'm just very nervous about doing so."

My jaw drops open. "Flynn Lancaster is nervous?"

"Extremely."

I take his hand in mine and bring it to my lips. "What's wrong?"

"I have to share something with you, and I need you to let me get it out before you say anything."

I nod. "I can do that."

He sighs, his eyes searching for mine. "What do you want to do in two weeks after you graduate?"

Tilting my head to the side, I reply, "Look for a job?"

"And what would you say if you could have an interview with the head of the archives department at the Natural History Museum in London?"

My eyes widen as I let the words sink in. "What?"

"Before you jump to conclusions, I did not use any of my methods aside from asking Ms. Sinopoli if she would write a letter of recommendation and Cassandra if she could help me put together your résumé."

"How?"

"Perseverance."

My eyes narrow. "Flynn, elaborate."

"What I mean is that I checked every single day for openings. I was getting quite desperate, really, because I knew you'd never forgive me if I used any other method, and truly, I wanted to show you that your résumé was more than enough to get what you wanted."

"Okay...and?"

"And one day, I saw the listing and sent your résumé, and with Ms. Sinopoli's recommendation, you got through all the interview stages."

"I did?"

"We talked, and they know you have two weeks left at

Bear Creek and clearly want to read your dissertation, but they kinda love you." Flynn's lips lift up.

"You're kidding me."

"I would never joke about something so important to you."

"Flynn..."

"I had to try, Talulla. Please don't shut me out. Let's talk about it."

I grab his hands in mine from across the table. "I'm not angry."

"You're not?"

"I'm shocked," I say, shaking my head in disbelief.

"I know it's a lot, and I'm so sorry I didn't tell you earlier, but I also didn't want to say anything until it became real and possible."

"And now it is?"

"Well, they did ask this morning if you'd be interested in an in-person interview."

"So they knew they were not talking to me all this time?"

"Yes, I made it clear from the beginning," Flynn says, squeezing my hands.

"And they are still interested in my application?"

"Extremely."

"I can't believe it."

"It's true, sweetheart. They loved everything they saw."

"Okay, but what would happen to us?"

"Us? What do you mean?"

"It's on the other side of the planet, Flynn."

"Would you want me around?"

"Of course I would, but I also would never force you to go somewhere you didn't want to go."

"Talulla, I'd follow you to the end of the world. Why

wouldn't I come with you to London? Did you forget that's where I was born?"

"Of course, I haven't forgotten it. The sexy accent is a dead giveaway."

"Sexy, you say..."

"Oh, come on. You know it."

"What do you say, little hunter?"

"That you gotta find a better pet name, or I won't let you get on the plane."

"You're saying yes?"

"I'm saying thank you."

"I did nothing."

"Incorrect. You give me everything, Flynn. You listen to me and take care of me, even when I protest about it. You're there. Always. And I didn't think I could ever feel this way about someone. Being able to trust you is one of the most beautiful feelings I could ever imagine."

"You're the spark lighting up my soul, Talulla. I'd do anything to make you happy."

I get up from the chair and reach for him. "Can I take care of you now?" I say, getting to my knees, my hands reaching for his belt buckle.

Flynn's hands grab my wrists. "You're a vision."

"Yours," I say, sliding the belt off and pulling his trousers down just enough to free his length.

FLYNN

I didn't expect Talulla to take the news with such maturity. Not because she isn't mature, but because I went behind her back and tried to do something nice. Maybe that's why she isn't mad about it. She understands I did this for her.

Now she's on her knees in front of me, ready to suck my cock, and all I can think about is how it will feel when I come on her face.

"Mine," I say as she licks the head. A groan escapes my mouth as she continues to move her tongue on my shaft. Up and down, licking as if it were ice cream.

She takes me all the way in, and I fist her hair, keeping her head in place as I move my hips, matching her pace.

"Such a good girl," I growl, moving faster, her moans of pleasure making me harder and harder as I hit the back of her throat with each thrust. "If you continue to take me like this, I'm not gonna last much longer."

She comes out to breathe, her hands never leaving my balls and length. "Then you might want to take me to bed if you want to fuck me."

"I'm pretty sure you know I can come more than once."

"Can you? You're getting older. I don't know how long you can last."

"Get up," I say, my eyes getting darker as she follows my orders. "Bend down over the table."

"And why would I do that?"

"Because you're getting spanked for your colorful tongue."

"You love it."

I grab the back of her neck and push her down onto the table. "And you're going to love my hand on your ass."

"Yeah, I probably will." She chuckles as she prepares for what's coming.

I squeeze her ass cheeks and then go for the hit. I spank her hard, the sound making my ears ring, and her moans make my dick pulse as I stare at her skin turning red.

I push her thong to the side and align the head of my cock with her entrance, feeling her wetness coat the tip.

"The way you're always ready for me is the biggest turn-on ever." I slide my length in and groan at how her walls contract as I start moving in and out of her.

"Oh god," she moans as my movements get harder.

"That's my girl. Look at you taking me so well," I say, spanking her once more. Her pussy keeps squeezing my cock with every hit. I keep one hand on the back of her neck, and the other starts playing with her clit.

Her pants are getting rougher and rougher, and with the sounds she's making, I know she's close to orgasm.

"You're gonna come for me now, darling," I say as I continue to torture her bundle of nerves. "And then you're gonna make me come in your mouth."

"Oh, fuck." Her sounds are getting more frantic, and as she erupts, the walls of her pussy contract even more, trying to keep me right inside her as she comes undone.

I continue to thrust into her, and as I get close, I slide out of her. Her groans of disapproval make me chuckle. "On your knees," I say, pumping my length as I wait for her to follow my orders.

She drops to the floor and sticks her tongue out, her eyes closing as I slide my dick in her mouth. Talulla's cries of pleasure make me want to fuck her for the rest of the night, but the sight of her here, ready for me, makes me empty myself down her throat in minutes.

"Fuck, you take me so well," I say, slowing my pace but keeping her head in place as I let her drink every last drop of me.

After cleaning up, we lie in bed, her body entangled with mine. "I can't believe Cassandra helped you plan all this and didn't tell me anything."

"I have a slight suspicion she has known for a while. Even before I did."

Talulla's laugh brightens up the room. "Of course she knew." Then she turns to look at me, her blue eyes searching for something. "Are you sure you're okay with this?"

"Darling, I have the plane tickets already booked."

With that, her mouth crushes against mine, her plump lips bruising from the continuous contact and sucking. Because we can't stop being with each other, not when everything is finally falling into place—our worlds colliding together to create a new one just for us. Her face heats and turns the perfect shade of red.

"I think I have the perfect pet name for you."

"Finally tired of *little hunter*? Because I am."

I click my tongue. "You'll always be *my* little hunter."

"You're insufferable," she says, rolling her eyes at me.

"And you're a brat."

"You like me this way."

"I do, very much." I chuckle. "And you seem to enjoy it when I spank the brat out of you."

She chuckles as she tries to get away from my embrace. "Maybe..."

"You're my world. You know that, right?" I wrap her in my arms once more, the bedsheets dropping to the floor.

"You've said it a few times," she replies, her breath mixing with mine. "So what happens now, fangs?"

I turn to open the nightstand's drawer and grab a dark red velvet box. I open it and turn it toward her. Talulla's eyes widen as they drop to the delicate gold chain with a red stone pendant set in the middle.

"Is that—" she starts saying, but I finish the sentence before she can find any possible reason why she doesn't deserve jewelry.

"Time to start our life, my beautiful red ruby."

Bonus Chapter

FLYNN

Ten fifty-eight.

Fifty-nine.

Eleven. Fucking. O'clock. On a fine Friday night.

Nine missed calls, and let me count—thirteen texts. All from me. All unanswered.

I stare at the screen of my phone until it turns black.

Again.

And *again*.

I swear I've been doing this on a loop for the past six hours...because she was supposed to be back at five.

Five sharp.

This woman is driving me absolutely insane, and the worst part? I can't even get mad. Not really. Because I know exactly where she is, and I know exactly what happened—she lost track of time.

Again.

It's not new. It's not surprising. It's the third damn time this week, and yeah, it pisses me off—just a little.

Maybe more than a little. But what am I supposed to do? Blow up her phone harder? Storm out and scold her? Sit here like a damn idiot checking the time every three minutes, hoping to hear the front door creak open?

But I'm not mad at her. Never at her. More at the circumstances.

Talulla has been studying, writing, and researching

nonstop for the past six months. No breaks. No breathing room. When she's in one of those hyper-focused modes, I learned pretty damn fast that she forgets basic things. Like drinking water. Sleeping. Even fucking eating.

And that worries me.

A lot.

She throws herself so deep into her work that it's like the world around her disappears, and I'm just standing here watching her body burn itself out in real time.

Why couldn't I have been mated to someone with a halfway decent sense of self-preservation? Someone who maybe remembers lunch? Or that humans need rest?

But no.

Of course not.

I had to fall for the daughter of the most famous vampire hunter alive—brilliant, fearless, and somehow managing to survive on caffeine, adrenaline, and pure stubborn willpower, with horrendous, undiagnosed ADHD.

God help me.

I actually snort at the thought of her trying to convince me she's *totally* fine. Like, sure, Talulla. You're thriving. Radiating health. Peak human condition.

Spoiler alert: she is absolutely, one-hundred-percent *not* fine.

She hasn't even trained in weeks, and she adores training. I know she does. She pretends she doesn't, but she fucking loves it. It gives her confidence, and it's extremely arousing seeing her in a ring showing exactly how deadly she can be.

But nope. She's obsessed with this paper—completely consumed by it. Don't get me wrong—I adore her for it. The way her brain works, the way she throws herself headfirst into something she believes in—it's one of the million things I love about her.

Something I haven't admitted to her. Not out loud, at least. I wouldn't be this pathetic if I didn't love Talulla.

But I'd prefer if she didn't, you know, *die* from starvation in the process.

That would be ideal, actually.

She'll look me dead in the eye, pale as a ghost, eyes twitching from too much screen time and zero sleep, and insist she's "in the zone." As if that explains why she hasn't eaten a real meal in two days and thinks coffee counts as hydration.

She drives me fucking crazy, and somehow, I still want her to do what makes her happy. Which, apparently, is this. Trying to kill herself with studying.

This is exactly why I've been asking her to come to my apartment after she's done at the library or with Ms. Sinopoli. Not just because I miss her—though, god, I do—but because at least here, I can *see* her eat. One full meal. That's the bare minimum I'm clinging to now.

If she's under my roof, I can make sure she sits down for five minutes, breathes, maybe even remembers what actual food tastes like. It's not much, but it's something. A little piece of control in the middle of this chaos she's drowning herself in.

She thinks I'm being extremely dramatic. Or clingy. Maybe both. But really, I'm just trying to keep her alive.

Dinner tonight is officially downgraded to more of a midnight snack at this point.

I pass a hand through my hair, trying to calm myself down, trying to breathe like a rational person who isn't two seconds away from pacing a hole in the floor.

She'll be here soon.

No need to rush over there. No need to barge into the library like some lunatic boyfriend on the edge.

She's fine. She's just late. Again. Like always.

Unless...

A thought comes to mind.

A very pretty one.

I cover the *mititei* I've made for her and secure all the food in the fridge as I plan how to prepare and accomplish this little idea I just had.

I can't help but grin as I unroll the sleeves of my black silk shirt and button them at the cuffs.

Time to bring an appetizer to my pretty red ruby.

TALULLA

Just another five minutes, and I can call it a night. I can't feel my ass anymore, and that means I've been sitting in the same position for, well, too long.

But I'm so close to the end. The aroma of parchment and ink becomes a secondary distraction as a tobacco vanilla fragrance catches my attention.

Flynn.

I raise my head and, sure enough, the perfectly dressed blond vampire I get to call my own is staring intensely at me. His icy-gray eyes sparkle as the fluorescent light coats his porcelain skin.

Gods, he's gorgeous. I swallow some air as his hard look continues to penetrate my being.

"What are you doing here?" I ask, my eyes widening when I realize he's not a vision and that he's really here. At the library. On a Friday afternoon. "Is everything okay?"

The corner of his lips lifts up. "You didn't come home, and you didn't check your phone."

"What the—"

"It's almost midnight."

My jaw drops. "No way," I say, looking at the clock. "Flynn," I start. "I'm so sorry, I just—"

"You're studying," he says, before slowly walking to my side of the table, whistling a melody, his fingers tapping on the polished surface. "I'm not upset, Talulla. I just wanted to make sure you were okay."

I start rushing and putting my books away, but his hand grabs one of my wrists. "I'll get my stuff, and we can go. I'm so sorry."

"It's a very calm place."

"What?" I ask, as my eyes stay on his hands still holding me.

"The library at Bear Creek," he starts. "Very, very calming. I see why you could get lost in your thoughts here."

I shrug. "I just find it easier to concentrate when everyone is doing the same thing."

He nods and finally lets go of me. "Stay here, little hunter," Flynn says before getting up. He starts walking to the table where two guys have been studying. Then he moves to the following one and the one after.

"What are you doing?" I question him in a loud whisper.

"Making sure of something before we continue your study session."

"What?"

"Just stay put, darling," he purrs. And fuck. His voice is like a siren's call that I can't help but follow.

Oh shit.

I focus on his look, the way he predatorily moves to every single person still present, and the way they react as he whispers something in their ears before locking eyes with every single person.

He's compelling everyone.

Every single person in this library is being compelled by Flynn, and I'm not doing anything about it.

Oh, fucking shit.

His smirk grows bigger and bigger the more I continue to stare at him and at what he's doing.

Heat grows between my legs, and I shift in my seat to get some sort of friction. I don't know what he has planned, but it's definitely not innocent at all.

Flynn finally gets to all the people in the room and then paces to the front door and locks it from the inside. No one comes in. No one goes out.

"That's quite the safety hazard," I joke as he marches back to me.

"Nothing will happen while I'm in here," he states as he reaches me. I'm still sitting as he comes to my side and reaches for my chin. "You've been in here for over six hours."

"I really am sorry for losing track of time."

He tilts his head a little. "I know you are, and I'm going to say again that I'm not mad at you, Talulla, not when you're working on something so important for you."

"We really can just go home now."

"After I show you something."

"Is that why you compelled the entire place?"

He shrugs, the smirk never leaving his lips. "I wanted you to be comfortable."

"What?"

"Lie on the table, Talulla."

"Excuse me?" I ask, shifting my weight from one foot to the other. "We're in public, fangs." I gesture around the place.

He snorts. "Don't act so surprised. Your cunt already knows what's coming. Now, be a good girl and lie on this table."

I swallow air and slowly get up from my chair. Flynn follows my every move as I do as he asked, and I position myself right in front of him. "I can't believe you wanna do this here."

"I want to take you everywhere, all the damn time."

"That would be so unproductive, but very good in terms of working out," I say, using my fingers as quotation marks as I say the words *working* and *out*. "I do like to keep myself in shape after all. Can't lose my hunter body," I add, gesturing to my body.

"Are you going to behave as I fuck you now, or do you need me to gag you?"

My mouth drops open. "You wouldn't dare."

"Lie on the table, red ruby."

"Or what?" I challenge him, crossing my arms over my chest as my pussy throbs at the thought of him taking me here as everyone else watches us.

I don't even have the time to react as Flynn grabs me by the hips and sits me at the edge of the table. "I think you enjoy being punished." He shakes his head as his hand travels up my leg. "You want to feel my marks on you, don't you?" he asks, and I can't help but nod as his fingers reach my stomach, then my neck, and stop on my lips. "Be right back. Do. Not. Move."

"Yes, sir," I whisper as shivers travel down my body. I follow his gaze as he walks toward one of the librarians and asks him to give him his tie.

Oh my fucking fuck, he is actually going to gag me.

Then he walks back to me and proceeds to twist the fabric to form a silk rope with it. "If you need me to stop, you tap anywhere on me, understood?"

I nod.

"Good." He smiles. "Now, let's begin."

The gentle touch is a juxtaposition of my vampire's desired intentions. Flynn takes his time tying the piece of fabric around my mouth, making sure it's tight enough to keep my lips parted, but never too tight to actually hurt me.

Flynn's dominance and need for control are never out of line, never something I wouldn't enjoy, and this moon-touched being knows exactly what my limit is.

And fuck, it is bliss having someone who accepts you the way you are and makes sure you're sated.

This vampire's craving for me is all I need to get ready for him. The pool of desire growing between my legs makes him smirk. "You little slut, you like the idea of being in public, don't you?" he questions, and I can't control the sounds I'm making as his fingers travel down my body. He grabs my wrists in one of his hands, and instead of tying those as well, he positions them on top of my head, keeping them together.

I can't help but moan through the fabric of the tie that keeps me from speaking.

His fingers find my folds quickly, and he doesn't hesitate when he forces two digits inside of me. "I'm not gonna be gentle, Talulla. You've been away all day, making me starve for you." Then, he slides out of me and brings his fingers to his mouth. "Mmm...exquisite as always."

The sounds that come out of me are wild as he continues to praise me.

But Flynn doesn't just give.

He takes.

He marks.

And, fuck, do I adore him for it.

The perfect level of pain that becomes the most beautiful bliss.

His hand, which is still half in his mouth, quickly comes down hard on my core—a perfect slap on my clit that makes me gasp.

My hips jerk up, wanting more contact with him.

"Look at you, dirty girl." He chuckles. "You want to be claimed, don't you?"

I nod fast, my eyes closing as he continues his ethereal torture.

Then, he finally unbuckles his belt and unbuttons his pants. His look is predatory and ravenous.

He spits on my clit, and before I can get a full look, his mouth is sucking it, and his tongue thrusts inside my folds. I can't help but touch him. My hands reach for his head, keeping it in place, and he lets me. This dominant being, who always needs to be in control, is now letting me hold him.

Because he might say he was starving, but he knows very well I've been dying to feel his marks on me as well.

Flynn lets me meet his thrusts with my own as I move my hips, following his rhythm. My orgasm grows faster than ever before, and right when I think he's actually going to let me come, he gets up.

Because it wouldn't be Flynn if he just let me have it so easy. I roll my eyes as an anguished groan comes out of me.

His chuckle grows just like my despair. "Turn around, red ruby."

I do as I'm told, and as he preps to drill into me, I turn my head and notice him looking at the people around us. A guy in his early thirties is looking right at me, and Flynn noticed it. He's in a trance, his mouth slightly open as he watches everything.

"What's your name?" Flynn asks, and as I look up, I see he's talking to the stranger.

"Jo-Jonathan."

He snorts. "Well, Jonathan, enjoy the view of how you're never going to fuck my Talulla." Then, in one quick motion, he's inside me.

My eyes fall shut as he starts to move inside me. Fast and hard. Gods, he's going to actually break me in half.

My moans get louder and louder. More high-pitched as he hits that spot inside me perfectly. Every. Single. Time.

His hands dig hard into my hips as he thrusts deeper and deeper with every movement. "By the heavens, how the fuck can you feel better every time I take you?" Flynn asks as his hands move up to my nipples. "There is nothing in existence that could ever possibly compare to what you are to me." This is when he decides to pinch one of my nipples and my clit at the same time.

I explode.

He lets me shatter.

"This..." he starts as I continue to come, hard. "Is the feeling I will never be tired of."

The waves continue to rush through me, and he doesn't stop. He can't. Not when he needs to prove to me that he will always give me what I need the most.

Flynn takes the tie off and lets me turn to face him. My arms automatically wrap around his neck, and I bring him down to me. His body collides with mine, never breaking the rhythm. He never stops fucking me, taking me, making me his altar to worship anytime he can.

This is where we excel. Like this. Molded into one being.

"Jesus Christ," we hear someone say, and Flynn looks up, back at Jonathan.

"Enjoying the view, Jonathan?"

"I..."

"Flynn, please," I beg as I feel another orgasm build.

"What is it, little hunter?"

"Don't bring Jonathan into this, please."

My vampire chuckles, and his lips find mine. Tobacco and vanilla envelop me completely, and I forget about what we were talking about just a moment ago. "I think I might carve Jonathan's eyes out if he doesn't stop jerking off under the table," Flynn says, his voice a firm whisper that sends chills down my spine.

"Do you know how hard it would be to clean up? And don't get me started on the kind of story you'd have to make up for it."

"I'm very creative," he replies before claiming my mouth once more.

"That you certainly are."

"I should have known someone would actually take his dick out and try to ruin our fun."

I snort. "Won't it be so funny to see his face and everyone else's when they go on with their lives and he finds himself with very sticky pants and hands?"

The grin that he gifts me is a mix of amusement and pride. "You're truly my perfect match."

"Down to the wooden stake in my boots."

"Take it out."

"What?"

"The stake. Take it out."

"Why?"

My vampire brings his lips to my ear and whispers, "Because I want to fill you up as you pierce my flesh."

My eyes widen. "But—"

"Be a good girl and do as I say."

My mouth closes shut. I take the stake out, and after I position it just slightly off-center to his heart, Flynn starts fucking me again.

"Now, little hunter. Stake me now."

I feel his cock pulsate inside of me as I sink the piece of wood into his chest. His look of pure ecstasy fills my entire vision, and I can't help but come as well as his blood drips on my skin, warm and cool at the same time.

He stills inside of me, and we remain like this for a moment that seems to last forever.

"That was incredible, Talulla."

"I can't believe you just made me stake you," I say as I look at his chest, still dripping, his eyes on me as if nothing absolutely wild happened.

"It was a little staking, nothing serious," he mutters as his lips caress my forehead.

We both chuckle as I carefully take the piece of wood out of him. My hand raises to his pec, making sure the wound closes.

Flynn grabs my palm and brings it to his mouth, his tongue out and ready to lick all the blood off me before planting a kiss right in the middle. "I'm okay, darling. I'm all healed," he reassures me, positioning my hand back on his skin to show me the hole is now completely gone.

"Enjoy the show, Jonathan?" I say out loud, my eyes never leaving Flynn's.

No response.

"I think we broke him," Flynn replies, now starting to lick the blood off my breasts.

I can't help but moan again as his tongue circles around my nipples, his fangs tickling my skin. Such a fucking tease.

"You're making me want to feel those teeth deep into my skin, fangs."

He growls as he continues to clean me off. "That is an event for another day."

"Tomorrow?"

He chuckles. "Get dressed, Talulla. I have dinner ready for you at home."

"You're just going to avoid the question?"

"I'm just postponing it," he says, his lips crushing onto mine. "For now, at least."

"So that's a maybe?"

"I did say it's an event for another day, didn't I?"

The corners of my lips lift up. "You did."

He helps me dress and collect my books, and then he says, "Let's go home, darling. You've been working all day."

"I do need to work a little more after dinner."

"You need sleep."

"Yes, Grandpa."

Flynn snorts at my comeback. "I should punish you for that."

I can't help but grin. There it is. What makes us *us*. The teasing, the flirting, and the absolute devotion we have for one another. "You definitely should, fangs. I've been a very bad girl. Staying out so late...studying."

Flynn's hand catches mine as a growl escapes from his mouth. He's ready for round two. "You know exactly what to say, don't you?" We rush out of the building, stop to look at the window for a moment, and enjoy the rest of the people going back to their chores.

Jonathan looks confused as he looks down at his unbuttoned pants, and I can't help but laugh.

"I can't believe I just let you fuck me in the library."

"That's what you do, Talulla. You accept me for who I am and embrace every little broken piece of the vase."

"You're not broken, Flynn. You never were."

"I'm not anymore, no," he says, cupping my cheeks with his hands and forcing me to look up at him. "You wove every piece back together with golden threads."

No words come out. Just my refined and utter devotion to his mouth, and his eternal essence. Because for the first time since we laid eyes on each other, I truly think he believes his words.

And for the first time, maybe, I also feel like a healed soul.

Broken fragments finally glued and molded together to create a new piece of artwork.

Look Out For:

RED RUBY

Book two is coming soon...

AVAILABLE JUNE 2026

Acknowledgments

Well, here we are again, and holy shit, I can't believe I get to do this another time.

To my mom and brother, thank you for your constant support in everything I decide to do. I'm so lucky to have you as my family.

To Chiara and Marco, thank you for giving me shelter when I was struggling with the end of this book and my mental health. Family really isn't just about sharing blood with someone, and you showed me that.

To my person, Mitchell, you're the reason I write romance. Thank you for showing me what true love is. I can't believe I wrote this down. You turned my stone-cold heart into something warm and fuzzy.

To the Love N. Books Press team, thank you for believing in my story and giving me the opportunity to let my characters shine. To say that I'm forever grateful is an understatement.

Connie and Mell, thank you for always being there for me, even if I end up in my bubble and forget about the rest of the world.

To Monica, thank you for letting me create the perfect baddie for you, and for all your insight on Romanian culture.

Kaila, you get a special thank you for pushing me to explore these characters and this story after I sent you that short story that one night. This journey wouldn't have happened without you. I am so lucky to have you in my life.

Noémie. Girl, I don't even know where to begin... I can't even explain how thankful I am to have found you.

I'm so grateful to have had you work with me on this project and more importantly, to have you do life with me as my friend.

To the Emilio's coven, you know who you are, thank you for letting me vent, making me laugh and the continuous support, this author thing would be so dull without you.

Elena, what can I say to you, cocorita of my heart? I don't even know what my life looked like before you, and honestly? Don't even want to think about that. Thank you for being an anchor in this vast scary sea we call life.

Here we get to my soul sister. Go away, mister, she is mine. Tj, I don't know how many times I've told you this, but I don't care because I wouldn't be here if it wasn't for you. I would have zero books. I would have zero everything if you weren't in my life. Thank you for being the best critique partner and friend I could ever ask for. Thank you for listening to my crazy venting moments and letting me talk on the phone for hours upon hours, thank you for always cheering me on when I doubt myself, and thank you for always giving me advice when I need it.

Last but not least, to my readers, I couldn't do this without you, and I know it's cliche and all that, but it's the reality of things. You gave me a chance, and I will be forever grateful for it. I hope this story brought you some sort of spicy contentment and, more importantly, raised your standards about love once again. Thank you for letting me live my dream.

Lots of love and bite marks,
Letizia

Letizia Firmani is an Italian author with an incurable obsession for anything fantasy or romance-related. Her first approach to writing was through music, and she actually dreamed of becoming a songwriter for most of her life. After majoring in Photography while consuming a very healthy amount of fan fictions, Firmani finally decided to give novel writing a go when the world shut down. Letizia spends most of her time daydreaming about fictional characters, putting hot sauce on things that definitely don't need it, and crafting your next favorite book boyfriend. She splits her time between Italy and Canada with her partner and an ever-growing number of cats who may or may not be plotting world domination.

www.letiziafirmani.com

www.ingramcontent.com/pod-product-compliance
Lightning Source LLC
La Vergne TN
LVHW030917080826
845145LV00013B/2940

* 9 7 8 1 9 6 9 8 7 6 0 6 6 *